Love Letter
for
a Sinner

by

Lynn Shurr

The Sinners, Book Five

Love Letter for a Sinner

Cover Art by *Diana Carlile*

The Wild Rose Press, Inc.
PO Box 708
Adams Basin, NY 14410-0708
Visit us at www.thewildrosepress.com

Publishing History
First Champagne Rose Edition, 2013
Print ISBN 978-1-62830-141-0
Digital ISBN 978-1-62830-142-7

The Sinners, Book Five
Published in the United States of America

The waitress reappeared with two fresh cups of coffee in a new holder. Rex fished a bill large enough to cover the orders and a generous tip from his wallet. He waved away the offer of change. Hesitating a minute, he clarified his question. "I meant, are you a virgin?"

Tricia, rising with the cup holder grasped in both hands, nearly spilled her burden again. "Now *that* is too personal a question. I have to go. The beignets are cooling."

He stood, too, and said, "Let me carry the coffee. Take the beignets. I suspect I'm more coordinated than you."

"Your concern and compliments overwhelm me. I can handle this, thanks." She might have if one of the pigeon-terrorizing tots hadn't dashed in front of her flushing a bird directly into her face. The second order of coffee crashed to the ground splashing her ankle to knee.

Rex got down on his and immediately swabbed the scalding beverage from her skin with a handful of paper napkins. The little Asian girl returned. "More coffees, sir?"

"Yes, same order. You have any ice back there? We don't want her to blister."

"Right away!"

Tricia stared down at Rex's wide back straining his red Sinners knit shirt. His tanned arms with their heavy biceps worked up and down her legs. How many women would love to have Rex Worthy at their feet? No matter because if Layla saw her, she was dead meat or in this case cold, stale beignets.

Dedication

In memory of Linda Houle

Chapter One

Joe Dean Billodeaux, aging quarterback for the New Orleans Sinners, but still a star both on the field and now in motion pictures, stomped into the trailer assigned to him on location in New Mexico. Damn but he hated making movies. Now, he liked making commercials, especially local ones in Louisiana where people understood his Cajun accent with no problem. He touted everything from automobiles to zydeco albums, including his own hot and spicy barbecue sauce that funded Camp Love Letter for sick and handicapped kids. He had turned down the offer to sell a drug for erectile dysfunction as damaging to his reputation, but only that one.

Joe slapped his black Stetson against his thigh to remove the pretend dust from its brim before tossing it aside. The words "fake" and "tedious" came to mind regarding moviemaking. Football might be just a game, but he took real hits and the action ran mostly non-stop and exciting. Jesus, Mary, and Joseph, his character died in the first ten minutes of the film, yet they did the scene over and over until he figured the man would have croaked from boredom, rather than being shot in the back by cattle rustlers.

Between each take, some woman rushed over to spray his face with water because he needed a more sweaty look, or to powder his clothes with extra dirt for additional grit. And they kept changing his lines, which had shrunk to about half a dozen. He had no trouble learning them, but his Cajun accent tended to come out whenever the director shouted, "Roll!" He got credit for sitting a horse well, and that was about all. He'd thought making a western would be fun, but no. Put this on his agent's list of things he would not do along with ED medications. Fake and tedious.

Figuring to shuck his dirty, sweaty clothes and take a shower, Joe slammed open the door to the small bedroom. Not fake, those large, perfect white breasts with their pink nipples staring at him from the mattress, and he should know from his youthful womanizing days when he'd had plenty to compare. This rack was attached to his co-star, Layla Devlin, sprawled seductively naked on top of his covers. He couldn't seem to lift his gaze to her violet eyes or pouty lips. The nipples puckered in happy anticipation or maybe from the gust of cold air he'd let into the room.

His arms braced against the frame, Joe stood frozen with one foot inside and one outside the sill. The little brain below the waist urged him forward. The brain in his head, rapidly losing control, ordered him to step back. He'd made a vow to his wife, Nell, never to cheat on her, and so far so good, until now.

"Aren't you coming in, Joe? I'm getting cold and need something to warm me up," the devil, uh, Devlin woman said. She kept her voice low and throaty and played with a coil of her long blonde hair, the color toned down for the movie and still crimped from being in braids for her role. Nell wore her dark hair very short and did not play with it at all.

Joe made a grab for his cell phone on a nearby

shelf and wrenched himself back into the short hall. He retreated into the bathroom and locked the door. Squatting on the lid of the commode, he hit the speed dial for his wife. Layla's voice, higher and more penetrating, called after him, "You needn't shower. I like a sweaty hunk of a man. Come as you are. Let the fun begin!"

Pick up, Nell. Pick up. She wouldn't if their ten children were having lunch. House rules, no phone calls during meals. Joe consulted his wrist and remembered no watch because that would be anachro-whatever for the time period of the movie. Filming started at the crack of dawn, and tables full of food and drink dotted the set. People ate when they felt like it between takes. Four rings and at last, his wife answered. In the background, water splashed and the delighted voices of Camp Love Letter kids shrilled.

"How's it going, my favorite handsome movie star? Are women throwing themselves at your feet?"

"Don't you even say dat—that. Layla Devlin is naked in my bed. I had lock myself in the bat'room, bathroom. How do I get rid of her?"

"Not tempted?"

"I'd be a liar, me, if I said no, but I don't want her messing up our lives, our kids' lives."

He pictured his little wife, whom he called Tink, short for Tinker Bell, though she hated being compared to anything tiny even if the description fit. She sat poolside supervising the campers, maybe giving their eldest sons, Dean and Tommy, now nearly seventeen and sixteen, a break from lifeguarding. He needed her to save *his* life or at least his vows right now. Joe pled, "What should I do?"

"Put me on speaker phone, and let me have a friendly chat with Layla."

Hoping his co-star might have taken the hint and gone, Joe cautiously exited the bathroom. Nope, she still lay on the bed but had rolled onto her back allowing her breasts to pool to either side of her chest. Her toned arms rested behind her head and her left leg cocked above the right as if accentuating her bikini wax job. He couldn't help but notice what hair she had left down there was golden brown, not blonde. She resembled a painting over a bar in a gentlemen's club. Defensively, he held out the phone with the speaker button depressed. "My wife wants to talk to you."

"Really?" Layla's finely plucked brows rose in her stunningly beautiful face.

"Indeed I do, Miss Devlin," Nell said. "Let me say I admire your work on screen. You certainly are an up-and-coming young actress. I am sure you wouldn't want to mar your career by getting involved with Joe Dean Billodeaux."

Coolly, the actress answered, "Why would that be?" She didn't bother to cover herself though she put down the provocative leg. He wished he could do the same with his third leg pulsing against his jeans.

"First of all, Joe never uses a condom. He is Catholic and a firm believer in no birth control. We have ten children and no prenup. If I catch him having an affair, I plan to take him for all he is worth, but I will turn over custody of the entire brood to him and his new love. I do hope you enjoy children, because he'll probably want more. You can kiss that tiny waist good-bye, and you will need a boob job after you nurse a few of his babies. I know."

4

Layla's alabaster's skin flushed the entire length of her body, then became even paler than before. In her current role, she portrayed the mayor's daughter who had come to the ranch to flirt with Joe's on-screen son played by a twenty-three year-old. It was possible for him to have a son that old, Joe guessed. Forty stared him hard in the face this year.

After the rustlers killed the father, they made off with the girl as well as the cattle. Once the script let Joe rest in peace, his son pursued the thieves and redeemed the girl, kind of a thin plot. However, Layla put on quite a show as her tight corset and layer after layer of clothes were stripped away, symbolic of her return to savage nature, the director claimed. Because they shot out of sequence, Joe witnessed a few of these scenes. Sex sells without any deep inner meaning, he thought.

Layla groped to cover herself as if she might get pregnant through eye contact. "Is all this true, Joe?"

"*Mais*, yeah, sugar. We got ten kids, and we never use condoms. I am a Cat'lic, me. Don't you never expect to get no abortion, neither."

Layla slid her long legs to the edge of the bed and robed her body in the top sheet. Her complicated costume from the very first scene lay at her feet in a tangle of stays, long lace sleeves, a high collar, and numerous petticoats. Hairpins littered the floor. Joe wondered how long she'd been here while he died over and over again under the hot New Mexico sun. Her dresser would have to put her back together again because he sure wasn't going to help her climb back into that outfit. He stood aside as she gathered the jumble and made certain the sheet covered her like a well-tucked sarong. Barefooted, she padded from the room. Joe scooped up the high-buttoned footwear no one could put on without a shoehorn and deposited them on top of the pile before she made it out of the trailer. The humiliated actress glared at him.

"Look, *cher*, it ain't because you're not gorgeous, but maybe you should try working up some passion with your co-star Brandon. He's more your..." Joe almost said age, but backed away from that thought. "Brandon is more your type."

"Brandon Deal is gay. He hasn't come out yet, the coward. He's afraid it might hurt his career."

"Oh, you been to his trailer, too?"

Without answering, Layla Devlin huffed away to her own domain where some poor soul would have to put up with her tantrum and get her camera-ready again.

Joe closed the door and locked it. He headed back to the bedroom and picked up the phone. "You still there, Nell?"

"I certainly am. I hope that commotion was Layla leaving."

"Yes, you terrified her, Tink."

"I told no lies." Joe could hear the muted laughter in her voice. "That's the first time I ever heard you use your cute Cajun routine to scare a woman off. Very effective."

"Yeah, and they say I can't act. But you forgot to mention how your cancer treatments left you sterile, and since I'm so faithful we don't need to use condoms. Not to mention you only gave birth using in vitro to half of those ten children. All the rest came to us this way, that way, all ways, as the traiteur told us they would."

"Don't remind me. That old woman threatened us

with two more." Talk of having a dozen children always sobered Nell.

"Not threatened. Madame Leleux had the sight. She saw what she saw." A sudden thought caused him to wrinkle his still-handsome brow. "You'd never leave me and kids, would you?"

"If I caught you cheating, I'd do worse than that. But, I'd never willingly abandon you and the children."

"No need to worry, but Tink, seeing that girl naked made me horny. Wish you were here."

An enormous splash drowned out her answer. A whistle sounded. Dean's voice grown deep and manly shouted, "Hey, no cannonballs! You want to drown the little guys?"

Nell had to repeat her answer. "Me, too, Joe. Me, too."

Chapter Two

Weary, Joe entered his trailer the next afternoon. The director had finally called his death scene a wrap. All he'd had to do was stare with his dark eyes wide open and the New Mexico sun glinting off the silver strands in his black hair while his mouth hung slightly open adorned with a trickle of fake blood as the cameras homed in on his beard-stubbled face. A stunt double having the same wide span of shoulders and narrow hips as his own did the actual falling backwards into the dust because his Sinners contract forbid him to engage in any dangerous activities. Joe felt he could have pulled off the dive with ease. He'd been sacked often enough in his eighteen-year career.

He still had to face doing the opening scene with Layla again. The part where he'd herded a few head of cattle into the corral and leaned over the neck of his mount to latch the gate went perfectly. The animal wrangler provided him with a great cutting horse as long in the leg as Joe, very like his horse, Lazy Boy, back home but not as flashy. Rascal could do tricks, too, like fall down dead in the shooting scene. He might make an offer for the animal since L.B. was getting long in the tooth, not that his stud couldn't still service a mare if given the chance.

Joe opened the door of the small refrigerator and plucked out an icy, dark Turbo Dog beer. They'd asked what he wanted stocked in his trailer and got it for him all the way from New Orleans. He chugged it down and considered having another. Might get him through the dialog with Layla, now more awkward to perform than before she showed up in his bed. Nope, better stay sober. Joe Dean Billodeaux did not drink when he had a tough game ahead, not since the early years of his career. He'd take a nap until some flunky called him back to the set. Plenty of flunkies around the set. Layla Devlin had a personal one, a pretty blue-eyed girl appropriately named Patsy. Joe might be willing to bet poor Patsy had borne the brunt of the star's anger after yesterday's rejection.

His bedroom door sat ajar. Sure he'd closed it before going out, Joe moved cautiously into the room. A scorned woman like Layla Devlin might just put rattlers in a man's sheets, and here he was without a real gun that fired actual bullets. The holster slung low on his hips held a weapon loaded with blanks.

Good Lord, not another naked woman, this one wrapped in a blanket with only the very top of her dark hair exposed for the moment. He almost wished it had been snakes until he saw Tink's big brown eyes twinkling at him as she did a slow reveal of her pixie face, then her small, full breasts. Joe knew she wouldn't go any farther down the road, self-conscious of her C-section scar from having the triplets. Guilty about that for having pushed her to have so many babies at one time, he told her over and over that the scar didn't turn him off. Hell, he had scars everywhere from playing football and having surgeries to repair torn muscles and ligaments. Nell said that didn't count. Scars, a little silver in the hair, deeper lines in a man's face, only made him more distinguished. They caused a woman to look old. She kept her hair the same dark brown as the day they met and wasn't adverse to small nips and tucks to stay attractive for him.

An impish smile played on her lips. The little lines at the corners of her eyes crinkled. "Glad I'm here?"

"Oh, baby, yes!" His gun belt fell to floor with a clunk. Joe stripped his leather vest, sweat-soaked shirt, jeans, and modern briefs in record time, forgetting about his boots and spurs until they entangled his feet he was that eager. As he bent over to escape their snare, Nell stroked his backside with her small hand. He thought the hardness of his erection might poke a hole in his gut if he weren't careful. Vaulting onto the bed, he joined his wife under the covers and said, "Top or bottom?" He liked to be considerate that way because it made no never-mind to him. He enjoyed sex any way it came with Nell. Now that he knew Brandon Deal to be gay, having the guy weep over his body and hug him to his chest in the death scene became off-putting, but that scene was over and done. Tink had come all the way from Louisiana to play.

Then, his wife said those dreaded words. "Let's talk first." A little sap left his woody.

"Could we talk after?" he bargained.

"No. I got on a five a.m. flight to get here, and I might fall asleep afterwards. I want to go over what we discussed before you came out here one more time. You promised me and the children you would retire from football at forty."

"I always keep my word."

"You do, but we want you to retire with dignity and grace. No embarrassing yourself with cell phone pictures of your genitals sent to pretty women. No trying to prove you're still young by driving fast sports cars or going to drunken parties."

"I got that out of my system when I *was* young."

"Some men feel the need to repeat those years." Her soft fingers moved up and down on his erection turning it hard again.

"Not me." Joe closed his eyes and thought how great he'd scored a psychologist for a wife. No need to take his problems to the team shrink, Dr. Funk, who had once diagnosed him as a sex addict. Ha! He'd proved Dr. Mind Fuck wrong.

He'd married a woman who climbed aboard and moved over him until he forgot what they'd been discussing. He thought Tink, being tiny, liked to pretend she could dominate him. He let her believe that until the last moment when he rolled over taking her along for the ride and drove deep inside her body until she clenched around his penis and he let go with an ejaculation he'd been saving up for a week.

Afterwards, they slept until the knock came on the door followed by the shout of, "Ten minutes." Joe put on his grubby clothes and went out to be sprayed and dusted again for what he hoped would be his final encounter with Layla Devlin. Not like Nell to sleep through any noise or disturbance. Her mother's ears were always cocked and listening for trouble in their household even in the dead of night. Maybe knowing she'd left the children in the good and competent hands of their staff which included a devoted housekeeper, a ranch manager with commando skills, a nurse who was a former nun, and a bona fide English butler, plus any friends and Sinners past and present who helped with

Camp Love Letter allowed her to rest obliviously for a change. He realized the strain raising ten kids put on Nell, and she still volunteered her psychology skills at the health clinic. After this year, he'd be around to help more. She had his word, not that it wouldn't be a struggle to give up the life he loved on the football field.

****

The open carriage came to a stop near the corral. Joe dismounted from his horse and strode over to address its occupant, Layla in her fancy duds, her pale face shaded by a white parasol. He removed his hat respectfully. "Howdy, Miss Beth. What brings you out this way?"

"Just passing by," Layla said in the faintest of Southern accents. "I surely could use a cooling drink, and I believe you might as well. Is Jody here? I could ask him to join us." Her violet eyes looked deeply into his in a way that said she had no interest in his fictional son.

"Uh, I t'ink he's in da barn."

"Cut! Joe, you aren't playing a Cajun. Put those 't-h's' back in the words and leave out the 'uh'. Again," director Quentin Sibley said.

"I-think-he-is-in-the-barn."

"Cut! No good. This is a simple sentence, but I want you to say it like you know what Layla is up to."

"I do," Joe said.

This time Layla delivered her lines as she leaned forward. The tight corset pushed her breasts up to new heights—about the level of Joe's eyes from where she sat in the carriage. Joe botched his single sentence again. Cut!

12

"Layla, you want the son. You aren't supposed to come on to the old man," Sibley directed. A red Sinners ball cap worn backwards protected his shaved head from the early June rays beating down on all of them. It might be a dry heat, but you could still bake tortillas on a rock. Joe licked his parched lips. Give him Louisiana air wet as a sponge any day. Old man. Now he was sorry he'd given Quentin the hat.

"Could I speak to Joe for just a minute?" Nell stood at Sibley's elbow. How long she'd been watching him struggle, Joe had no idea.

"Who the hell are you and what are you doing on my set?" the director said graciously.

Nell held out her hand. "Mrs. Joe Dean Billodeaux. Love your movies."

She didn't. Joe knew that for a fact. Having too much sex and violence, they never got a showing in their home theater. She'd been against his taking this bit part, but the money spoke, and he thought he'd have fun playing a cowboy. After all, he did enjoy doing a cameo in a football movie called *The Big Score*, but then, he'd only had to play himself, accent and all, for a few minutes.

"I believe I can help if you will let me have a word with Joe." Nell reclaimed her hand from a rather aggressive shake.

"Anything, anything if it gets this fuckin' scene wrapped." Sibley waved a remarkably hairy arm exposed by his tight, black T-shirt and gave her free rein. She stepped carefully over cables and around cameras. Upon reaching Joe, Nell tugged his shoulder down to her level. She whispered in his ear and walked away without giving Layla the briefest acknowledgement. This time her husband delivered the line with a suggestive drawl. The cameras kept rolling as the carriage driver, a black servant, helped Miss Beth down. Both men watched Layla sashay toward the barn, and Joe shot one of his sure-to-get-him-laid grins straight into the lens.

"Now that's a match won't never happen," he remarked to the driver.

"The mayor won't have none of it, but I brings her where she want to go."

Shaking his head, Joe moved away heading back to the corral. Cut. At this point his double usually stepped in to take the bullet in the back as the rustlers swept across the scene to abduct Miss Beth and raid the cattle, but that scene was in the can, thank *le bon Dieu*. Tomorrow, he could go home. Or maybe not.

Joe walked over to his wife watching her admire his long stride. They'd never let their sex life shrivel despite having all those kids, but their privacy certainly suffered. He squeezed Nell's waist. "I'm done here. What do you say we take a few days to ourselves before getting back to Chapelle?"

"I've always wanted to see Acoma Pueblo," Nell said quite seriously.

"Not what I had in mind, sugar, but we can work that into our plans." Then, she smiled.

Twirling her parasol as if it had saw-edged blades on its rim, Layla Devlin stalked to them and sized Nell up with those violet eyes capable of portraying a myriad of emotions on command. At the moment, she favored hatred. "You are short and old like some sort of aging Tinker Bell."

"Oh, I wouldn't aggravate Nell. She might be little,

but her vertical leap is something to behold when she's worked up. I'm the only one allowed to call her Tink." Nell strained against Joe's grip on her waist. "If I weren't holding her back, she'd scratch your pretty eyes out in a minute."

The movie star stepped back nearly tripping on her long skirts. Layla shielded her precious face with the parasol. They laughed at her, which didn't help one bit in allaying her anger. Quentin Sibley strolled over to their group oblivious to the tension. A man who liked to be in control, he swung one arm around Nell's shoulders separating her from Joe and drew Layla in with a hand to her tightly-corseted waist.

"Tell me how you got Joe to deliver his line. I might need to use that technique on other actors."

"I'm afraid it won't work on anyone else. I simply said to use the tone he brings out when he knows our twin teenage daughters are up to something. Treat Miss Beth like the spoiled child she is, I said."

Layla Devlin's eyes narrowed, the better to point her laser beams at Joe's wife. Quentin roared with laughter and releasing Nell, slapped his knee. The actress shook off his other arm.

"Yeah, all but three of our ten are teenagers, and four of those are girls. That's why fathers get gray." Joe took off his Stetson and raked his fingers through his still thick black hair shot through with enough silver it seemed to spark in the afternoon sun. The unruly curl that always escaped to his forehead made an appearance as sexy as ever regardless of a streak of gray.

"Really?" Layla said with her full lips sullen and mean. "I thought you were only getting old. Didn't the Sinners draft Rex Worthy right out of Texas A & M to take your place last year in case you couldn't make it through another season?"

"You haven't seen Rex Worthy on the field very often now, have you? He won't be getting playing time this year either. Besides, I think that boy ain't right."

"Do not tell me another gorgeous guy is gay!" Layla punctuated that statement with a stamp of her high-buttoned shoe, which might have been charming if she weren't such a bitch.

"I'm not sure about it, only he tells everyone who asks that he's still a virgin. What kind of man does that? Most will tell a lie in the other direction if they are, like how many women they've bedded," Joe offered.

Layla jumped right on that statement. "So you were lying about all those women you had early in your career and how great you were in bed."

"I never claimed to be great. The ladies said that. Now that I am…more mature, I regret the way I carried on with women, but I haven't been a virgin since I was fourteen."

"A football player and a virgin." Layla grew thoughtful. "I'm a big fan of the Sinners. When does football season start again?"

"September for the real games."

"We should be finished filming *Savaged!* by then, and I could use a rest. I do so adore New Orleans." Oddly, her southern drawl had returned. "Would you show me around and introduce me to some of the players?" Her gloved hand reached out to touch Joe's arm.

He moved behind Nell and circled his wife's waist with his hands. Nell rose up on her toes as if she might spring at any moment. Layla backed off.

"Sure, the two of us would be happy to show you around. You can come to the ranch and meet the family. I'll invite Rex, too," Joe said over Nell's head.

"That would be so—pleasurable, I am sure." Layla's violet eyes darkened to a shade Nell would refer to as passionate purple when she told the story to her friends.

Quentin Sibley, not a man who liked to be ignored, dusted his perfectly clean hands together. "We're through for today. What say we all go out for a big steak dinner this evening, say seven. I'll book a private room so we won't be bothered by the public and bring Brandon Deal along. All the ladies want to meet him."

"Sorry, we have other plans, but great working with you, Quent." Joe offered a hand grimy from being on the set.

Sibley shook it rather gingerly. "Wish I could say the same. You got the look, Joe Dean, but not the talent, sorry to say. Keep your day job."

"I plan to."

Sibley moved off spouting orders to those who waited on his every word. Layla turned to follow, but Nell could not resist sending one last jibe her way.

"And Miss Devlin, Joe is still great in bed."

Chapter Three

Nell lay curled against Joe's chest absorbing his warmth and lulling herself with the steady beat of his heart. Her husband slept. She did not. What she had to tell him wouldn't wait much longer, but for now she let him rest. He'd gotten a small break from summer training camp and come home more tired than she'd ever seen him. Shortly, he'd be on the road again doing preseason games, though Rex Worthy, trying to show what he could do, would be on the field more than her husband.

For now, she took comfort in the memory of their free time in New Mexico. She'd begun to think of it as their Last Honeymoon with sex more frequent and imaginative than any since their courtship days and early marriage. Because she wanted to see Acoma, Joe arranged for them to stay the night on the steep mesa with its cluster of ancient adobe houses. Not a luxury adventure, they spent the night in a cool, mud-walled room with one tiny window and used the outhouses lined up around the rim of the drop-off. Their hosts were generous and hospitable. She recalled that night sky filled with stars from end to end so close it seemed you could walk upon the path of the Milky Way as the natives believed their dead did in ancient times. Soon, she might be taking that road.

Death stalked her mind tonight. She recognized the

symptoms: tired all the time, nausea, vomiting, bloating. Cancer had reclaimed her, this time not leukemia, but possibly ovarian. She could hide her illness from Joe away at training camp and the children who were self-absorbed like all kids, especially the teenagers, but not from her housekeeper, Corazon, or Nurse Wickersham. They urged her to make an appointment with a doctor, a specialist. She decided to see her good friend and partner at the clinic, Dr. Arminta Green Bullock, better known as Mintay, and get her advice on how to proceed. First, she wanted to tell Joe and prepare him for the diagnosis. Once confirmed, they would break the news to the children together. To think she said she'd never leave them and now might not be able to keep that promise.

Nell rolled aside and brought her knees and arms into a fetal position. She attempted to cry quietly, but Joe awakened. He stretched his six-foot-three frame the length of the bed. "You okay, Tink?"

"I have something on my mind." She tried to make her voice less weepy and kept her back turned from her husband. "Tomorrow, I'm going to see Mintay for a checkup. My cancer might have returned in another form."

Joe sat up, the sheets sliding down the smooth muscles of his chest marred here and there with small scars acquired on the playing field. They rarely bothered with nightclothes but kept some handy in case the children knocked. "Come here. Let me hold you."

"Not scared of catching cancer like you were when we first met?"

"You know I got over that." Since Tink stayed rolled into a ball, he turned her over and tucked her against him.

"I was in remission when we met. Now it's the real deal."

"You don't know that yet. I'll call Coach and tell him I'm not coming back tomorrow. Let Worthy do the passing if he's so keen. I want to be with you when you get the diagnosis."

"Thanks."

Her voice sounded so anguished he wanted to shed a few tears, too, but he held steady for the both of them. Joe rubbed her back until she dozed. He swore he didn't close his eyes for the rest of the night. What if he lost her? What would he do? How could he cope with ten kids?

****

Only Dean, their eldest, noticed anything awry. "Dad, shouldn't you be leaving for training camp? I mean, you don't want Rex Worthy to get the jump on you. This is your last chance for the Super Bowl."

"That's right. This year is one for the thumb. I'm going after that fifth ring with all I got, believe you me."

Too bad Dean wasn't ready to step into his place on the Sinners team. Already six feet tall at nearly seventeen and being scouted by college teams, his firstborn had a brilliant future ahead of him. Reassured, the boy piled into the van driven by Knox Polk, their ranch manager, and, let's face it, bodyguard, with the rest of the brood. By tonight, his family's world might be much less secure.

Joe insisted on driving to the clinic. Nell looked far too haggard from lack of sleep and possibly her condition to be trusted behind the wheel. They took the double cab truck because his legs cramped in the little red compact car she kept for errands and quick trips into town. As he lifted her into the big vehicle, he noticed for the first time the roundness of her belly, the thickness of her waist under the loose blouse she wore. He should have been aware of that last evening, but as usual, he was up for fun and games in the dark, never considering Nell might not want to participate. She'd rarely turned him down in all the years of their marriage except when really ill. Terribly ill.

Her arms and face remained thin, her large, brown eyes underscored with blue shadows. She'd barely eaten any breakfast. A fast growing tumor, then, because he swore in June when Nell visited the set of *Savaged!* she'd had her usual spunkiness and small waist. What a great week that had been, maybe their last for a long time, but she would recover. He'd pull out all the stops to see she got well.

They didn't speak as they rode into town. Afraid jostling might hurt his wife Joe concentrated on avoiding potholes, the curse of all Louisiana back roads. Nell caught on when he swerved across the center line once too often.

"I'm not in any pain, Joe. It's just the nausea and vomiting that's causing me trouble."

He tried to make a joke of it. "Not on my leather upholstery, please." She didn't laugh.

Joe cleared his throat. "Look, if you do have cancer, I'll hand in my retirement papers tomorrow."

Nell laid a cold hand on his thigh and gave it a squeeze. "I know that is the greatest gift you could offer me, but don't. I'd only feel worse taking away your last season, and we have plenty of friends who will help with the children if I'm in the hospital. I hope Nurse Shammy will be able to care for me at home most of the time."

That she'd thought all this out, never saying a word until last night hurt him worse than being buried under two linebackers. "I wasn't with you when you had the triplets and should have been."

"My choice. I wanted you to finish your game. Besides, you delivered our twins. How many men could say that?"

What a long history they had together. He'd thought they would have a long future ahead after he retired. Joe parked in front of the clinic and helped Nell down as if she were a branch of flower petals easily broken and bruised. Running ahead, he opened the clinic door for her and lingered in the opening after she passed.

"I got a few errands to run. Mintay won't want me in with you while she does the exam anyhow."

Joe saw the disappointment in her eyes, but knowing it would be only temporary, he could handle it. "I swear I'll be back for the diagnosis. Don't let the doctor tell you anything before I arrive."

Nell nodded. "Sure, no problem. See you in a little while." She moved toward the examination rooms with her shoulders squared.

Joe rushed back to the truck. Nell probably thought he couldn't handle the situation, but he had lots to accomplish in a short time. First stop, the church of Ste. Jeanne d'Arc where he lit every candle on the Mary altar and prayed, "Mother Mary, spare my wife from cancer" each time a flame ignited. He left a large check in the donation box on his way out.

Next stop, Ike's Barber Shop, a place he hadn't set foot in since he could afford three-hundred dollar haircuts. A place sporting a traditional red-and-white-striped barber pole outside and three chairs inside, Joe Dean had lost his childhood curls here to Ike's scissors right before he started kindergarten. His daddy had put his foot down and said no son of his would go to school looking like a girl. His mama cried when Daddy brought the locks of black hair home in a bag for her to keep, but not Joe. He hated those curls and kept them severely in check since then, all except that one always flopping on his forehead—but the ladies seemed to love it, especially Nell.

Framed pictures of his football exploits decorated the walls above a selection of sports and fishing magazines months and years out of date. As Joe well knew, they covered the girlie magazines that made Ike's place popular with teen boys despite being so uncool. The air smelled of the talcum powder the elderly barber brushed on the shaved necks of his all male customers and not of the scented shampoos and hairspray in unisex salons. His daddy still came here once a month for the same cut he'd worn all his life. Only Ike occupied the shop today. The other two chairs were rented out to barbers who worked hours busier than a Monday morning, busy being a relative term. With his bifocals on the end of his nose, Ike sat in one of the chairs reading yesterday's paper, but he pushed up when Joe entered his shop. Were the barber's hands shaking just a little? Didn't matter for what Joe had in mind.

"Why Joe Dean Billodeaux, I swear you haven't been in here since college. Your daddy keeps me up with all your doings, though." Ike gestured to the publicity stills framed on the walls. "I tell everyone how I give you your first haircut and how you cried."

"Did not!" Joe stopped himself.

Ike had a twinkle in his faded blue eyes. Born Harold Eisenhower, of course he'd been nicknamed Ike after the president and general. The man's hair had long since thinned and turned white, but his sense of humor remained intact. He'd learned the Cajun patois from a grandmother and could tell a pretty risqué joke the in local French, another reason he remained popular with older men. "Got ya!"

"You sure did, Ike. Do me a favor and shave my head."

"Why, you got the ringworm? The ladies are gonna be so, so sad when they see you're going bald."

"No ringworm! I'm doing summer training right now. The heat is getting to me."

Joe wouldn't allow Nell's illness to become the subject of barbershop gossip. She'd lose her hair to chemo, but she wouldn't be alone. This is how a real man showed his support. He took a seat in one of the chairs. Ike flourished a plastic cape over his clothes and plugged in a pair of clippers. The barber started in the back. The floor became host to small piles of black hair spangled with silver. Ike kept up a professional chatter.

"You know this place used to be a beauty parlor way back, Irma's Kuts and Kurls. I bought it out in the Sixties from Irma's daughter and everyone says to me, bad time to open a barbershop, but not so much around here. Not too many hippies in Louisiana. Now the Eighties, those were some good times for the mustache trims." Ike worked his clippers up the sides of Joe's head until only a short Mohawk remained down the center. "Maybe you want to keep this. It's real stylish right now."

Entirely spitless with shock, Joe managed to get out a, "No, take it all off." Jesus, his ears looked huge.

Ike worked the clippers from the back. The last to fall—Joe's single unruly curl. It landed in his lap. "You mind if I keep the clippings? They're gonna be worth something if you get that fifth Super Bowl this season. Think you got a chance? Or do you want to take them pretties home to your mama like last time?" Again the wicked twinkle in the eye as Ike dusted his customer's shoulder with a whisk.

Joe fingered the fallen curl. "Keep all of it except this. You got a bag I can put it in?"

"Sure thing. You want a wax and buff, too?"

"I—ah…" Joe had no idea if Ike joked again. "No, gotta get going. What do I owe you?"

"Fifteen dollars, but I can retire on locks of your hair if you win this year."

"Count on it," Joe said, barely hearing his own words. His head appeared white as brand new soccer ball against the rest of his darker complexion.

Ike broomed the clippings into a dustpan and slid them into a large plastic bag. He handed Joe a smaller one for the curl and accepted a twenty, no change wanted. Joe walked out into the eighty-degree heat of a late July Louisiana morning. Sweat instantly beaded on his bald head. He made a dash for his truck and raced it to one of the Dollar Stores that had popped up on the outskirts of Chapelle. He wouldn't chance being seen in the Walmart this way. Couldn't go in that place without meeting six people you knew.

The store carried Sinners gear. Every place in town did, even the Winn-Dixie and the new art gallery. The black knit cap with the Sinners red devil logo on it cost more than a dollar. He picked two off the rack, tucked them under his arm and headed for the goal line, the cashier at the front of the store. Christ in heaven, here came Miss Lolly and Miss Maxine, the biggest gossips in town, beating him to the counter with a buggy full of cheap canned goods. Joe jammed one of the caps down over his head before they saw who they cut off at the checkout.

"Joe Dean Billodeaux, is that you? Fancy meeting Nadine's rich son in a Dollar Store."

"Miss Lolly, Miss Maxie. I can't resist a bargain just like you."

Miss Lolly nodded. Her red-lacquered hair did not move an inch. She addressed the bored black woman at the counter who waited for the old ladies to unload their cart. "I remember the day we did a novena with Nadine praying for a son. That's his mama, Nadine. She already had four girls. Joe Dean Billodeaux would not be on this earth if it weren't for us."

"Uh-huh," the clerk said laconically. Not a football fan evidently. Good.

Joe helped them unload the cans as fast as he could. Sweat trickled down his neck from under the knit cap with the price tag hanging from the side. The cashier shoved baked beans and canned corn into plastic sacks. Joe reloaded the filled bags into the cart as Miss Lolly fumbled with a change purse containing a wad of one dollar bills. She counted out the total carefully.

Joe intervened with a debit card he knew had at

least five-hundred dollars on it. "Let me get this, ladies. Add on these two hats. I want to wear the one I got on home, so just scan the other twice, okay?"

"Fine by me." The cashier swiped the card and waited for the results.

"Don't the Sinners give you caps, Joe Dean?" Miss Lolly said.

"Ah, yes, but I like these better." The cheap acrylic made his head itch. He refrained from scratching. No sense in encouraging ringworm rumors.

Meanwhile, Miss Maxine with her unlikely shoe polish black hair and sharp dark eyes to match stared at his head. "I never realized what big ears you have, Joe Dean. Wouldn't have noticed before my cataract surgery."

All the better to see you with, my dear. The words from *Little Red Riding Hood* came to his mind. How many times had he read that one to the kids and then played the wolf with them afterwards?

She turned toward the clerk. "You know what they say about men with big ears, or is it big thumbs or big feet?"

The cashier, a big white grin decorating her face, returned Joe's debit card. Miss Lolly tittered and informed her, "Joe Dean has nothing to prove. He has ten children."

"Three are adopted and one is Nell's niece." Why did he hastened to say this? Perhaps because the clerk now looked at him as if he were a wife abuser. "Here let me push your buggy for you ladies. Did you call a cab?"

"No, we drove as usual. The big, black one over there." Miss Maxine pointed a witch-like finger at an elderly Lincoln Continental the size of a small ocean liner. It held its own among the SUVs, trucks, and sub-compacts on the lot.

"T-Bob gave us a very good price on it after Miss Lilliane died. It has hand controls, you know. Still lots of good years on it, Aldus Thibodeaux says, if we change the oil regularly. Of course, mostly we use it for church and the grocery store."

Miss Lolly opened the vast trunk with a key, something he hadn't seen in a while. Joe stashed the bags inside and slammed it shut. "You have a good day, ladies."

"Such a nice boy," Miss Maxine said.

"He wasn't always," Miss Lolly replied in a whisper loud enough to startle a few birds off the electrical wires.

Her hearing must be going. Joe could have sworn the old women were past eighty when Dean came into the world, but he must have been mistaken or they would be in heaven or elsewhere criticizing their fellow man or woman by now. He hurried to his truck eager to get on the road before they did. One more stop, and he'd return to the clinic later than he wanted having run into this pair.

Back in town, he parked on the church lot and cut across the street to Pommier's bakery, hoping and praying they still had some hot beignets left. Nell seldom ate greasy foods, but Joe knew women facing chemo should build themselves up prior to treatment. He wasn't the first man on the Sinners team to have a wife with cancer. Last year, huge Demetrious Mallet, his new nose guard—the replacement for Calvin Armitage who retired after a remarkable twenty years in the NFL—sobbed in the locker room when he learned his wife had breast cancer. The Demon already had a shaved head and could not make the grand gesture, but his wife survived. So would Nell.

Joe made sure the cap covered the top half of his ears before entering the shop. He asked the squat, swarthy baker, "You have half a dozen beignets left, LeJeune?"

"Only what I put aside for myself before I go home to get some sleep. We got petit fours and pig ear pastries."

"No, thanks. Nell hasn't been eating much lately. I wanted to tempt her with something special."

"She can have mine absolutely free. She does good work over at the clinic. Never takes a payment. She treated my mama for depression after I got married."

"I don't want to take your breakfast."

"Hey, I got a whole bakery to choose from, me. I'll put 'em in a bag."

LeJeune Pommier handed over a white paper sack already showing grease spots on its bottom. The scent of an inch of powdered sugar coating the donuts wafted from the opening.

"You tell Miss Nell to enjoy from me."

"I appreciate it."

Last stop, the clinic. Leaving the beignets in the truck, he went inside to find Nell already sitting in Mintay's office. "Sorry I took so long."

A little testy, Nell replied, "Why are you wearing that ridiculous hat with a dangling price tag? It's supposed to go up to ninety-eight today. I told Mintay to take another patient since you were late."

Joe avoided the hat question. "How did the

examination go?"

"She did a pelvic exam, collected blood and urine. Asked about my symptoms like any doctor."

"And?"

"She had her doctor face on. I couldn't tell a thing."

Dr. Green, also known as Mrs. Rev Bullock in the community, bustled in with her white lab coat flying open. Her black hair always worn in a short, practical bob swung a little with her momentum. She kept herself trim and tried in vain to downsize her husband, a former cornerback with the Sinners. To Joe, her green eyes set in a light mocha complexion appeared amused. A slight smile curved her lips. His optimism bubbled up the way it did when his team was two scores down, but he knew they could still win. He clenched Nell's hand harder than intended and ground her small bones together. Intent on the verdict, she didn't flinch.

"I am going to recommend you see a specialist."

Nell's shoulders slumped. "Should we consider aggressive treatment at MD Anderson?" she asked, mentioning the awesome cancer treatment center in Houston.

"I don't think so. You might want to consult Dr. Stewart at Ochsner since he delivered the triplets. Nell, I am ninety-nine percent sure you're pregnant. I used one of the test kits we keep on hand for worried teenagers. It came up positive, but I suspected as much." Mintay's smile burst forth radiant with joy with for her friend. "Congratulations."

"But, I'm sterile from my previous cancer treatments. This can't be."

"I can only say the human body is still a mystery.

Maybe all those hormone treatments you had for in vitro jumped-started something in your system."

"Not possible. The triplets are ten. Too many years have passed. I'm almost forty. This is absurd."

"Sometimes as we near the end of our reproductive life, a woman's body will go into overdrive as if it wants one last chance. Usually, I warn my patients to take extra precautions once they get to forty. In your case, I thought that was unnecessary. Must have been that wild week you and Joe had in New Mexico, both of you all relaxed and loosened up. No responsibilities or children around." Mintay issued a small sigh. "How I'd like to snatch Rev away from his congregation for a week of heaven. Ain't gonna happen. Last time we managed a getaway we went to Samoa for Adam and Winnie's wedding five years ago."

"You want more than three children? I thought you and Rev had completed your family." Nell massaged the hand Joe had crushed.

"Lord, no! I only want what leads up to them with no interruptions."

"Could I ask a question here? When is her due date?" Sweat trickled down the side of Joe's face.

"Mid-February, I'd guess. The obstetrician will give you a firmer time after his exam."

"Good, not Super Bowl week then."

"No, unless she is carrying twins again, and that is a possibility. Nell is larger than most women this far along if she conceived in June, and older women have twins more often. They frequently come early as you know."

Joe shivered. Nell put a hand to his forehead. "Are you sick? Do you have chills and fever? Is that why you're wearing the dumb hat?"

"No, I had a frisson, me. I tell you number eleven and twelve are on the way exactly like Madame Leleux predicted."

Nell removed her hand abruptly. "Not that old woman again!"

"We can do an ultrasound next week if you want," Mintay suggested. "Settle it once and for all."

"I know already." Joe swiped the knitted cap from his head and mopped his face with it. Both women stared, then burst into unrestrained, nearly hysterical laughter.

"What have you done, Joe?" Nell pulled a tissue from the box on Mintay's desk and blotted her eyes.

"I wanted to show you my support if you had cancer." He took the little snack baggie from his shirt pocket. "I saved my last curl for you. I thought I'd go to LeClerc's jewelry store and find a gold locket to put it in. Then, you'd have part of me to hold whenever you went for treatments. You know I don't dance around in the pocket too long. I either throw or go. This time I went too far."

Nell transferred to his lap and put her arms around his neck. "You are the most amazing, loving man." She followed that statement with a long-lasting kiss to his lips that made the doctor squirm with discomfort.

"I could put the two of you in an examination room if you can't wait to get home," Mintay suggested wryly.

"No, thanks. We can wait, but I'd still like to have that locket in case you aren't around when the babies come, Joe."

"I will be. I swear it."

"Don't swear. We can't imagine what life will

bring us."

"That's for sure true. Too bad Madame Leleux is dead, but we could ask her granddaughter."

"No, thanks. She might see more than twelve children in our future."

Joe set Nell on her feet more carefully than he'd handled her when he thought she had cancer. He leaned across the desk and gave Mintay a kiss on the cheek that might have made the mild-tempered Rev jealous. "Thanks for the good news. Let's go buy a locket, Tink."

Joe escorted his wife to the truck without once letting go of her elbow. He placed her inside the cab, latched her seatbelt, and offered her the white sack full of beignets. "You haven't been eating much, so I brought you a special treat."

"No, Joe! Just the thought of grease when I'm pregnant…"

He barely got her out of the truck in time to save his upholstery.

Chapter Four

"Take the bench, Joe. Let Rex do the passing to the receivers. He needs the practice more than you." Coach Marty Buck, his silver crew cut gone white and acquiring a small pink bald spot at the back, hadn't changed much during Joe's long career. He still blew his whistle with vigor and motioned his franchise quarterback to come off the field.

With reluctance, Joe tossed the ball to Rex Worthy and trotted to the bench. The Sinners worked on completing their final day of training camp today, the last of the two-a-day practices, the last of playing outdoors in the stinking heat. Party tonight! Joe doubted if he had the energy for that, but he'd go out for a drink or two with the guys. Rex Worthy would go back to his room and pray for a good season, no doubt.

Over by the ice pile kept to cool off huge, overheated linemen, the Sinner's kicker and punter goofed around scooping up ice chips in plastic cups, making snow cones with juice from the Gatorade cooler. They headed his way and took seats on either side of their quarterback. Joe striped off his helmet and let it dangle from his hand.

"Here, you look like you can use this." Howdy McCoy, the kicker, offered him one of the improvised snow cones. It said something that Joe accepted it.

The punter, Brian Lightfoot, offered him a Sinners

ball cap. "You should cover that bald head before you get heatstroke. Really, Joe, the scalped look is so not you. What *were* you thinking?"

Brian was gay. His comment only made this more obvious. Though his sexual orientation made Joe uncomfortable, as long as the fellow could place a punt where the team needed it, he didn't give a damn who the man slept with. Others simply wrote it off saying all kickers were odd in one way or another. A thought occurred to Joe as he watched Rex Worthy throw a hard but not particularly accurate pass across the field.

Joe slapped the cap on his head. "Brian, does your gay-dar still work, I mean since you got married a while back?" Three years ago, the punter had given the straight life a chance and took boy-hipped, small busted, tall Venetia Hardcastle as a bride. Not that the woman was unattractive, just not Joe's type. Brian always described her as having elegant lines and said nothing bad about his now ex-wife.

"You know how that turned out, but we produced one beautiful daughter. As for the gay-dar, it never quit working, part of the problem."

"So, what do you think about Rex Worthy?"

"While I am sure gay men hang posters of him on their walls, no, definitely not. He's too Jesus-freaky."

"But a guy that age who admits to being a virgin. Something's got to be wrong with him."

"Nothing wrong with loving the Lord or being a virgin, Joe." Howdy McCoy spoke up. He'd been raised as a strict Baptist, but was a little more relaxed now having married a Catholic, the birth mother of one of Joe's adopted kids. "Rex is okay. He's just not much fun."

"Someone should loosen him up. He needs to put some sin into being a Sinner. It might improve his game." A second later, Joe wished he'd kept his mouth shut.

Players stopped their drills at the far end of the field and stared. One of Rex's better passes bounced off the chest of a wide receiver looking toward the sidelines. Practice stopped altogether as Layla Devlin minced her way over the turf on four-inch heels. Her personal assistant wearing running shoes walked a few paces behind holding a battery-operated fan trained on Layla's bare back. The actress wore one of those tops that tied around the neck. Her unfettered breasts jiggled with each step, but her violet eyes hid behind over-sized sunglasses. She'd gone back to light blonde since wrapping *Savaged!* Joe noted, and wore her hair in a high ponytail. At one time, she would have been exactly his type.

"Speak of the devil, and here she comes," he muttered.

Howdy, always a gentleman, said, "Now, Joe. You shouldn't speak that way about a lady."

"She's no lady. I found her naked in my bed while I was making that movie. I can testify those knockers are real."

"Spill!" Brian declared. "What happened next?"

"Nothing. Nell scared her off, but I didn't like her enough to screw her anyhow."

"Was a time liking the woman didn't matter to you, I've heard." Brian sucked on his Gatorade snow cone. "I'd like to see those famous eyes up close."

"I think you will get your chance. She's coming after me again."

36

Layla made it as far as the fifty-yard line before Coach Buck barked, "Who the hell are you? Get off my field. This is a closed practice."

"Layla Devlin, so charmed to meet you." She held out her hand as if she expected Coach to smack a kiss on it.

The three men on the bench sat close enough to hear. Her southern accent had come back though Joe knew Layla had grown up in Iowa, the dull state, she'd told him. He waited for Marty Buck to throw her wagging behind out of the stadium. While Coach did not take the extended hand, he did appear to be drooling a little. Usually, he only frothed at the mouth when really angry. "Good to meet you, too, but I have a practice to run."

"Oh, don't mind me. I'll sit here on the bench beside Joe. We are *old* friends. I stopped by the Superdome to book a skybox for the entire season, and they told me where the team held its camp. Metairie isn't that far away so we simply drove on over here to watch, not to interrupt."

"The guards let you in?" Coach questioned.

"I *am* Layla Devlin. They recognized me. Continue coaching. Don't mind little ole me." Leaving Marty Buck with his mouth hanging open and no words coming out, Layla swayed toward the bench with Patsy, her assistant, in tow.

Since Howdy and Brian both stood up as she approached, Layla slipped easily into a spot next to Joe. Her assistant clambered over the bench in order to keep the fan cooling the star's back.

"Aren't you going to introduce me to your friends, Joe?"

"Howdy McCoy, the kicker, he's married. Brian Lightfoot, the punter."

"*Enchante, mademoiselle.*" Brian executed a small bow over her hand with the same panache he showed when executing the perfect punt.

Layla took in his dark good looks and long, muscular legs. "Gay?" she asked.

"Alas, but not without appreciation for the fair sex. Might I ask to see your famous eyes?"

Flattered, Layla pushed her sunglasses to nest in her thick blonde hair and gave Brian a seductive wink. His large, luminous eyes drank in the sight. He put his hand over his heart. "Wait until I tell the rest of the boys! I know a transvestite who does you in his act. Lee will be so jealous."

Howdy shifted his feet. "It's mighty hot out here. Could I make a snow cone for you?"

"How cowboy charming. I feel as if I'm still on the set of *Savaged*! That would be lovely."

"Would the other lady like one, too?"

"Oh, Patsy is fine back there."

"Tricia," the assistant murmured, her voice barely heard over the whirr of the fan. Her brunette bangs stuck to her forehead with sweat and the rest of her long, straight dark hair straggled out of a large clip on the top of her head. Desperate blue eyes the color of the hot, cloudless summer sky squinted into the sun while a drop of perspiration formed on her pointed chin.

"I'll get two." Lanky Howdy picked up the cups and loped to the ice heap.

Coach Buck broke up the little confab. "Billodeaux, get your ass out here. Work with Worthy. He can't hit a target standing still let alone a running wide receiver.

Relieved, Joe tossed the ball cap aside and picked up his helmet. Layla's pouty lips, slick with a glistening lavender gloss, dropped open. "Did your mean little wife make you shave off your hair to do penance for wanting me? You truly are much less attractive bald. I didn't notice those big ears before at all."

"I didn't want you." Joe rarely lied, but would never confess how his cock and balls had betrayed him momentarily. "We thought Nell's cancer had returned. I shaved my head for her to show my support." He strapped on his helmet immediately.

"That explains the poor fashion choice!" Brian Lightfoot marveled. "Nell is okay, though?"

"Yes, she's fine, pregnant with twins the natural way, but fine."

Howdy arrived bearing the snow cones. "Here, Miss Devlin. And one for you, Miss Patsy. I think you need some fluids, too. Did I hear you say Nell is pregnant again?" Howdy shook his head causing his auburn hair to fall across his face. His sprinkling of freckles was obscured by the redness of his fair face in the sun. "You still got it, Joe. Brave, too. Cassie and I decided to quit after having the two kids—and Tommy of course. Congratulations."

Mention of Tommy didn't make Joe feel any younger. His adopted, redheaded son was nearly the same age as Cassie when she'd given birth to him. "Thanks," he muttered.

"No joke, then, about your never using condoms. Good thing I haven't come for you, Joe. Patsy, higher up on my neck!" The assistant adjusted the fan to allow the breeze to part Layla's hair and cool the slender column of her throat. Patsy sipped the snow cone gratefully.

"You gonna jaw with the fans all day or come out here and show the kid how to throw a perfect spiral, Billodeaux?" Coach shouted. He added a blast of his whistle for good measure.

Joe started moving, but before he got very far, Brian cupped his sensuous lips and shouted, "Nell is expecting twins."

That broke up the practice as word spread up and down the field. The players crowded their quarterback with back slaps and congratulations. Coach Buck took off his hat and stomped it into the grass. "Are we going to practice, or what? First preseason game next week, and don't tell me they don't count. Back to your drills!" As the men retreated to their posts, Coach said, "You never cease to amaze me, Joe."

"I plan to give you an amazing year." Joe paused for a second. If Layla hadn't come to seduce Joe, who did she want? Howdy had moved down the bench a few feet as if he might be her target.

The star's voice trilled, "Which one of you lovely men will point out Rex Worthy to me?"

Brian waggled a graceful finger at the backup quarterback who had congratulated Joe and gone right back to work drilling footballs into the ground yards from where they were supposed to go. Good on the short hard pass, great on running the ball, but hopeless on the long throws where Joe excelled. Joe picked up a football, showed his handhold, cocked his arm without releasing, and gestured to Rex to do the same. He called out a route to the wide receivers and waited for them to get down the field. Both threw their balls at the same time. Joe's landed in outstretched arms as softly as a baby being rescued from a high fall. Worthy's pass bounced off the helmet of his target.

"Getting better," Joe said. And better. Layla Devlin had come for Rex Worthy.

Chapter Five

Since Joe made no offer, Layla Devlin arrived at the post-practice party on Brian Lightfoot's arm. As had become the custom, the team took over Mariah's Place, the nightclub in the French Quarter that Howdy McCoy purchased for his long-lost mother several years ago once he got over the shock of discovering she earned her living as a fading torch singer and part-time waitress in Vegas. Despite her own dubious morals, Mariah Coy watched out for "her boys" making sure none of them went home too drunk to drive or took up with the wrong kind of woman—at least not in her club. Having given up her house in the Musicians' Village, she now lived over the night spot, closing down the place evenings and sleeping most of the day.

"Good evening, Billy," Brian said to an elderly fixture in the club.

Mariah's shaking white-haired personal bodyguard returned the salutation. He co-habited with the singer, but how much hanky-panky he had left in him was debatable. Still, Billy hand-selected the other guards to take care of Mariah's Place and never went upstairs without Mariah on his arm.

"Who is this beauty, Brian? You thinking about taking a second wife?"

"May I present Layla Devlin, star of stage, screen, and television? I merely escort her for the evening."

Billy squinted his watery blue eyes. "A looker, but she can't hold a candle to my Mariah. Better take a seat. The music is about to start."

As Layla intended, Brian paraded her to the front of the room with Patsy trailing. One of the lesser Sinners gave up his seat for her while the punter lounged against a wall and the assistant faded into the shadows. By attending with Brian, Layla signaled her interests rested elsewhere. He rarely stayed long before departing for the kind of bars he preferred.

With a hat a la Frank Sinatra pulled down low on his forehead, Joe made no move to get closer. He leaned against the bar next to Howdy McCoy. Rex Worthy sat on his other side nursing the single beer he'd had in his hand since they arrived after Joe insisted he needed to learn how to be part of the team on and off the field. He and Howdy planned to depart after a couple of drinks and Mariah's opening song, leaving Rex to deal with Layla. Best to let the team blow off steam without their leader, Joe thought, not admitting to himself how exhausted he became after the two-a-day practices. As for Howdy, nothing suited him more than going home to his family.

The lights dimmed. Dry ice swirled in the spotlights illuminating the stage. Clad in gold sequins, Mariah Coy burst through the red velvet curtains. Her slinky dress barely covered her large, enhanced breasts. As usual, she wore one of her outrageous red wigs and high heels that jacked up her height considerably. In a voice roughened by years of smoking, she introduced herself, the band, and segued into her signature song, *Fever*. She bent way over during certain parts of the song, giving a treat to the men in the first row—and

Layla Devlin to whom she gave a green-eyed stare. Mariah didn't care to be upstaged by anyone in her place.

"I wish she'd give up the cancer sticks," Howdy muttered. "Her lungs aren't getting any better. I told her she can't smoke around the grandchildren and that helps some."

"Mariah can't change any more than my mother will stop butting into my life. She's going to be some mad when she discovers the team found out about the twins before we told the family." Joe finished his drink decisively and waved away a refill.

"Nadine won't hear it from me." Howdy set aside his beer as the song came to a conclusion. "Let me say goodnight to Mom before we leave." He made his way to the side of the stage to be buried in Mariah's big bosom as she kissed him on the cheek and dragged him into the spotlight.

"This is my son, Howard McCoy, kicker for the Sinners. Here's to a Sinners' Super Bowl. One round of drinks on the house!"

Another beer appeared at Rex Worthy's elbow. "That's really Howdy's mother? I mean I knew Mariah Coy was his mom, but she's so different from him."

"Not like yours, huh?" Joe tossed back the free drink. Howdy was driving.

"My parents were missionaries."

And only ever did it in one position strictly to produce Rex Worthy, Joe thought, but did not say. "Well, we can't all be as lucky as Howdy with a celebrity for a mother. I'm leaving."

"Me, too, I guess."

"You stay a while and mingle with the other guys

on the team. Try not to be such a stiff, okay? The more they like you, the more they want to protect you on the field."

Not that the boy couldn't take a hit. Though six-three like Joe, Rex was built like a bull through the chest and shoulders. He could ram his way out of the pocket and down the field. Maybe his bulky muscles impeded long throws. That's what Joe figured. Rex affected one of those three-day stubbles that made his broad face appear tougher and some ladies adored, but not Nell. She didn't much like beard burn. Since Rex wasn't into the ladies, he probably just didn't like to shave. Brown hair, hazel eyes, nice enough looking guy to attract women, but as a Sinner that wouldn't be a problem even if he was ugly as a dog's butt.

"If it will help my game, sure, I'll stay."

"All right then. Don't do anything I wouldn't have done at your age."

"That gives me quite a bit of leeway," Rex answered with some discomfort.

"Damn right. Come on, Howdy, take me safely home," Joe said as his kicker approached wiping Mariah's lipstick from the side of his face. As they moved to the exit, Layla made her move toward the bar and Rex Worthy. Heaven help the kid. He wouldn't know what to do with her.

Rex remained unaware of the actress closing in on him, but Mariah Coy's green eyes followed her the whole way. He tried to start a conversation with one of the linemen on his other side by asking what church he attended, but the guy simply grunted and moved to join some of his buddies at a table. Mariah introduced the guest singer for the evening. As the music started again, couples hit the dance floor, making Layla and her entourage for the evening weave among them.

Finally, she slithered into place next to Rex and crossed her lengthy legs. Now, he couldn't help but notice her. A wonder she could sit in those tight, white skinny jeans. The high wedge sandals on her feet showed off toenails painted the same glistening lavender as her long fingernails. She wore a deep purple tank top covered by a transparent shirt dotted with small violets, a symbol of shyness that didn't suit her at all. Rex wondered what marvel of engineering held her breasts up, reprimanded himself for impure thoughts, and took a long draw on his second beer.

Standing behind the actress, Brian Lightfoot issued an introduction. "Rex, this is Layla Devlin, the actress. She wanted to meet you."

Layla tossed her loose blonde hair over her shoulders and waited for his adulation.

"Sure." Rex supposed he should say he liked her movies, but he'd never seen one. They had a reputation for being steamy and inflaming.

When he forgot to offer his hand, the actress put hers on his shoulder. "My, you are so tense after that workout today. Her other hand landed on the opposite shoulder. The lavender nails dug into his muscles. She slid off the barstool to get closer and more or less forced herself between his legs. Her breasts rubbed lightly against his chest, and her nipples hardened against the tank top. All the while, Layla pinioned him with her unusual eyes.

"It appears my escort service is no longer needed. You still back there, Patsy? I doubt Miss Devlin will want you for the rest of the night either. Can I drop you somewhere?" Brian offered.

"Yes. No. I mean I'm still on duty. Sometimes Miss Devlin needs my assistance to get back to her room. Please call me Tricia, short for Patricia," the assistant said.

"As you wish, Trish." Brian removed one of his cards from a small metal case with an art deco design on the top. "Have a pen?"

"Always. For autographs and such."

Tricia delved into a huge black handbag filled with organizer pockets, and offered one blue and one black. Brian selected the blue and neatly wrote his cell phone number on the back of the card. He pressed it into Tricia's hand. "In case you need any assistance. New Orleans isn't the safest of cities. Might as well take this seat since Miss Devlin isn't using it."

"Thank you." The PA perched on the edge of the barstool with her feet clad in sensible black pumps tucked on the rail. She centered her bag on the lap of her classic little black dress. When the fat, bald bartender offered her the free drink, she shook her head, barely moving the chignon of dark hair pinned at her nape. "No, I'm working."

"Want flat Coca-Cola then?" the barkeep asked. "The johns don't know the difference."

Her face flushed. "Not that kind of work. I am Miss Devlin's PA."

"That's what they all say," he joked. "Hold up a hand if you change your mind."

Rex leaned back to escape the relentless pressure of nipples pushed against his chest. He reached an arm out, grasped the beer bottle, and took a big swig. The suds went down the wrong way, and he began to cough.

Brian Lightfoot slapped him on the back a few times, causing Rex to lean in toward Layla again, not sure which one made him more uneasy. At least, his spasm removed her hands from his shoulders.

"If you are settled, I must be on my way, much as I'd like to stay and see how this plays out. Good night and good luck to you all." With a final impish pat to Rex's back, Lightfoot departed their company.

Rex cleared his throat. "Sorry about that. It's so smoky in here. I can't abide smokers." He eyed Howdy's mother holding out a cigarette for Billy to light.

"Good that I don't smoke, then. I only snort." Layla cocked her head at Rex and smiled. Registering the horror on his face, she backpedaled. "That's a Hollywood joke, darling. I believe in keeping myself pure inside and out. I go for regularly scheduled detoxifying sessions."

Behind Layla's back, Tricia coughed once. "Sorry, the smoke." She waved a hand before her face when Rex Worthy smiled her way. He had a good, honest smile, strong unstained teeth with nothing feral about them despite the beard stubble surrounding his lips, the kind of grin her brothers back on the farm sported when they teased their only sister. She found herself answering it with one of her own, quickly wiped away when her boss turned around suddenly.

"Patsy, I need the little girl's room. Rex, please save this seat right next to you and order a cosmopolitan straight up for me like the gentleman I know you are." Layla sashayed in the direction of the restrooms. Tricia followed.

As soon as the door shut behind them. Layla

positioned herself before the mirror over the sinks. She fluffed her hair, smoothed on more lipstick taken from the tiny purple velvet bag swinging from her wrist. "This isn't working, Patsy, but why?"

"He might be shy. You are coming on awfully strong. Or maybe he is the kind of man who likes to take the lead."

"Every man wants Layla Devlin—except that jackass, Joe Dean Billodeaux and the so very gay Brandon Deal. I believe I could seduce Brian Lightfoot without any trouble however."

"Maybe."

"I need to be more relaxed. My pills, Patsy." Layla held out her palm.

Tricia found the bottle of prescription meds held securely within a loop in her large bag. "Take one and don't drink afterwards."

Layla shook out three and swallowed them dry one at a time. "Now I do need that cosmo. I don't have to pee." She stalked out of the restroom without using the facilities.

"But I do," Tricia said to the closing door. She hurried knowing what a train wreck Layla Devlin could be if unsupervised. In the few minutes it took to wipe and wash, Layla had plotted a collision course before Tricia returned to the bar. The cosmopolitan glass sat on the counter drained to its last dark pink drop, and the bartender worked on preparing another.

Rex Worthy, his broad brow creased, said, "Shouldn't you slow down a little, Miss Layla?"

Layla, her smile already a little lopsided along with her posture, answered, "You'd take good care of me if I got sick. I know that. I can trust you."

"Well, sure. I'd help any lady in distress, but..."

The second cosmopolitan arrived and joined the first in Layla's stomach. "Another!"

Tricia shook her head at the bartender. "We need to get her back to the hotel. She took some pills that aren't to be mixed with alcohol. If you'd help me get her into a cab?"

Rex immediately offered an arm. Layla wrapped it tight around her waist. "My hero."

They struggled to the exit with Layla boneless in his grasp. The bored paparazzi, lurking outside Mariah's Place as usual when the Sinners were in town, perked up as the door opened. So far the evening had been a bust with Joe Dean going home early in the company of Howdy McCoy who hadn't given them any fodder since his famous sophomore kicking slump years ago. A large presence hard to ignore, Rex hailed a cab and got an instant response. He hauled Layla between the tightly packed parked cars along the street, put her inside, and held the door for Tricia.

"Thanks, Mr. Worthy. You can go back inside now. I'll take it from here."

"Noooo! I want Rex to take me home," Layla wailed. Her armed snaked out of the cab and grabbed the quarterback by the oversized belt buckle he wore with his jeans. She jerked him forward making him bang his head against the top of the doorframe. Cameras flashed.

"Shove her over and get in quick," Tricia directed. "Driver, the Windsor Court...fast!"

"The Windsor, guys," the closest paparazzo shouted. His comrades raced for their cars.

Inside the taxi, Layla attempted to open that great

big belt buckle. Tricia leaned over and shoved her hands away. "Do not molest him, Layla."

"Maybe he wants to be molested. Could be he wants to get laid for the very first time—like a vir-er-gin."

As they drew up before the Windsor Court Hotel not all that far away, Tricia piled out with a red-faced Rex following. He dragged Layla from the seat and draped her over her assistant while he paid the cabbie, then both hauled her to the entry of the luxury hotel.

"Do you need help getting her to her room?"

"Absolutely not! Tip the doorman for some help. I won't have your image sullied by her."

"My image doesn't matter if you need me." Rex tucked the tongue of his belt into the buckle.

"I can handle it. And here come the men of the yellow press. Get back in the cab quick and make a run for it. We will be fine."

"I'll call tomorrow and see how she is."

"Don't. Go, go, go!"

Accustomed to obeying that kind of command, he did. The doorman had a strapping bellhop ready and waiting. The best shot any of the photographers got was of Layla being carried onto an elevator that accessed a private floor by a paid employee of the hotel. Ah well, better than nothing.

In the safety of their suite where the bellhop deposited his load in the bathroom, Tricia got out the brown bottle of ipecac syrup from her black bag. She held it to Layla's lips. "Drink."

"Oh, come on, Patsy. I was only acting. I thought he'd come up to the room, but you queered that deal." The actress laughed. "Queer deal like Brandon Deal. I am feeling a little woozy though."

Tricia yanked the star's head back by her long hair and held the bottle to her enhanced lips. "Drink or I will pour it down your throat."

"All right already!" Layla chugged the contents of the bottle. It worked fast. She made no effort to vomit in the toilet but instead spewed her two cosmopolitans and heaven knew what else over the front of her assistant. Wiping her mouth on the back of her hand, she said, "Let that teach you to get between me and what I want, Patsy."

Chapter Six

Joe sat at the breakfast bar in his New Orleans condo. Nell, dressed in a nightie and robe that parted a little over her baby bump, bustled around the small kitchen putting a meal on the table. She'd absolutely forbidden him to go out for greasy beignets. Instead, she slapped down bowls, spoons, a carton of milk, and boxes of cereal, shoved the basket of fruit his way, and poured him a cup of dark roast coffee made the way he liked it. She wrinkled her nose at the smell. Another thing she didn't tolerate well when pregnant: coffee, especially strong coffee. Her plate held two slices of dry whole wheat toast, her cup, an herbal tea. Dr. Stewart at Ochsner had confirmed both the pregnancy and the presence of twins in her womb yesterday. No surprise to Joe. Even years gone, Madame Leleux knew her stuff when it came to predicting births.

While Nell showered earlier, Joe put a Sinners cap on his bald head and sneaked downstairs to ask Greg, the doorman, for a selection of the latest tabloids. A few days had passed since the end of summer training. Coach magnanimously offered a short break to the team before they went on the road tomorrow for the first of the preseason games. Nell would head back to the ranch with the good news, but she wanted to wait until Joe returned before telling their family. For that reason, he held the scandal sheets low on his lap.

A smile crept past his guard. Not all the rags showed that great picture of Layla's hand snaking out of the cab to jerk Rex Worthy by his belt buckle, and only one photographer caught him hitting his head on the roof of the taxi. The headline was particularly sweet. *Virgin No More?* He'd ridden up in the elevator with Brian Lightfoot returning from a light jog, but the punter couldn't answer that question either. Unlike Howdy, Rex was not his best friend and unlikely to pick a gay man to confide in at any time.

Secretly pleased by the headline below the fold as well, Joe took care to keep that one hidden. *Joe Dean Scores Again!,* it read. The tabloid had used a file photo portraying him with his sexiest grin. A few years old, he had less silver in his hair and not as many lines on his face. Reliable sources reported the quarterback's wife to be pregnant with twins and asked another question—*Super Bowl Babies?*

"What's so amusing?" Nell asked.

Before he could answer, the phone rang. Saved by the bell—or not. Caller ID indicated his mother. She started right in on him directly after he said hello.

"You know how I like to go to the grocery early while they got everything fresh. What do I see at the checkout? My own son grinning at me because his wife is expecting twins. What for you don't tell your own mother first before the newspapers? I thought you was out of those eggs you paid Nell's sister for long time ago."

"We did it all by ourselves. Look on it as another miracle, Mama."

"Since Madame Leleux said, I knew you had two more coming, but I figured they would be like Teddy and Stacy, kids you might adopt, though you never did adopt your niece."

"Stacy didn't want to be adopted. Loyalty to her parents, I guess. Being her guardians is good enough."

Mawmaw Nadine never kept her voice low. Nell picked up words of the conversation here and there. She looked as cross as he imaged his mother to be. "What have you done?" his wife mouthed at him. Trying to look innocent, Joe shrugged. Nell ripped at the papers he held on his lap. Her eyes took in Rex Worthy being seduced, then slid below the fold. "Hang up," she said.

"I apologize, Mama. Word got out unintentionally. You should have been the first to know. Look, we haven't told the kids yet. Would you keep it quiet for us?"

"Sure, because I can keep a secret unlike my own son. Well, makes no never mind now. You know nothing brings me more happiness than a new baby in the family. Two new babies is even better. You done good, Joe. Tell Nell she needs to get plenty of rest and give up the sex, okay."

"I will. Always great to hear from you." Reluctantly, he put away the phone, the only thing standing between him and Nell, a woman as steaming as that cup of hot tea by her hand. He checked to see if she'd taken all the papers off his lap. No, he still had a layer for protection.

"You told the team first!"

"Not exactly. Brian was ragging me about my shaved head. I explained about how we thought you had cancer, how I wanted to be really supportive. Then, when I said you were fine, the second part sort of slipped out."

"We weren't even sure about the twins until the ultrasound yesterday. I'm surprised these papers don't know the sex and the names already." Nell shoved the tabloid in his face. Good, she'd forgotten about the tea.

"Well, neither do we. The doctor couldn't tell yet, and I don't need to know. It only matters that they are healthy, right? Even Dean doesn't care if we have more girls than boys since he discovered how great the opposite sex could be. The twins bring all their friends home. It's a pretty good selection."

"We are not raising Dean to be a teenage Lothario like you were."

"No, no, I didn't mean that! I meant to say he'd be happy to have two little sisters. All the kids will be."

Nell dropped the papers, hitched herself onto one of the high stools, and buried her face in her hands. "No, they won't. All but the triplets are teenagers. They will be mortally embarrassed by this." Tears oozed between her fingers.

"Don't cry, Tink. Think of all the free babysitters we have on hand." Joe let the rest of the tabloids drift to the floor and took Nell on his lap. "It's gonna be fine, sugar. Fine and dandy, you'll see. Look, I didn't plan to spend today driving back and forth to Chapelle, but we can. We'll get there before the kids come home from school and call a team meeting when they arrive. One snide comment about us being too old for more kids, and they get stall-cleaning duty for a week."

"Okay," Nell sniveled.

"It's just your hormones talking right now. You know how you get when you're expecting."

If Nell didn't remember, Joe certainly did. She had fits of jealousy, one of which had lead to their twin girls being delivered in the bathroom of a motor home, and chafed at being confined to bed rest for her multiple births. This would be another long haul with a large load, but he'd become wise enough in the ways of marriage never to say those words.

"You'd be tetchy, too, if you were about to swell up like you'd swallowed two watermelons whole while half the women in the world chase after your husband. I see Layla Devlin is in town."

And so it began. "After telling me how unattractive I am bald, Layla only showed interest in Rex Worthy." Joe retrieved one of the tabloids. "See, she made a move on him the other night."

Nell scanned the article. "Well, unless they did it in the taxi with her assistant watching, I'd say Rex is still a virgin. By the time the paparazzi arrived, he'd left and some bellhop hauled her wiggling ass to her room. Poor Rex to be pursued by a woman like that. I mean he is entitled to his principles. You should help him get rid of her."

"How, by throwing myself between them?"

"No! Some other way. You'd help any other guy on the team." Nell reached up and removed Joe's Sinners ball cap. She leaned back in his embrace. "Layla is right. You look terrible bald. Would you consider keeping your head shaved for the next six months until I have the babies?"

"I'd do it for cancer, but not for more kids. I don't want to frighten the new babies with my huge ears."

Nell closed in on one of his lobes and nibbled. "I think I am almost over the morning sickness phase of pregnancy and entering the horny phase."

"Last thing my mama said was we should lay off

the sex."

"When have I ever listened to your mama?" She gave that earlobe a really long suck and shifted her position from sitting on his knee to wrapping her legs around his back. Nell rubbed against the erection she provoked in his jeans.

Joe could have cited a few incidents where his wife gave in to the steamroller tactics of Nadine, but he held his tongue because Nell stuck hers in his ear. He stood, taking his wife with him, and moved toward the bedrooms. They only got as far as the Madame Pompadour room, as Nell liked to call it. All pale blue brocade and gold accents with a crystal chandelier over the large bed and white, spindly-legged furniture intended for female guests, their daughters fought to stay here when they visited. Their mother never told them it remained as a relic from their father's womanizing days.

Her baby bump hadn't gotten big enough to prove any impediment yet, but Joe went as gently as he could considering that Nell raked her nails across his back under his fitted black T-shirt to spur him on. He'd only managed to get his bottoms off when the urge struck Nell really hard. Earlier in the summer with cancer on her mind, Nell's lovemaking had been preoccupied and routine. He should have caught on then that she worried about something, but since sex was always good for him, he'd missed it. Now, she came quickly once, and then again waiting for him to finish, very satisfying for both.

Now they lay waiting for their heartbeats to return to normal and watching the morning sunlight dance in the crystals of the chandelier and shed little rainbows across their half-naked bodies. "I needed that," Nell said.

"It was great for me, too. Shower together?"

"Sure, I could use another one after getting hot and sweaty." Nell rolled off one side of the bed. "Meet you there." She paused to regard the brocade bedspread they'd never turned down. "That will have to go to the dry cleaners." She didn't seem at all upset.

The doorbell rang and sent his Tink sprinting for the bathroom. Joe groaned and got into his jeans commando. What now?

Brian Lightfoot stood on the other side of the door with Howdy McCoy hovering behind him, one of the disadvantages of having a condo in the same building as other members of the team. Brian exuded a scented body wash and wore his long, dark hair slicked back wet, both proof that he'd cleaned up after his run. Howdy, clad in grungy sweats and sporting a light, reddish stubble on his face, looked like a man dragged from his bed a little too early.

"May we come in? I hope we aren't disturbing anything," Brian said.

A little flushed, Howdy added, "We waited until the headboard stopped banging against the wall, then waited a few minutes more before we rang. You could hear that noise all the way out in the hall."

"Good thing I own the entire floor then." Reluctantly, Joe allowed them to enter.

Brian held out a peace offering. "I brought beignets, still warm."

Nell's head poked from the bathroom door. "Save some for me." She retreated again.

Getting to the point as if he were really, really

tired, Howdy said, "My mom called me from the club around closing time. She doesn't like the looks of Layla Devlin and thinks we should protect Rex from her wiles. Just try to get back to sleep after the images she left in my mind. Then, Brian comes along singing the same song this morning."

"Not that Rex is a dear friend, but having met Miss Devlin close up I'd say she is a nasty piece of work. She treats her nice assistant worse than a slave and sleeps with all her leading men. Good thing you only had a bit part, Joe."

"She tried with me and Brandon Deal and went back to Hollywood frustrated."

"Unsatisfied. That explains why she's after Rex. Imagine what the tabloids will say if she actually takes his cherry." Brian snooped in the cupboards looking for just the right plate to serve the beignets.

Clad in a cute yellow terry exercise outfit with an elastic waistband, Nell whizzed by and snatched the beignets from his hands. She dumped her dry toast into the sink, rooted in the bag like a truffle pig sniffing out powdered sugar, and refilled her plate with two of the donuts. "I'm over my morning sickness," she declared.

"What about the grease?" Joe said.

"A little grease never hurt anyone. Help yourselves to coffee."

Only Howdy took her up on the offer. Joe reheated his in the microwave.

"Not that I don't get a charge out of your mother, Howdy, but why is she so concerned about Worthy's innocence?"

Joe's kicker took a deep swallow of his brew. "Maybe because she couldn't protect mine."

Joe claimed the beignet bag before Nell dove in for seconds and fished a couple pastries out for himself. "Last time I checked, Rex Worthy was a grown man capable of handling his own problems. He must have fended off women in college. Maybe he reads the Bible to them until they fall asleep, and he can sneak away from their beds. If he does want to change his status, I must say Layla has some prime goods." As punishment for that statement, Nell purloined one of his beignets. Or maybe she was simply ravenous from great sex. He'd go with that idea.

"Rex wants to wait until marriage like I should have done." Howdy sorted through the powdered sugar in the bag to see if he could unearth another beignet before Nell got them all and found one.

"Still full of Baptist guilt after marriage and two kids? Do you really regret having practiced a little beforehand?" Joe questioned.

"Not so much, but I respect his position. I'd like to help him out. He doesn't have many friends on the team."

Joe sighed over his plate and sent a cloud of powdered sugar into the air. "Got any ideas?"

Brian fastidiously brushed the sugar fallout from the sleeve of his casual pink shirt open at the throat to show off his evenly tanned olive-toned skin. "We could find someone for him to marry quickly."

Joe shook his head. "Easier said than done."

"Not if we flood the market with all the nice, eligible young women we know. We have them over to the ranch for a barbecue sort of like a secret Bachelor show," Nell suggested, her mouth ringed with white sugar. "Are all the beignets gone?"

"Have mine." Brian handed over a single donut, the last in the sack. "My ex-wife might know someone. We are still on great terms. An elegant woman but too old for Rex."

"I think Cassie's youngest sisters are around Rex's age," Howdy offered.

"Some of your many nieces might be available. Ask your mother. It will give her something to do besides butt into our life." Nell delved a finger into the beignet bag but came up with nothing but a white-coated pinkie that she sucked as avidly as Joe's earlobe.

"Okay, fine by me. You know I'm always up for a barbecue. We'll invite our usual friends as a cover, maybe during the break between the preseason games and the start of the regular season," Joe capitulated.

"Not too many of the younger team members. We want Rex to have lots of choices without having to compete too hard," Nell cautioned.

"I have to invite everyone on the team, but if I tell them families are coming and only beer and soft drinks will be served, the single guys will leave early to get some action in the clubs before midnight."

Glumly, Joe poured more coffee and hid his face in the mug exposing the top of his shaved head to the others. To think he had to save the virtue of his own replacement. What a bitch that would be, or which bitch would it be might say it better. Nell stared at him as if she read his mind. Mentally he corrected that statement to, "Which nice young lady would Rex Worthy choose?"

Chapter Seven

Unknowing that his teammates discussed his fate only a few blocks away, Rex Worthy sat at a table outside Café du Monde enjoying his own beignets and café au lait. With the heat and humidity of New Orleans still keeping the tourists at bay, he could sit in peace without being bothered by autograph seekers. The locals, used to seeing Sinners players around, pretty much respected their space. Wearing one of the plain red team caps minus the winking devil logo and some expensive shades did help to preserve his anonymity, but his size could not be hidden easily even behind a planter with a short, thick palm tree in it. The palm appeared to have sprouted a pair of very broad shoulders along its trunk.

He watched what's-her-name, Tricia—or was it Patsy—scurry by almost colliding with his table and getting in the takeout line. She seemed as harried as ever, but looked kind of cute in modest shorts, a not-too-tight pink T-shirt with the women's breast cancer logo on it, and her usual running shoes. Today, she wore her dark hair long, straight, and loose over her shoulders with her bangs brushing the tops of her eyebrows. Not as leggy or busty as Layla, he found the PA to be pleasantly slim, but not stick thin like lots of women nowadays, and a nice height for a woman, neither too tall nor short. Pretty blue eyes not as exotic or unnerving as Layla's.

Having invoked the actress's name like a demon in his mind, Rex hunched his shoulders hoping Layla Devlin did not lurk nearby. The woman left message upon message for him at Sinners headquarters. He tried to make clear to the actress when he answered one of them that he'd be out of town for the preseason games. She should go home to Beverly Hills and not wait around for him to be available. Obviously, Layla remained New Orleans, but she didn't appear to be with her assistant. Relaxing, Rex stretched out his long, thick-thighed legs and leaned back in his chair.

Having fulfilled her mission, Tricia retraced her route with a sack of beignets and two cups of coffee in a holder. As intent on making good time as an UPS deliveryman, she forged ahead without looking and stumbled over Rex's outstretched feet. He caught her elbow, thus preventing a face plant, but the coffee cups went soaring like missiles, their plastic caps flying off and their contents spraying like unused rocket fuel.

"Oh, no! Oh, no!" Layla's assistant cried.

"It's only spilled coffee." Rex raised his sunglasses in case she didn't recognize him. "Rex Worthy, remember?"

"Yes, yes, I noticed you when I arrived but thought you would prefer your privacy, Mr. Worthy. She only gave me a half hour to get here and back. Those donuts better still be warm, she said. Now I have to go back in line."

Tricia's blue eyes glanced woefully at the large family that had been behind her. They still worked on their order. Who wanted juice or milk? Who was old enough to drink coffee, a huge debate evidently? How many beignets to order to feed their horde?

Rex raised a hand. A small, oriental girl in a white jacket hurried to his table. "Need a refill, sir?"

"Not for me. Could you bring two au laits to go, please?"

"Sure thing." She rushed off to personally fill the cups.

"Why don't you sit down and catch your breath, Patsy."

"Please, please call me Tricia, short for Patricia, Welles. I hate Patsy." Nervous as the nearby pigeons being spooked by the smallest of the children waiting in line, she sat on the edge of one of the metal café chairs.

"I can understand that. Call me Rex. Mr. Worthy is my father. Actually, he's Reverend Worthy. Could I ask you a kind of personal question? Why do you put up with Layla Devlin? She treats you like dirt."

It registered on Tricia that any other man would have said shit. Again, he reminded her of her brothers. Their mama did not allow foul language at home, though she knew the boys used it behind her back. On the Welles farm, people shoveled manure when Mom was around.

"Because we come from the same dirt, I guess, and then there is the matter of money. I grew up with Layla in Iowa, only she was Louise Dillman then. She lived in town. My family farmed out in the sticks. We went to school together, had the same goals, and often got in each other's way. I played Maria in *The Sound of Music*. The teacher directing the show cast her as the Baroness the Captain was supposed to marry."

Trying to keep up his end of the conversation, Rex said, "I've seen the movie many times, my mother's favorite. Isn't that what they call type casting?"

"Yes. In the church play about the Bible, I'm the Virgin Mary. Layla played Salome. The minister had to ask her to tone down her dance for John the Baptist's head."

"Are you?" Rex asked.

"What, a Baptist? No."

The waitress reappeared with two fresh cups of coffee in a new holder. Rex fished a bill large enough to cover the orders and a generous tip from his wallet. He waved away the offer of change. Hesitating a minute, he clarified his question. "I meant, are you a virgin?"

Tricia, rising with the cup holder grasped in both hands, nearly spilled her burden again. "Now *that* is too personal a question. I have to go. The beignets are cooling."

He stood, too, and said, "Let me carry the coffee. Take the beignets. I suspect I'm more coordinated than you."

"Your concern and compliments overwhelm me. I can handle this, thanks." She might have if one of the pigeon-terrorizing tots hadn't dashed in front of her flushing a bird directly into her face. The second order of coffee crashed to the ground splashing her ankle to knee.

Rex got down on his and immediately swabbed the scalding beverage from her skin with a handful of paper napkins. The little Asian girl returned. "More coffees, sir?"

"Yes, same order. You have any ice back there? We don't want her to blister."

"Right away!"

Tricia stared down at Rex's wide back straining his

red Sinners knit shirt. His tanned arms with their heavy biceps worked up and down her legs. How many women would love to have Rex Worthy at their feet? No matter because if Layla saw her, she was dead meat or in this case cold, stale beignets. For now, she needed this crappy, shitty job a long way from the farm and her mother in Iowa. "Get up!" He did, the knees of his khakis wet with milk and coffee.

Their waitress returned with the beverages and a plastic bag of ice chips, setting them on the table. "The manager says no charge." Rex tipped her again with a couple of bills.

"Sit down, Tricia, and hold the ice against your burns."

"It isn't that bad." Still, she sat, accepted the bag of ice, and applied it to her slightly scalded skin. "Boy Scout?"

"Eagle Scout."

"It figures. Look, I really need to get back."

This time he stood and clutched the coffee holder before she did. "I'll escort you safely back to the hotel."

"Really, you shouldn't. If Layla sees you…"

"I'll say hi as nice as can be."

Tricia touched the side of the bag with the beignets. Cold. She simply didn't have the heart to order more. "Let's go and get this over with."

They walked side by side with Rex managing to hold the coffees in one hand and still keep the other free to shoot out and steady her every time they approached a patch of cracked sidewalk. Lots of cracked sidewalk in the French Quarter.

"You were saying you grew up with Layla. How did both of you end up in Los Angeles?"

"We wanted to study acting at UCLA. Neither of us could afford to pay rent alone. I got a job as a part-time waitress and brought home leftovers. Layla found work as a lingerie model and covered our housing. Her photo shoots paid really well, but when I inquired, I was found lacking."

Rex glanced quickly at her chest and away again. "They look all right to me."

"Yes, but just all right, average, normal. Layla's are spectacular—and real."

Rex swallowed hard as if remembering Layla's breasts pressed against his chest. "Money isn't everything. You shouldn't have to expose your body to earn a living."

"Not so true in Hollywood. I got commercials calling for fresh, perky girls whose mothers told them about feminine hygiene products. Layla started getting small parts almost immediately, scoring almost every time she had an audition. Then, she met a director, a much older man who liked having her on his arm. Micah Stanley, you might have heard of him. Her career took off. She left me in the dust. We both ended up quitting college."

"I understand how that might have happened, but why do you work for her? Why not go home and be with your family?"

They crossed busy Canal Street without mishap. A streetcar clanged behind them making Tricia jump, but Rex continued on without spilling a drop of coffee. She admired his steely nerves. She did not enjoy city life and confessed only to herself that she would always be a farmer's daughter at heart. A homeless man held out a plastic cup and asked for change. Rex paused to empty his pocket.

"You shouldn't do that, you know. He'll probably buy liquor with it."

Rex shrugged. "Or maybe a hot meal. Only the Lord knows."

"Right."

"You were saying why you work for Layla and take all that abuse."

"I wasn't saying, but if you must know, about the time I thought of going home and getting a teaching degree, my mother was diagnosed with breast cancer, fairly advanced. She never wanted to squander money on a mammogram."

"Did she beat it?"

"We don't know yet. After two years, the tumors came back. She'd doing a second round of radiation and chemo right now. Dad's insurance isn't the greatest. Farmers have to buy what they can afford. Layla pays me an obscene amount to be her dogsbody. She enjoys tormenting me, and I can endure it for as long as my mother needs my financial aid."

"That's why she calls you Patsy when she knows you dislike it."

"That and the obvious meaning of the word. It's nothing new. She called me that in high school when we were rivals for various parts. Better than her nickname of Dildo—because of her last name, Dillman."

"You called her a dildo?" For the first time, Rex appeared shocked to his core. He stopped in mid-stride, but the coffee only sloshed a little in the cups.

"No! That's what the guys called her. She certainly proved them wrong. They voted her in as prom queen."

"What were you? First runner-up?"

"Not even that close. I was valedictorian. Oh, if my classmates could see me now." Tricia rethought her words. She stood on the sidewalk with one of the most eligible men in the NFL surrounded by an exciting if unnerving city most of the folks back home would never see. He carried coffee for her. "We should keep moving."

They arrived at the doors of the Windsor Court Hotel. Rex would have continued inside, but Tricia held up her hand. "Stay, Rex. You seem like a really nice guy, so let me tell you something. Layla is determined to have you—yes, in the biblical way. She's planning to get a condo here and wait you out since her next project doesn't start shooting until spring. Run, hide, do not let her get near you. You went out of your way for me today. Heed my advice."

"Not much out of my way. I live right over there in the Warehouse District."

"Don't tell me where! Layla will get it out of me one way or another. I appreciate your help today, but here we part ways.

Her sunny skies blue eyes gazed up at him so seriously he finally said, "Okay. Too bad, though. I think we get along great."

Tricia shook her head and sent her dark hair flying. She placed one hand on his biceps and said mock seriously, "Sorry, our love can never be."

Under her fingertips, his muscles bunched as he gripped the coffee holder too hard. The cups began to tip. She got her hands under it in time and gently removed it from his grasp. "Joking. I did enjoy meeting you, but you need to run along."

"Yeah. I guess you're right. I hope you mom is better soon."

"Me, too. Bye, Rex."

He continued down the block leaving her with a last view of a really fine pair of taut, rounded buttocks. She bet he had stamina, lots of stamina. The doorman opened the way for her. She rode up in the elevator thinking over and over, "Our love can never be." As she entered the suite, Layla pounced and grabbed the sack of powdery donuts. The actress sank her fangs into one of them as Tricia set the coffee on a table.

"Cold! These are cold, Patsy." Layla slung the square pastry at Tricia's chest. It bounced off in a cloud of white. She crumpled the bag and tossed it into a wastebasket. "Now I'll have to order room service because I am ravenous. What took you so long?"

"I spilled the coffee and had to get more. It should still be hot, very hot."

"Are you sure that is why you are late?"

"I can't think of any other reason."

"I called downstairs and asked the doorman if you were in sight only a few minutes ago. He said he thought you were coming down the street accompanied by a young man. Which young man? Who do you know in this city?"

"I ran into Rex Worthy at the café. He insisted on carrying the coffee because he's a real boy scout." Tricia gave it up. Layla would have found out somehow, some way, probably by interrogating the doorman later in the day.

"Why didn't you invite him to come up?"

"Oh, I did. He was busy." Tricia stared hard at the pattern in the rug beneath her feet.

"Liar! If you don't help me get what I want, I will fire your sweet ass, Patsy, and your mama will stop getting that top notch care I finance. Understood?"

"Understood."

Chapter Eight

Joe surveyed his barbecue party held in honor of the end of preseason and the start of the real football season tomorrow. Only a couple of minor injuries for the team and more wins than losses as Coach tried out his newest team members and various strategies. Joe usually played only the first half if that. Then, Rex took over usually running the ball or settling for short passes and hand-offs since most of his long ones ended up as incompletes or interceptions. It went without saying that the get-together would break up early and allow all the players to return to New Orleans at a reasonable hour and completely sober. Also unsaid, the project to get Rex Worthy laid or engaged or married.

Although his backup offered over and over to help with various preparations or games for the children, the women treated him like King for a Day. You would have thought Mardi Gras came early the way they had him seated under the oaks in a fan-backed cypress yard chair with cold drinks on hand and a plate of food in his lap, making him easy to find as each one trotted up their candidates for Mrs. Rex Worthy. The guy didn't have a clue. Joe wouldn't call him a poor guy because the selection provided exceeded average by a long shot.

At least his sister, Lizzie, had been a little less obvious in strategically positioning her youngest daughter, Lisa, right next to Rex when Joe brought out

Rascal, the trick horse, for a brief show. Thanks to Joe and not to Lizzie's alcoholic husband, Lisa had gone to nursing school, recently graduated, and found work at one of the Lafayette hospitals. All men fantasized about sexy nurses, and his niece brought the goods. She owned the Billodeaux eyes like large pools of melted dark chocolate. Her curly black hair rioted untamed around her face. As far as figures went, she wasn't tall but very nicely stacked. With her sandaled feet resting on the bottom rung of the corral fence and her cute little rump clad in white short shorts thrust out a bit as she leaned her bare tanned arms on the top bar, Rex couldn't help but notice her. They struck up a conversation. Good.

In a few years, his fifteen-year-old twin girls would resemble Lisa. Joe checked their whereabouts with a father's eyes. Nell said no dating until next year. He agreed. In fact, he'd be happy if they didn't go out with guys until college, maybe not even then. There they stood side by side being ogled and amused by Prince Dobbs, the teen dressed like a gangsta and hung with gold chains.

Xochi, his adopted Mexican daughter, stood with them hanging back a little, shy ever since she'd burst into bloom at the age of twelve and boys couldn't seem to raise their eyes from her well-developed bustline anymore. He'd only seen her birth mother once, lying dead in the sand and cactus near her home in Laredo. A beautiful woman with thick, black hair and large, dark eyes staring at the sun, the flies already drinking her blood. Xochi favored the mother and not her father, his deceased reprobate cousin.

He could hear giggles as Prince clowned for his

daughters. Even Xochi smiled a little. Unfortunately, the boy had his mother Sharlette's tawny good looks and not his former tight end's more lumpish features. Yes, Joe knew all about male fantasies, especially involving twins. He'd have a talk with the kid before the day ended.

For his performance, Joe mounted Rascal and rode around the ring at a quick pace a couple of times. He gave the horse the nudge to rear, and Rascal performed it as well as Roy Roger's Trigger ever did. Dismounting, he stepped back a few paces and said, "Bang, bang!" while pointing a finger at his mount and making a subtle roll over gesture with his other hand. Rascal dropped to his side and played dead so convincingly some of the smaller children in the audience started crying. Joe gave the signal to stand immediately. Rascal got up and shook off the dust of the arena to a round of applause.

Joe slipped him a sugar cube, turned and walked away. Rascal, following close behind, head-butted his master a couple of times, then exposed his big teeth, and nipped the cowboy hat from Joe's head. At least, his scalp had a dark shadow growing on it now, nothing like its former glory, but better than bald. The crowd laughed as Joe and Rascal did a little tug of war until the horse got the signal to release the hat.

After that, Joe asked Rascal to bow for the folks. The horse went down on his knees and touched his nose to the ground. As the applause sounded, the corral gate swung open and admitted the Billodeaux's adopted son in his bright red wheelchair. The boy came alongside Rascal and heaved himself into the saddle. Rascal rose. They cantered around the ring and ended the show with

Rascal rearing and pawing the air again. Maybe Teddy needed a wheelchair and crutches to get around, but he'd developed great strength in his thighs and clung on like a cocklebur hidden in the yellow fur of their ranch dog, Macho, who added his barks to the clapping. Rascal knelt by the wheelchair, and Teddy got himself settled again. And that was the real reason Joe Dean Billodeaux purchased a trick horse.

After the show, Nell, Sharlette Dobbs, and Cassie McCoy corralled Rex and escorted him to that chair under the oaks. Besides food and drink, the backup quarterback now had a court of lovely young women seated at his feet: Sharlette's college student daughters, both as great-looking as their mother, and two redheads, Cassie's youngest sisters who despite their mother's hope would never be nuns. Lisa joined the harem.

The duo of wannabe supermodels Brian borrowed from the Amberello Agency's New Orleans branch managed by his ex-wife stalked over as if they walked the runway and leaned gracefully against the trunks of the live oaks with their bony pelvises thrust forward in tight stretch cropped pants. Espadrille sandals added to their lanky height. Considering their thinness, both had out of proportion breasts or very good padded bras under tank tops with spaghetti straps resting on their rather knobby collarbones. They went by Katya and Tatiana, no last names, cousins they claimed. The models tossed their streaky blonde manes and made pouty lips at Rex while looking at him with rather predatory blue eyes. Otherwise, they seemed terribly bored as eating and socializing didn't interest them.

Brian Lightfoot sidled up next to Joe where he stood by the riding ring keeping an eye on Dean and

Tommy giving pony rides to the little kids. The oldest of the ponies had galloped off to that big pasture in the sky, but his eldest sons tended to rush Buttercup and Boo who were getting on in years, too. Male teen hormones dictated that they wanted to ditch their duty as fast as possible and scope out the college girls in attendance—as if they had any chance with Rex Worthy on the scene.

"Is our man showing any preference?" Brian asked.

Joe studied Rex and his bounty of women. "Not as far as I can tell. What a smorgasbord of beautiful, young women. If he can't find something he likes on that buffet, there *is* something wrong with him. I'm not too sure about those Russian models you brought. I thought we specified nice girls. They look at him like starving Siberian wolves."

"They probably are starving. Maybe not nice, but possibly naughty. I thought Rex might like an alternative. Venetia says neither one will make it to the top in modeling. If they'd left their breasts alone, they might have had a runway career, but now they are too top-heavy for that, yet too skinny below to make it in lingerie. Fit only for car shows and convention hostesses. She thinks they'd like to find a rich husband and retire."

"Backups don't make that much."

"Come on, Rex got a hefty signing bonus after he took Texas A & M to the BCS Bowl, and he certainly isn't spending it on a wild lifestyle."

"Most likely gave it all to charity." The phone in his hip pocket buzzed with a call from Knox Polk out at the gate left open today so friends could come and go as they pleased. The ranch manager made sure no one else tried to gain access to Lorena Ranch. "Yeah, Knox, what's up?"

"I got two women in a rented convertible out here. The driver claims to be Layla Devlin that actress you worked with a while back. Are they invited? They ain't on the list."

Joe reached up to rake his fingers through his hair but found his head still too closely mowed and only the spike of a cowlick where his unruly curl used to be. "Layla is here," he told Brian. "How did she find out where Rex was?"

Brian shrugged expressively. "Not from me. Who knows what happened after I left them at Mariah's Place? Maybe she found a way to microchip him. However, I'd let her in if you want to avoid an ugly scene. This is not a woman who holds back when thwarted."

"Yeah. Let them in, Knox." He shoved the phone back in his pocket and moved forward to greet the occupants of the red convertible, top down and moving at a speed along the lane unsafe for small children and pets.

This didn't prevent Macho, barking in basso, from chasing the vehicle. As the car jerked to a sudden halt to avoid running over small, fluffy Titi, the other Billodeaux dog yapping her little heart out, Joe noticed Rex standing up and taking a sudden interest. Making apologies, he waded through the women at his feet. So, he wanted Layla after all. No accounting for bad taste, the same kind of taste he'd had many years ago.

Joe reached the new guests first. He crossed his arms over his chest and raised an eyebrow. "What brings you to Lorena Ranch, Layla?"

Layla shoved her oversized sunglasses up to rest on the scarlet silk scarf covering her hair and delivered one of her famous sultry stares. "I went to Sinners headquarters this morning, and they said most of the team was out at your place having a barbecue. I could only imagine you thought I'd left town because you failed to invite me. You did say I'd be welcome to visit the ranch. Everyone knows you live near that Podunk little town, Chapelle, and everyone in Podunk can give directions to your place. Besides, this marvelous machine comes with GPS."

Rex ambled over to join them. "Hi, Tricia. You like dogs?"

The PA had her fingers engaged in scratching Macho's ears as he hung his big head over the side of the convertible. The dog drooled on the bodice of her pale blue sundress, a retro outfit with a snug bodice, flared skirt, and wide straps showing very little of her back or bosom. She didn't seem to mind the dog slobber. Macho inched forward to rest his jowls on her shoulder. "Yes, we had one just like him when I was a kid on the farm."

"Is it safe to get out?" Layla asked. "Patsy has the big one under control, but that little ankle biter might attack." The Bichon Frise stood at Joe's feet issuing a low growl that came out sounding more like a purr.

"In both cases, their bark is worse than their bite. Sure, get down. Food is in the pavilion. Brinsley will bring you a cold drink when you decide where to sit." Joe nodded in the direction of the family's butler clad in a white linen suit and serving longnecks and soda pop cans from a silver tray. He added class to any affair.

Joe moved around the convertible and hauled

Macho off his new best friend's shoulder. Hanging on to the dog's collar, he opened the door for Tricia and offered her a hand, nearly treading on Rex in the process. Layla called from the driver's seat, "Rex, darling, would you help me out?" She offered a graceful, languid hand.

"Sure, Miss Layla."

He hustled to the other side and lent his support as the actress swung her long legs out of the car and balanced on her high heels worn today with black leggings and a snug, red tunic top that came to her mid-thighs. The lace edging of a black bra and a great deal of breast showed above the scooped neckline. An iron cross on a chain filled the gap below the chin and above the cleavage. Smaller matching crosses dangled from her earlobes. Somehow, the effect came across as more satanic than Christian. Rex failed to remark that she'd gone to the trouble to wear the team colors as well as religious symbols.

Layla opened her arms wide to give him a good view. "See, I wore Sinners' colors to a Sinners' barbecue."

"Yes, ma'am, you surely did."

She squeezed his stubbled cheeks. "I told you to call me Laaay-la. Can you say that?"

"Um, Laaay-la."

"Good boy. Now I could use that drink. Driving with the top down dries the mouth." She emphasized her statement by licking her lips, today coated in vermilion. All the red in her wardrobe reflected up into her lavender eyes giving them an unholy gleam like an extra in a vampire movie. Rex walked off with Layla on his arm, but Joe swore the kid had crossed his fingers on the other hand behind his back. Was he hoping to get lucky with the movie star or warding off evil? No telling.

Tricia followed behind as obediently as the two dogs tailing Joe back to the barbecue pavilion. The people entered. Angling for a handout or an accidently dropped wiener, the canines waited by the screened door shut in their muzzles. The bevy of young women grouped around Rex's deserted chair disbursed with less hope on their faces than the animals. The Russian models went to examine the convertible and lounge against it as if working an auto show. They soon attracted some of the younger, unmarried Sinners. The other girls joined the circle of matrons and very young children.

Precious Armitage, a large, very black woman who never met a plate of food she didn't like, pointed a barbecued turkey drumstick at the pavilion. "First, my girls is too young when Adam Malala is looking for a wife. Now they both too old when we trying to fix up Rex." A drop of sauce fell on her broad bosom covered by a purple and green flowered caftan. Precious wiped it off with her pinkie and sucked it away.

"Like any of us have a chance when Layla Devlin shows up," Asia Dobbs, slumped at her mother's feet, said. Arlette Dobbs agreed. "You tell it, sistah."

"I don't know why you dragged me and Kathleen up here from New Orleans if you knew *she* was going to show up," Nora Thomas, one of the redheads, complained to Cassie.

"I had no idea Layla would be here. Did you, Nell? Maureen, stop chasing your brother with that stick!" she yelled before Nell answered. She could never take her eyes off her daughter for a second.

"She was not invited. I'd sooner let a rabid dog into my yard." The little boy on Nell's lap picked up on the angry tone and began to wiggle. He held out his sturdy arms toward his mother, and Nell returned the blue-eyed boy with the feathery blond hair to Stevie Riley. He bore the imaginative name of Arjay in honor of Revelation Jeremiah Bullock, their good friend with a name no one wanted to stick on a child.

"Come to Mama, my surprise baby," Stevie said to her second son.

Mawmaw Nadine, who always had an opinion, added, "A child conceived at forty is a *Dieudonne,* a gift from God like Nell's new miracle babies." She patted her daughter-in-law's stomach.

"Well, my husband calls this boy the next great wide receiver for the Sinners. I wish he could be here today, but he's off one of his lecture tours." Stevie checked on her other two children, as Nordic looking as their parents, rampaging around the picnic with Nell's triplets.

"I guess we were silly to suppose Rex would prefer one of us to a movie star," black-haired Lisa said wistfully as she leaned against her grandmother's chair.

Mawmaw Nadine bristled. She leaned into a patch of sunlight making her gray hair gleam like a steel helmet above her strong features. "You my grandbaby, *cher* heart, and as good as any woman here. Now, all you skinny gals go get something to eat. You been holding in your stomachs all day to impress Rex. No telling when one of you will faint."

"Maybe if we swooned in the barbecue pavilion, Rex would give us mouth to mouth," Kathy Thomas suggested wickedly.

"I'd be happy to do that if you pass out," Dean Billodeaux said as he approached with Tommy, the pony rides completed for now as they claimed the horses needed a rest. "I have lifeguard training, you know." He gave her that sure-to-get-you-laid smile inherited directly from his father. The college girls ignored him.

"Yuck! Kathleen and Nora are my aunts," Tom exclaimed, making Cassie, his birth mother, laugh.

"Well, they aren't *my* aunts any more than Stacy Polasky is my real cousin."

Hearing her name mentioned as she supervised the nearby fun jump, Stacy, his parents' ward, stuck out her tongue at Dean and called out, "I'm glad I'm not your real cousin!"

At fourteen, the girl had coltish legs and a pink and white complexion still entirely blemish free. She shook her blonde curls in a way that drove the boys at her private school mad. Dean spent more time being mad *at* her. They simply could not get along. Also helping with the jumper, tall, big-boned and dark-complexioned Riley Bullock looked at Dean with longing in her wide brown eyes. She patted down her frizzy hair which nothing seemed to straighten. Stacy elbowed her. "Stop that! He's a jerk."

Nell sighed. "Dean, Stacy is part of our family. Stacy, Dean is not a jerk, just a teenage boy. Both of you watch your language." She withdrew a paper from the pocket of the maternity jeans she was already compelled to wear and consulted her notes. "Boys, almost time for the dragon boat races. Go help Adam."

"We don't get to eat?" Dean complained.

Both he and Tom could swill like pigs at a trough and never gain an ounce. How Nell envied their teen metabolism. "You had lunch before you started the pony rides," she told her sons.

"He's a growing boy. You go get second lunch, Deanie," Mawmaw Nadine said.

Precious Armitage heaved out of her chair. "Come on, girls. I could use a second helping, and if Layla Devlin is still in there, I'll clear her out your way." Built pretty much like her husband, a retired nose guard, she could do it, too.

"She isn't," a quiet voice informed them. Tricia Welles stood beside the group with a plate of food clutched in her white-knuckled hands. "When the butler refused to bring her a double dry martini because only soft drinks and beer were being served, she dragged Rex off to the barn through the other doorway of the pavilion. Could someone go rescue him? I can't because Miss Devlin said to get lost for the next hour or so. If I interrupt anything, I might be fired."

"Poor baby. Brian told us all about how that bitch treats you, only he always says it be-yotch. You sit down right here in my place," Precious Armitage offered.

But Nell, small yet always mighty, stood with fists on her hips and belly slightly protruding. "Not in my barn," she said.

Chapter Nine

"Rex, honey, close that ole barn door." Layla studied the layout, the box stalls, the hayloft, as carefully as if she blocked out a scene in her next movie.

"I'm not sure Joe wants it closed. Gets pretty hot in Louisiana in September. You need some cross-ventilation. Some people who keep horses air-condition their stables, but others think it spoils the stock," Rex babbled.

"Shut it!" Layla shot a violet laser glance at him over her shoulder but added more sweetly, "Only for a little while. The breeze coming through stirs up my allergies." She peered into each stall as Rex obeyed her. Most stood empty since the horses grazed in a nearby pasture, all except Rascal chewing a measure of oats, his reward for a good performance. "I wonder if any of these are clean. In *Savaged!* I'm gang-raped by six bandits in a barn, but we had fresh straw for the scene."

"I'm real sorry about that," Rex said.

"We were acting. I should get an Academy Award nomination for my effort. So what do you think? Are they clean or not?"

"Joe keeps a tidy barn, but someone didn't finish the job." Rex nodded to a wheelbarrow full of horse apples coated with rice hull bedding occupying the center of the aisle in front of Rascal's stall. "Why don't

I dump that in the manure pile for him?"

"Because that's not what we're here for." Layla lit on him like a fly on the contents of the wheelbarrow.

"Right, you wanted to visit your old friend, Rascal. I could dispose of the droppings while you do that."

"Rex, I have no interest in Joe's trick pony or any other livestock. In these heels, I'm almost as tall as you are. Why don't we forget about the stalls and make your first time doing it standing up? I promise the results will be spectacular." Layla backed him against a stout upright supporting the barn roof and ground her hips against his groin.

"It's getting really hot in here. I should open the barn door."

Layla licked the beads of sweat off his upper lip and rotated her hips harder. "So nice to have a young man with a rock hard dick after catering to Micah Stanley's wilted lily. He can only get it up if I give him a BJ. I might come just doing this."

"Me, too. Let up, Layla. Please."

A mighty shove of the barn door allowed the September sun to stream into the stable like a spotlight aimed right at the couple. From the force applied, Rex expected to see Joe looming in the entrance. Looking over Layla's shoulder, he had to drop his sights to small, pregnant Nell.

"Get off that innocent boy, you whore!"

Layla turned to face her accuser. Rex covered his crotch with both hands and hung a head turned so red it showed between the strands of his brushed-back brown hair. Nell marched forward, hands fisted, and Layla retreated until she came up against the door of Rascal's stall.

"We came to visit Rascal. One thing led to another. Boys will be boys," she blathered.

Hearing his name and expecting treats or adulation, Rascal raised his sorrel head from the oats and came up behind the actress. Delicately, he bared his teeth and seized the red silk scarf on Layla's head pulling it down around her neck and sending her three-hundred dollar sunglasses skittering across the rough and dusty floor.

"What the hell." Layla slapped a hand to her bright blonde hair.

Rascal followed up with a decisive head butt. Not having Joe's weight and teetering on very high heels, Layla plunged forward facedown into the wheelbarrow of manure. Kicking her feet in the air to regain her footing only drove her deeper into the filth. Bracing her hands forced her arms in to the armpits. Being a gentleman, Rex suppressed his grin but snorted a few times through his manly nose as he grasped the star's shoulders from behind and hauled her out. Nell felt no need for reserve. She laughed so hard she doubled over her swollen belly.

"You! You gave that animal some kind of signal to humiliate me," Layla shrieked through her mask of stinking brown. Both of her prominent breasts had left dents in the pile and now resembled twin dung hills sporting a light frosting of rice hulls. The blonde hair surrounding her face had turned the color and consistency of brown licorice whips.

Nell took a deep breath to steady herself. "No, Rascal sometimes has a mind of his own. Hence, his name. His trainer warned us to watch out for pranks." She looked toward the door as someone blocked the sunlight.

Precious Armitage with Sharlette Dobbs and Mawmaw Nadine stood there like linemen ready to defend their quarterback. "I skipped my second helping because I thought we might need a few of us to pull you off her. Not good for those babies, Nell."

"It's a wonder you didn't bring Stevie and Cassie, too."

"They is running after their little kids. We beyond that now. You need any help?"

"No, Rascal took care of her for me. I never got near her."

"Let me get that horse some carrots off the vegetable tray," Sharlette drawled.

"You are all vile people! Rex and I were enjoying a private moment before you barged in. He was loving it." Layla tossed her hair and sent bits of filth flying. Rex jumped away.

"Not in my barn, you slut. Clean up, go, and never return to Lorena Ranch. You can shower at the pool. I'll try to find some clean clothes to fit you." Nell's fists opened into claws.

"Good luck wit' that," Precious said. "Not a thing you or your girls got is gonna fit over them boobs. I always bring an extra caftan on account of my big shelf catching dribbles. I'll go get it for her. No need to return it. I have a whole wardrobe full of them."

The sunlight streamed in again as Precious left the scene. Three small shadows replaced hers. Nell's ten-year-old triplets took in the scene. "Uh-oh," Trinity, the smallest of the bunch, said.

Lorena, the only girl, did the explaining. "Honest, we cleaned all the stalls, Mom. Only when Jack and Josee Riley showed up, we sorta kinda forgot to dump the wheelbarrow. That was Mack's job, anyhow."

"Thanks for ratting me out, Lori," Mack, the largest of the three, retorted. "Now I'm in double trouble first from yesterday and now from today. I'll never get off barn duty."

"Yes." Nell compressed her lips to hold in a smile. "You will have to be punished for this. Just look at Miss Devlin all covered in sh—manure. She hardly looks like a famous movie star, thanks to the three of you. I'll think of some fitting chore tomorrow. Meanwhile, why don't you go with your grandmother? I believe she has something special for you."

"Yes, my *cher bebes*. How about three extra large slices of my coconut cake?"

"Do we have to eat our vegetables first?" Trin asked, as this was always a pre-condition for getting sweets.

"Not today, honey. Come wit' Mawmaw." Nadine shooed her three youngest grandchildren, soon to be supplanted by newborn twins, before her.

Layla pointed a long, scarlet-lacquered nail at Nell. A glob of dung fell from its underside. "You are rewarding them for this. You should be ashamed."

"Me? No. Their grandmother spoils them terribly."

"I want Patsy! Someone send her in here."

"I'd be so happy to do that for you. I'll show her where you can shower before you leave. Ta ta." Nell left with a trail of laughter burbling behind her.

Layla's anxious assistant appeared moments later. "Oh, my." Tricia pressed her fingers hard against her lips. "Is that what I think it is?"

"You ought to know, farm girl. It's shit, shit, shit exactly like this entire day. Get your bag from the car and clean me up before I go out there."

"I'll fetch it," Rex offered.

"Thank you, Rex, darling. Please hurry."

He moved out of the barn as fast as if he were carrying the ball toward the goal line. He returned in less of hurry blotting the corners of his bright hazel eyes with a paper napkin after laughing so hard he cried. "Here you go." He turned the large handbag over to Tricia and lingered in her general vicinity several feet from the besmirched Layla. "I think I'll go help with the dragon boat races if you don't need me. Sorry you're going to miss them. Have a safe trip back to New Orleans. Maybe you should drive, Trish, since Layla is upset."

"I will. I'm sorry about the way things worked out."

"Me, too. It would have been nice if you could have stayed."

"If the two of you are finished, I need some assistance here. That's what I pay you for, Patsy," Layla interrupted.

"Of course. I have wet wipes for your face and hands. I think we can use the scarf to cover your hair. The ends are kind of grungy, but we'll tie then underneath. Still, I wouldn't get too near anyone. You do reek."

Layla seized the package of wet wipes and tore through them, throwing each used tissue on the barn floor as she finished with it. Her makeup came off with the muck, and the sticky strands of her hair went from dark to light brown in the process. "There, how do I look?"

"Fresh as a baby's bottom," Tricia told her. A

badly wiped baby's bottom. She picked up the tissues with her fingertips and deposited them in the wheelbarrow. "The pool house is in that direction. We follow the signs. They have plenty of fresh towels there, and I brought along a bar of your favorite scented soap and small bottles of shampoo and cream rinse from the hotel."

"Take a peek outside. Are any of my fans waiting for me?"

"No, I think everyone has gone down to the bayou for the boat races. It's all clear."

"Good." Layla made a point of patting her PA's shoulder with one ill-cleaned hand. Dirt from under the long nails made talon-like stains on the pale blue sundress. "Don't know what I'd to without you, Patsy."

They escaped to the pool showers. Tricia laid out her boss's make-up while Layla showered twice using up every ounce of the shampoo.

Precious delivered the caftan, orange with gold sunbursts, big as a beach umbrella, while the actress bathed and hurried off to catch the races. As they walked back to the convertible deserted by the Russian models, cheers rose from the river as the boats got underway.

"Put up the top. I don't want anyone to see me this way," Layla ordered. She laid her head, still wrapped in a towel turban, against the rest and closed her eyes.

"Sounds like they are having fun," Tricia remarked as she took the wheel.

"Not nearly as much fun as Rex and I would have had if Nell hadn't gotten in the way again. I'm beginning to hate that woman."

Chapter Ten

Two long, aluminum dragon boats bobbed on either side of the dock. Brightly painted and bearing snarling heads like the mythical beast on their bows, Samoan Adam Malala had convinced Joe to buy them for Camp Love Letter. "Good time fun," his cornerback swore. "Even the kids in wheelchairs can participate if they have enough arm strength." Most of them did. Now the boat races were a cherished part of any gathering on the ranch.

Those who had signed up to row sorted through a heap of life vests to find their size. The audience lined up chairs along the bayou. Adam, who had stripped down in the pool house, tied back his mane of frizzy curls and rolled up his lava-lava for the occasion, exposing his waist to knee tattoos with pride. Joe swore the man oiled his smooth, brown chest, or maybe he'd worked up a sweat since the temperature soared above ninety this afternoon. Joe, captain of the second boat, felt an urge to take off his own shirt and show the world he could still compete in the manly chest competition, but he had nothing to prove.

Adam fitted a vest on Teddy and lifted the boy from his wheelchair into the drummer's position. Those two possessed a special bond formed the day they met, both of them showing up at Lorena Ranch five years ago to seek out Joe Dean Billodeaux. Joe outfitted

Trinity and put him in place to provide the beat for the rowers in his boat. "Where's Riley? She's on my team."

"Right here. We're bringing the last of the kids from the jumper." Riley Bullock balanced Adam's robust young son on one hip while Stacy carried his little sister. Both children had mocha skin, their mother's green eyes, and an explosion of fuzzy black hair.

"That your baby, Riley?" Prince Dobbs jibed. "Looks exactly like you except for the pretty eyes." Joe's twin daughters stepped away from him, and Xochi turned her back. No giggles now. They'd grown up with Riley as a friend.

Stacy handed the toddler to Winnie, Adam's wife sitting with her sister Mintay and Rev Bullock, Riley's parents. The Rev fingered the gold cross on a chain around his thick ebony neck as if he needed a reminder not to shove the boy into the bayou, but Stacy saw no need to restrain her temper. "You are meaner than Dean," she accused Prince.

"That's nice to know, princess," Dean said as he prepared to take his place in his father's boat. Generally, he used the honorific Stacy had insisted upon when she first arrived at the ranch to mock her. "Yeah, Riley can't help what she looks like, so shut up, Dobbs."

Riley's mother wrinkled her usually serene brow. Dean's misspoken gallant defense only embarrassed her daughter more. If her child hadn't been as dark as Rev, she'd be blushing tomato red right now. Genetics had gifted Mintay's lighter skin and green eyes to her son who was competing at a debate competition in Baton Rouge today. Good thing her younger boy, the image of her massive husband at a younger age, had a football game in Lake Charles or Prince would have been knocked to the ground by now.

Before Mintay could think of the words to comfort her daughter, Winnie Malala took her son into her lap as well as his sister and pinned Prince with an emerald stare. Since marrying Adam, Winnie had gained a towering confidence she'd lacked before. "You'd better be saying my babies are beautiful, and Riley is, too."

"Yes, ma'am, that's what I meant," the boy said as Adam clamped a huge hand on his shoulder.

"You're on my team. Find a vest and get moving." The Samoan muttered something else possibly derogatory in his native tongue. He couldn't endure a rude child. His dark eyes did not leave Prince as the boy tripped over his sagging pants trying to get into the boat.

The awkward moment passed as the fully loaded boats moved out into the stream. Nell, puffing a little, arrived and took a seat reserved for her in the Bullock family group. "Glad I didn't miss this. I had to scrape Layla Devlin off Rex first. Actually, I didn't do the scraping. Rascal bumped her into a wheelbarrow full of manure, and she decided to leave." Nell laughed again.

"Wish I could have seen her face," Mintay said, well aware of the play the actress had made for Joe since she worked with Nell every day.

Precious Armitage pounded up to join them. "All covered in crap. Priceless, I tell you. Made me wish I was one of them paparazzi with a camera handy. Worth giving that ho one of my caftans just to see it."

Sharlette arrived on her husband's arm. "Did we miss anything? I went back to give Rascal his well-deserved carrots, and Ace was waiting for me."

"Nothing you need to worry about right now," Winnie told her as she cuddled her children.

A toy cannon blasted off a round, and Tommy dropped the rope tied to a tree across the water that held the dragon boats in line. The drums beat out a rhythm, and the paddles dug into the surface of the brown water. They dashed to the first bend in the river where a piece of tape stretched between two trees marked the end of the race. Adam's crew won by the length of the dragon's extended red tongue. The boats reversed and returned to the dock for the next round.

Adam slapped Joe on the back. "Sorry about that, my brother, but I could not go back to the islands if I lost to a *palagi*."

"No hard feelings. At least I didn't lose to Rex."

Joe took a long look at his substitute getting ready to captain one of the next boats with Howdy McCoy set to be his rival. His entire crew appeared to be composed of young women and teenage girls, all of whom needed his help getting into their life vests. Joe noticed the most competitive of his twins, Jude, already in place as the drummer. Quiet Annie, her other half, would do the same for Howdy and Tommy, who had traded places with Dean in holding the rope. Lisa, Arlette, Asia, Kathleen, and Nora boarded along with Xochi and the rest of Rex's crew. The Russian models had declined to sweat and sat with diet drinks in hand on the shore.

Joe went over to Howdy to offer a few tips and noted the despair on Tom's face. "Rex looks really strong."

"He's got a crew of women, Tom. We have a chance," his stepfather assured him. Being a kicker most of his strength rested in his legs, but he'd agreed to give this a shot and would.

"Pretty women, a whole boatload full," Tommy said as if he would never be that lucky. "We have Brian and a bunch of little kids." He eyed Lorena and Mack, Jack and Josee, already in their places and itching for the race along with a bunch of their other friends.

"Hey, this is so not my thing and so not my color," Brian answered regarding his orange life vest ruefully. "But I shall give it my all."

"You'll do okay, son." Joe patted Tom on the back and stepped away for the start of the race.

The tiny cannon roared again, the rope dropped, and Rex dipped into the bayou water with a powerful stroke that put his boat instantly in the lead. He seemed to be doing most of the work alone as the girls tangled paddles and lost the rhythm. With the tape growing closer, the young quarterback looked over his shoulder to check on his opponents not so far behind. The children rowed higgledy-piggledy but with great enthusiasm. To Joe, he appeared to slack off a little, just enough to allow McCoy's boat to pass at the last second. Overjoyed kids smacked their paddles together and cheered. Technically, the two winning boats were supposed to compete next, but Adam, considering the puny competition and the gasping Brian, decided to concede the victory.

Rex's team gathered around him and apologized for a poor performance by stroking his arms and patting his back. Asia Dobbs looked up at him through her long bangs and held out her thumb. "See, I raised a blister for you," as if she expected him to kiss it and make it all better.

Nell clapped her hands. "Listen, everyone. Corazon has a make-it-yourself sundae bar set up in the pavilion. Help yourselves." Her announcement set off a stampede among the younger children. Adam's offspring clamored for a ride on his back to get dessert. "I have to help Mr. Joe put the boats away first."

"Go ahead and take them for a sundae. Rex will help me," Joe said.

Adam hoisted his two little ones onto his back and made a game out of trying to outrace the others to the pavilion. Since none of Rex's escorts moved, Joe said, "Ladies, go get some ice cream while Rex and me put up the boats."

"We stay to watch Rex lift the heavy boats," Tatiana said.

"Yes, ice cream does not pass our lips," Katya explained.

"Then see if any celery sticks are left from lunch. Move." He waved them away. They caught up with Brian—his one-hundred-percent cotton lavender shirt plastered to his back by sweat, his white shorts and formerly spotless athletic shoes sullied by drops of bayou water—and helped him along.

Prince Dobbs slouched past right behind the teen girls he'd showed off for earlier. They ignored him. Joe caught the boy by the backwards brim of his ball cap.

"Dude!" Prince exclaimed.

"I know your father indulges you, son, but since I have lots of daughters, you and I are going over there behind that oak and have a talk about respecting women—and what happens to guys who don't. For God's sake, pull up your pants." Did he sound like an old codger?

Joe glared at the teen's baggy jeans sagging low enough to show off the top of his polka-dotted boxers. Prince wore one of the more lurid of the Sinners' souvenir T-shirts sold in the Quarter with a leering devil on it, nothing cute about it. Joe wished he could make the kid turn the shirt inside out as well as hike up his pants but supposed that would be going too far with someone else's child. "This way—dude."

Prince returned a few minutes later a shade paler than his tawny mother and wearing Joe's belt to hold the pants above his skinny hips. "Enjoy that ice cream, you hear," Joe called after him. "Come on Rex. Raise your end on the count of three. The boats aren't heavy, only awkwardly long."

He gave the count and with a grunt, they started for the boathouse. After settling the dragon boat on its rack among the canoes and paddles used for Camp Love Letter, they returned for the second vessel walking side-by-side. "So what do you think about your crew?"

"Oh, Lisa rowed the best, but the others were fairly useless. I thought the little kids would get a kick out winning so I held back at the end."

"Just don't ever do that during a Sinners' game. Lisa grew up paddling on the bayou, but the others are mostly city girls. What I really meant is do any of them interest you personally. Did you get any phone numbers?"

"A bunch of them." Rex patted the hip pocket of his jeans where some sodden napkins stuck out of the top. "But I can't really get involved with any of them."

"Why not? That's a prime bunch of women."

"They sure are, but you know, Kathy, Nora, and Lisa are Catholic. I can't marry a Catholic."

"Why not? Nell married one. We worked it out, got married twice, once in a civil ceremony, once in the church. The Dean, Tommy, and Xochi go to services with my mother. The twins, Stacy, and Teddy attend the Episcopal Church with Nell. We trade off the triplets every other week. Okay, it is complicated—like marriage. You have to put some effort into it."

Rex nodded. "I understand about effort, but my parents would be upset, really upset."

"Then how about Asia and Arlette? I think they're Baptists or maybe AME like the Rev. Either one strike your fancy?"

"Joe, they're black." Rex stared at the ground as if watching carefully for oak tree roots. He missed Joe's scowl.

"Not very black, and both beautiful like Sharlette. You have something against black people because some of my best friends are black." Joe wasn't just saying that either. His dislike of Rex Worthy increased a notch. "You'd better learn to respect black folks because our offensive line is totally dark, and they hold your career and health in their meaty hands."

"I do respect black people. They are our brothers and sisters in Christ. I grew up on a mission in Africa, played with them all the time."

"But your parents would object to a black girl?"

"Not them. My grandparents. I know they live in another time, but they made me promise not to go with any black girls when I got back from Africa. I was only thirteen, but I try to keep my promises and respect my elders. I respect you a whole lot, too."

Joe grimaced at that last remark but let it pass. "Yeah, I understand about keeping vows, but you can't let your parents and grandparents pick your wife, can you? My mother would have liked I marry a nice Catholic girl for sure, but I held on to Nell." Joe hesitated as a thought struck him. "Or do they choose a bride for you in your religion?"

"No, it's not part of the Methodist doctrine. We aren't polygamists either." Rex grinned broadly as they reached the second boat and heaved it up on their shoulders. The long distance between them cut the conversation short until they unloaded their burden in the boathouse.

"We'd better get some ice cream before it all melts. That leaves Tatiana and Katya. You have anything against atheistic communists or the Russian Orthodox Church, whichever way they jump?" Joe said as they paced each other to the pavilion.

"Atheists would bother me, but truly, I really didn't like the models. They seemed more interested in that red convertible and staying skinny than in me."

"I see your point. I don't much care for them either, and I dated a lot of models in my time. Most of them want to land a rich husband so they can finally have a good meal. You certainly took notice of the convertible, too. Are you really interested in Layla Devlin? I mean you can make your own decisions, but I'd warn you away from that one."

"No, not Miss Devlin. I…um…it was a really nice car." Rex studied those tree roots again as if he wanted to get a degree in botany.

"You should buy one. Have some fun with your money."

"That's kind of frivolous when people are starving all over the world."

"I guess you don't want any ice cream because starving children in Africa can't have any," Joe snapped.

"No, sir. I love ice cream."

They entered the pavilion where commercial-sized drums of vanilla, chocolate and strawberry waited amid a dozen scoops, most of them in use. Bowls of maraschino cherries sat on either end of the table. Hot fudge bubbled like lava in a crockpot. Tubs of whipped topping, some already scraped to the bottom sat here and there. The chocolate chips and jimmies of all colors were going faster than the chopped fruits and nuts.

Macho and Titi had gotten inside and lurked lapping up spills beneath the table. All the young women except Asia Dobbs and the models deserted their bowls and clustered around Rex again as if he were the Good Humor man come to call at their doorstep.

Asia ripped her thumb from the grasp of the camp nurse, fondly called Shammy but now officially Mrs. Clive Brinsley, as she applied antibiotic cream to her blister and joined the mob.

Joe sighed wearily. "Go get some then."

Rex moved to the sundae bar with his coterie of women making suggestions as to what he would like best—chocolate or strawberry. He chose vanilla of course.

Nell moved casually to her husband's side and whispered, "Well, which one does he like best?"

"He admired Lisa's prowess with a paddle, but other than that, none of them. No Catholics, no black girls, no atheists, and no skinny women."

"He's awfully picky."

"I thought maybe Layla since he ran over to greet her."

"Are you kidding me? When I opened that barn door, you would have thought Layla was nailing him to a cross by the expression on his face."

"Sometimes sex and agony are close to the same thing."

"Not in this case. What is the matter with him?"

Joe shook his head. "Only thing I can figure is he's a closeted gay despite what Brian says—or he's found somebody on his own and doesn't want to talk about it."

"All that effort for nothing. Okay, I give up—temporarily. I'll get Titi if you will haul Macho out from under the table. They'll both get sick if the kids keep feeding them maraschino cherries."

Nell went to lure the smaller dog away from the feast. Joe dragged Macho out by his thick, leather collar from under the table and shoved him through the doorway. Both animals pressed their noses against the screen wanting to get back in, but finally had to settle for licking the vanilla ice cream off their muzzles.

Families began to depart with tired, sticky children in tow. The two Russians informed Brian they'd found another ride home and went off with the rookie wide receiver and a new running back. Kathleen and Nora piled into the McCoy van with Howdy driving, their nephew asleep, and Cassie trying to hush her daughter who screamed to stay longer. Prince's parents returned Joe's belt, apologized for the behavior of their son relayed by others who had witnessed it, and boarded their three into a huge, red SUV. Lisa lingered near Rex until her mother collected her for the short drive home.

Once the young women departed, Rex got out the keys to the modest truck he drove and went to thank Nell for a nice day. To his surprise, she took him aside.

"Look, Rex, we think you need someone special in your life. Today we tried to help you find that person, but you found fault with some very fine young women. Exactly what do you want?"

"I explained all that to Joe. There's one other thing I didn't tell him because he'd make fun of me. I always thought I'd marry a virgin—and I don't think any of them are." His face pinked to match the remaining strawberry ice cream.

"In this day and age, that's pretty old-fashioned. I suspect only the girls under eighteen are still intact, and I'm not sure about all of them except for mine."

Neither noticed Joe listening in until he spoke. Slapping Rex hard on the back, he said, "I never did virgins. They're trouble and have no idea what they're doing."

"You never had one, even in high school? I mean I've heard the guys talk about your reputation." Now Rex had two red spots on his cheeks about the color of the maraschino cherry juice dribbled on the concrete floor.

"I went to parochial school where the nuns made sleeping with a virgin outside of marriage sound like a mortal sin. I guess it is. Anyhow, you'd end up getting married right out of high school and having a baby six months later. Plenty of the other kind of girls around to practice on."

"You think I need to practice?"

"Football, sex, everything gets better with practice. I think you owe it to your bride to know what you are doing. Or maybe you want to marry a virgin because she won't notice how inexperienced you are."

"Maybe," Rex agreed. "I gotta get going. I want to be in before curfew. We have a game to play tomorrow.

Chapter Eleven

Tricia stopped the rental car before the hotel lobby doors and gently prodded Layla awake. "We're back in New Orleans."

"Thank God, a return to civilization. I haven't seen so many screaming kids since my publicist forced me to visit that orphanage in Africa while I was filming *Plague!*. I made a generous donation simply to get out of there." Layla groped for her sunglasses and didn't find them. "I can't go out there without my shades."

"There's another pair in my bag."

Layla pawed around until she found them and checked herself in the visor mirror. "Not as flattering as the ones that pestilent horse ruined, but they will have to do. Why didn't you remind me to take the towel off my head before I went to sleep? I can't drop it now. You know what high humidity does to it. My hair will be all snaky."

"Just go up to the suite as quietly as possible. No one will recognize you. I'll return the car to the rental agency."

"Be quick about it. I want to go out tonight, and you'll have to help with my do."

Another grand evening of making sure Layla Devlin returned to her room alive. Tricia could not wait. The concierge opened the door of the convertible. Layla stepped out. A hot gust of wind inflated the orange and gold caftan as huge as a hot air balloon. The paparazzi appeared like crocodiles homing in on a drowning wildebeest. Layla raced for the safety of the lobby as fast as her lengthy legs and high heels could carry her, but the caftan swelled her rump to an enormous size for the cameras. The doorman prevented pursuit by the photographers, but Tricia waited to make sure the actress boarded the elevator with no problem before leaving.

Back on the street, she put the roof of the vehicle down again and sought out the interstate. With traffic too sluggish to allow her to speed, she simply pretended to be dashing away, pedal to the metal of the red Mustang, wind in her hair, far from Layla Devlin. Perhaps, someone else drove with her, someone kind and strong and too good to be true. A horn blasted as she cut off another car trying to change lanes for the airport exit. Rattled, Tricia returned the car and also to earth. Accepting a ride back to the hotel in the agency van, she prepared herself mentally for another night in hell.

Layla had already entered purgatory by the time her assistant arrived at the suite. Two small bottles of chilled white wine sat sweating and empty atop the bar while the actress, like another dead soldier, lay draped on a brocade divan with her reptilian locks spread out around her head and her body wrapped like a cocoon in the thick terry robe provided by the hotel.

"Patsy, I have a headache. I cannot go out tonight, but I expect you to see I get to the Sinners game tomorrow in tiptop shape."

"We put in a six-hour round trip drive out to the ranch, and neither one of us had much to eat since breakfast. You need food and some aspirin."

"Nothing. I had nothing to eat—or drink thanks to that surly servant." Layla laid a hand across her eyes as if the slight had been personal and never to be forgotten. She did have a long memory.

"Let me order something from room service. What would you like?"

"A cheeseburger, rare. I feel the need for red meat."

"You got it. Here's the aspirin. Why don't you lie down in a dark room until it comes?"

"I shall do that." Layla dragged her enervated and slightly tipsy body to the largest of the bedrooms and shut the door.

Tricia phoned in the order, cheeseburgers for both of them, and helped herself to a cluster of grapes from the complimentary and always full bowl of fruit on the counter. She removed a small cheese and cracker tray from the mini-bar and the little bottle of red wine in the back Layla neglected to find. She'd only had a few mouthfuls at the ranch before her boss summoned her to the barn. Tricia smiled to herself reliving the moment of Layla Devlin covered in shit. This evening might turn out decently after all.

The house phone rang, and she dove to answer it before the second bell. No need to wake the sleeping python. "Hello?"

"Hey, Tricia. It's me, Rex. I'm on my way back to the city and wanted to see if you, the two of you, got home okay."

"Pretty risky behavior for an eagle scout to drive and use a cell phone at the same time."

"Oh, I have one of those gadgets you set your

phone in with a speaker."

She imagined his earnest expression and nearly laughed. "Thanks for checking on us. Layla slept most of the way back. I sort of had fun driving the Mustang even if I did have to keep the roof up mostly."

"You'd like a guy who drove that kind of car, huh?"

"Actually, women aren't as impressed as men think by fancy cars. I went to my prom in my date's truck, and we had as good a time as Layla and her crowd in the limo. He got me there and back again safely without putting any moves on me, and that's what counted."

"Yeah, because sometimes seniors have sex on prom night. So you didn't?"

"I've heard that happens sometimes after the prom. You know, Rex, high school kids can have sex any night of the year." She knew, simply knew, that his ears burned red, but no way would she satisfy his curiosity about her love life, past or present. None of his business.

"Sure." He paused, groping for a change of subject. "You coming to the game tomorrow?"

"Layla has a box. I'll be there."

"Good. I hope I get to play in the game."

Tricia heard a sinuous stirring in the master bedroom. The tone of the phone changed as Layla picked up the extension. "I have to hang up now. Good luck, tomorrow." She dashed the receiver down before he could reply and identify himself. Sweet guy. He deserved her protection.

"Who was that?" Layla demanded.

Why lie? She'd spared the man direct contact with the actress who stalked him and that was enough. "Rex

Worthy. He wanted to see if we got back to the hotel okay."

"How nice he was concerned about me. Why didn't you keep him on the line?" Suspicion tainted Layla's voice.

"I thought you were asleep, and frankly, you aren't at your best right now. Save yourself for the game tomorrow. Oh, room service is at the door. Let's eat."

Layla devoured her cheeseburger, bloody in the middle, after setting aside the huge bun. She ate the fixings on one side of the plate, tomato, lettuce, and pickles like a salad, leaving only the onion slice behind. Afterward, she curled around her belly like a boa constrictor digesting a small pig and went back to sleep.

Tricia slowly ate her burger, cooked all the way through and topped with the extras including the onion, a simple meal, one Rex might enjoy. Where had that thought come from? Wherever, it had to go back into hiding right now. She'd enjoy the rest of her peaceful evening and look forward to the Sinners game tomorrow.

****

Layla's skybox filled to bursting with everyone she knew in New Orleans and texted in the last few days. Her acquaintances came down heavy on the side of musicians, mostly male, and a transvestite introduced by Brian who did a Layla impersonation and arrived in full, glamorous drag. Layla herself opted for a black team jersey ordered in the smallest adult size and bearing Rex's red number eight on the back. Never had a sports jersey fit so tightly or shown so much of a chest.

Layla paraded past the windows of the box

numerous times hoping the cameras would pick her up. Eventually, they did. She gave a cheery wave and turned her back to reveal the player she supported. The cameras panned to Rex Worthy warming the bench. His shoulders hunched as if he were protecting the back of his thick neck. On many levels, Tricia pitied him, always a bridesmaid never the bride, though Layla certainly wanted to give him a wedding night, another reason for her sympathy. After his warm-up, Rex had gotten on his knees and prayed. She wondered what he asked of God—for a Sinners victory or simply to be allowed to play.

With so many others around to entertain her boss, Tricia enjoyed the game. She had a little fetch and carry to do keeping Layla in booze and skewered barbecued shrimp, but otherwise enjoyed a paid respite from her job. The worst part of the day had been untangling and smoothing Layla's snarled hair into the loose waves the actress preferred. Tricia's knuckles still smarted from a quick strike with a hairbrush when the comb pulled too hard, a small price to pay for this wonderful day. She sat among the tattooed and the dreadlocked, the druggies and the ultra-talented, largely unnoticed. That suited her just fine.

The Sinners went to the locker room at halftime two scores up, both of them achieved with long passes into the end zone by Joe Dean Billodeaux. When the team returned, Rex threw the football into a net a few times keeping his arm warm. "Put in Worthy," Layla shrieked, though no one except her guests heard her.

She got her wish toward the end of the third quarter. Joe left the safety of the pocket and drew back his arm for another ground-eating pass. He got it off right before being smashed to the ground in a stealthy attack from his left side. His receiver caught the ball and ran it to the twenty yard line before being brought down. Shaking his head, Joe still sat on the turf. The medical men came out with their questions and held up fingers. How many do you see? The quarterback got to his feet to the cheers of his fans, but despite a brief argument about staying in the game, left the field for the locker room with the trainers. The camera panned to Nell, who preferred sitting on the fifty-yard-line among the team wives rather than a private box, and registered the concern for her husband showing on her face.

"Put in Worthy," Layla screamed again. Sitting beside her, the tranny, who went by the stage name of Lilah Divine, placed his masculine hands over ears adorned with rhinestone chandelier drops. The coach obliged his idol.

"Worthy goes in while Billodeaux is being checked for concussion," Al Harney, the announcer, informed the crowd. Anxiety did not grip the Superdome. The Sinners were two touchdowns up over a weak opponent who hadn't scored at all or even come close. Their rival's halfway decent defense kept the score from being worse.

Rex took his place and called the play. Tricia found she'd crossed her fingers for good luck. Two wide receivers went right and left toward the end zone. The quarterback fake pumped left drawing off some of the defense, then tucked the ball and began running. His heavily muscular thighs churned. He stiff-armed opponents with a decisive shove sending some to the ground. Faced with a barrier of two tackles between him and the goal line, Rex made a leap over their hunched backs, tucked into a roll, and came up with the football still firmly in his grasp. No showboating for him. He tossed the ball to the official and pointed one finger skyward giving the glory to God.

"That, my friends, is Rex Worthy's first touchdown in the NFL," Hank Wilkes up in the booth supplied, going on to fill in the color with statistics on the young quarterback's career at Texas A & M as the teams traded sides.

Joe Dean Billodeaux returned to the bench almost unnoticed. He shook Rex's hand and said a few words. Al Harney could not resist commenting that if Joe had been on the field, the fake pass would have been thrown, sharp and arrow straight to the receiver in the end zone—not to take away from Worthy's fine performance. "Two different kinds of quarterback, Hank, two different styles." No one would argue that.

"Patsy, I need a pen and paper!" Layla snapped her fingers.

Before Tricia could make her way to the front, the actress's transvestite double drew a small bejeweled pen and notepad from a sequined handbag. "Here you go, dear. Sending a love note to Rex? Yes, I saw your names linked in the gossip rags, but he really doesn't seem your type."

"Who does?"

"*Moi?*" The violet contacts the man wore glittered with speculation.

"That would be like making love to myself."

"Not if I take off the wig and boobs, honey."

Layla laughed. "I'll keep that in mind, but you are simply too easy. Let me see what I can do with the last virgin boy scout first." She finished her note, folded it over, and thrust it at Tricia. "See Rex gets this after the game."

"I'm not sure if I can reach him."

Don't come back to the hotel tonight if you can't."

"Harsh," the Layla impersonator said. "I like that."

"If I go now, I might be able to get a place near the entrance to the tunnel, but I don't know if Rex will see me. I can't guarantee..." Tricia insisted.

"Get going. As for you, my violet-eyed hussy, I might need your help with Rex. You have any contacts in the Quarter? I need some special meds."

"Anything for my favorite star. But forget Rex. Catch my show tonight. The Quarter will be rocking after a Sinners' victory." His lavender-painted lips formed a seductive moue.

Worried, Trish left the box and took the escalators down to the first level. She posted herself by the wall framing the tunnel where fans gathered hoping for a high five or an autograph from their favorite players as they passed. She stayed there crushed between a fat man and a groupie with neon orange hair for the entire fourth quarter while Joe Dean Billodeaux orchestrated another touchdown, this time handing off to a running back as if to prove his versatility. Before the game ended twenty-eight-zip, the Sinners, Tricia succumbed to reading the note.

Rex,

Come to the Windsor Court after the game to celebrate your first NFL touchdown. Say around seven. I am so happy for you."

A simple offer, to the point, unsigned, and very unlike Layla. Uneasily, Tricia fingered the pink, perfumed paper with little rosebuds in each corner. No matter. Rex probably would not see her. Then, she'd have to ask the neon-haired girl where the groupies went to meet the players. Could take all night to hunt Rex down. She'd suggest he pen a refusal on the note as proof she'd done her job. By the time she returned, Layla might be passed out or asleep. A girl could hope.

Reporters held both Joe and Rex back for brief interviews, but at last the two men moved toward the tunnel. Joe reached up to slap palms with a few children. The orange-haired young woman called out to Rex, "Hey, handsome, how do you like these apples?" She raised her black Sinners' T-shirt and exposed two small naked breasts adorned with nipple rings.

Joe did a double-take but kept on walking. Rex cringed and started to turn his head away, then noticed Tricia dangling the note over the barrier. He jumped up slightly to take it from her fingers and read it right on the spot. With that smile reminding her so much of her brothers, and Trish wished it didn't, he nodded. "Sure, I'd like that. Seven." Like the beta male in a pack, he trotted after Joe, the top dog.

Orange-hair covered her tits and shoved Tricia resentfully. "What have you got that I haven't?"

"A bra?" Trish ducked behind the bulk of the red-faced fat man who'd gotten an eyeful. Other retorts played through her mind—natural hair, nipples without holes. That kept her amused until she reached the box, finding it deserted. Only as she made her way back to the hotel alone did it occur to her that Rex assumed she'd written the note—and Layla intended it that way.

Chapter Twelve

The knock on the door sounded promptly at seven. Layla's orders that Rex Worthy be shown to her suite immediately upon arrival had been honored.

"Let him in, Patsy." Layla arranged her long limbs to maximum effect on the divan and made sure her nipples didn't pop from her décolleté. She'd chosen a bra that gave lift from below but allowed her Pride and her Joy, as she called her breasts, to be mostly exposed. After hearing about the trashy flasher and Rex's reaction, she'd decided to move cautiously lest she scare him off, at least in the early part of the evening. Pleased with the way the cerise silk gown clung to her curves, she had no need to worry about a panty line because she wore no panties. The less between her and her object, the better.

Tricia pushed the lever. Rex Worthy stood there immaculately groomed in a navy blue suit, white shirt, and red tie but still stubbled with a few days growth of beard. Regardless, an enticing aroma of lime aftershave wafted over her. He held out a bouquet of a dozen tightly furled pink roses wrapped in green tissue. "These are for…"

Layla executed a neat interception, passing between the couple and seizing the flowers. "How did you know? Pink is my second favorite color after lavender." She laid a chaste kiss of thanks on his bearded cheek.

"I didn't know. I..."

"Come in, come in and see what a wonderful spread we have for the two of us. Chilled oysters on the half shell, shrimp remoulade, cold rare roast beef with a dipping sauce, asparagus, a lovely basket of breads, nothing that needs to be heated up except me." Layla paused for a compliment that didn't arrive.

"Isn't Tricia staying? I mean I thought we were going out."

"You mean Patsy? She'll be on her way after she serves the drinks. I've gotten her a room on a lower floor for the night. This is a private party, just the two of us. Let's start with champagne and oysters. Patsy, open the bottle."

Tricia struggled with the foil and the wire and the stubborn cork while Layla escorted Rex to the divan. Stupidly, she dwelled on the fact that he had seen her in this same simple black dress, pumps, and hair in a tight chignon during that embarrassing episode in the bar. She must look like a member of a funeral party rather than a victory celebration compared to Layla who looked like a—slut. There, she'd thought it if not said it. The damned cork would not budge.

"We're waiting—impatiently," Layla called.

She tried again to open the bottle, but suddenly noticed the scent of lime and the heat of a large, masculine body behind her. Rex reached around her, almost an embrace, and worked the cork with his big thumbs. The festive pop sounded, and champagne foamed over the neck of the bottle. He stepped to one side, filled the two flutes waiting on a tray behind the suite's bar, and took a third glass from the rack above it. "I want you to celebrate with me, too."

"Rex, sit down. You're the guest of honor," Layla said. "Oh, I've forgotten to put your lovely flowers in water." She flounced, breasts a-jiggling, to the bar and gave him a playful shove back to the sofa. Turning the bouquet over to Tricia, she ordered, "Find a vase."

Tricia searched the cabinets for a container and finally found a tall, glass cylinder that would do. She turned to see Layla emptying a packet of crushed white powder into one of the flutes and stirring it with a long, red-polished nail. A sudden image of the witch in the tale of *Snow White* preparing the poisoned apple flashed into her mind.

"What are you doing?" she asked beneath the sound of the water running into the vase.

"The boy scout needs to relax."

Layla flashed a smile wasted on Rex who sat with his eyes closed on the couch, his large hands clasped tightly on top of his knees. Tricia thought he might be praying for deliverance.

"Are you trying to ruffie him?" she whispered.

"None of your business." Layla lifted the tray and carried it to the low table, carefully positioning the glass in front of Rex. Trish followed close behind her. "Oh, I forgot to bring the bottle. Surely, we'll want to make more than one toast." With a significant gyration of the hips, Layla returned to the bar.

Tricia grabbed the flute intended for Rex and shoved hers in his direction. When Layla returned, she held the ruffied drink as steadily as a chalice at communion. Raising the glass, she offered a toast, "To Rex's first touchdown in the NFL."

Displeased, Layla grumbled, "I wanted to say that,

but I am sure I can come up with something better." She touched her glass to the one Rex held, and he in turn clinked his against Tricia's flute. They drank, though only Trish, hoping Layla had no more doses of the drug, drained hers to the bottom.

"A second toast to a long and interesting evening full of new experiences," Layla offered with a pout. She topped off all the glasses. This time Trish merely sipped.

"Time to leave, Patsy. The key card to your new room is on the table by the door. I've had your belongings moved there. I'll call you when I need you. Feel free to sleep in tomorrow. Rex, shall we start with the oysters?"

"That's a bunch of food for two people. I think Trish should have some after two glasses of champagne."

"She's fine!" Layla snapped. "She only has to walk down a few flights and call room service if she wants anything."

"That would be a waste. What can I bring you, Tricia?" Rex set his drink aside and got up. "How about a little bit of everything/"

"No oysters!" The thought of the slimy gray globs going down her throat suddenly made her want to gag.

"Okay. A few shrimp, some beef and asparagus, a nice roll. Everything looks great, and hey, we got chocolate-covered strawberries for dessert, looks like." He presented Tricia with a neatly arranged plate. "Eat it all and slowly now."

Layla stalked to the buffet and downed several oysters, sucking them directly from the shell. "Try these, Rex. So delightfully salty. Wash them down with the rest of your champagne. I promise you won't regret it."

Rex humored his hostess. He doctored a couple of oysters with hot sauce and slid them between his lips, followed them up with saltines and the rest of his drink. Layla squeezed his arm. "We are going to have such a good time tonight."

Tricia did eat slowly hoping the food would offset whatever Layla put in the champagne. A half hour passed while Layla and Rex ate directly from the plates on the buffet. She began to feel woozy. Good, if she threw up, all might be well. Trish stood and wavered.

"I'm going to my room now. I feel very strange." She started to wobble toward the smaller of the suite's bedrooms.

"Not there! You're downstairs tonight, remember?"

"Not really." One of her legs buckled and Rex, the Eagle Scout, caught her before she hit the floor. He took her into his arms. Yes, he did, *swept* her into his arms actually. She patted his cheek. "Why don't you ever shave?"

"Tell you later. I should take her to her room and call the house doctor."

"No! Patsy is hearty country stock. She'll be fine," Layla said as if her assistant were a prime dairy cow.

"I'll sit with her until she feels better. You don't have to worry. Ah, thanks for the nice party, Layla." Rex moved to the door, scooped the key card from the table, and elbowed the door open. He shut it with a decisive kick and went directly for the private elevator. It took them nonstop to the ground floor. He checked the card for a number and summoned the next elevator going up.

The concierge rushed over. "Do you need assistance?"

"Just too much champagne, I think."

Tricia, bright-eyed, waved a hand in the man's face. "Yep, yep, too much champagne. See, Rex Worthy is carrying me in his very own arms. Wheeee!"

"I've seen worse working here. Do call the desk if you need help." The uniformed man went back to his post, and Rex entered the newly arrived elevator with his passenger.

At the door to her room, he propped Tricia against the entry while he fiddled with the key. No luck on the first try. A red light still winked at him. The hallway of Tricia's exile was significantly busier than the private floor. A weary family done in by a day on the town passed. The little boy had his face painted like a tiger. The elfin black-haired daughter carried a flower made of balloons that she held like a bridal bouquet.

Trish smiled at them broadly and waved. The little girl resembled a tiny princess, which brought *Snow White* to mind again. She felt a great urge to sing *Some Day My Prince Will Come*. After all, bluebirds circled Rex's head as he reversed the card and tried again. Must be a sign.

"I know that song," the tiny princess twittered.

Oops. She must be singing. Tricia covered her mouth with both hands and giggled.

"I know that player," the stocky dad in Bermuda shorts said.

"Taking advantage of a drunken woman," his blonde wife added. "What a phony." Her tiger-painted son growled.

Tricia felt moved to point out to the woman, "Your dark roots are showing. I bet you have pretty black hair exactly like your daughter. Hi, honey." She wiggled her fingers at the child and stared at the mother's prominent breasts. "Are those for real?" When the woman reddened, she added, "Didn't think so, but nice work."

To Rex's great relief, the light turned green. They stumbled into the open space with Rex nearly landing on top of Trish when she fell across the single king-sized bed in a significantly less luxurious room compared to the suite. He got up leaving her hanging half off the mattress and went to close the door. The two wide-eyed children backed by their furious mother stared from the hall as he gave them some privacy.

"Maybe you'd better stay down, Trish. I'm not a big drinker, but those two glasses of champagne sure went to your head faster than anything I've ever seen."

Tricia rolled over and sat up on the edge of the bed. "Not champagne. Ruffies. Layla wanted to make you relax, but I stopped her. You can be as uptight as you want now."

"Thanks for that, I guess. Should I call a doctor?"

"Nope! I feel great." Tricia nodded her head so emphatically the tight chignon at her nape unraveled and released her long, dark hair. "You know what? I think you like me more than Layla."

"That's the truth."

"She's on to us, probably spying on us right now. Better check for bugs." She got down on her knees, rump in the air, and peered under the bed, then upended a table lamp and left it lying on its side. "I don't see any, do you?"

Rex surveyed the room to make her happy. A large,

soft-sided suitcase, lumpy and overstuffed having been hastily and badly packed, lay on the luggage rack with her huge, black handbag on top. A small laptop sat on the desk. "No bugs. Really, you should lie down and rest. Mind if I use your computer for a minute?"

"Help yourself to anything you want." Tricia stood and twirled around with arms outspread, lost her balance, and collapsed on the bed again.

Living a clean life, never doing drugs, Rex realized how very little he knew about situations like this. He summoned up the internet search engine and typed in Ruffies. A site intended for teens offered the simplest explanation as he truly did not need to know its chemical composition or the laws regarding Rohypnol in various countries. He'd always figured ruffied girls passed out and got used by guys with no more morals than a tomcat on the prowl. Glancing over at Tricia who kicked off her pumps while singing that prince song again, he read over the effects.

Disinhibition. Check. Excitability or aggression. Check. Talkativeness. Definitely. Dizziness. Check. Drowsiness. Definitely not. Possible paranoia. Yes. Hallucinations. Can't tell. Stomach disturbances. Not yet. Urinary retention. No idea. Amnesia. He certainly hoped so or she'd be really embarrassed in the morning.

"Trish, do you need to use the bathroom for anything?" He turned her way.

She'd peeled her dress down to her waist. Must have had one of those built-in bras because her breasts were naked as two boiled eggs—but a lot more attractive. They weren't big and spectacular like Layla's or pierced, thank heaven. Nice and normal, neither too large nor too small, just the right size as he'd figured at Café du Monde.

He'd seen bare breasts at the strip clubs teammates dragged him to for celebrations, treating him to lap dances he didn't want but felt churlish refusing. African women at the mission weren't shy about being topless or nursing their babies in public, a natural act, not an erotic one his mother often said. Breasts were designed to nourish, not arouse. He felt a sudden need for nourishment, saliva pooling in his mouth. No, no, he couldn't take advantage of a drugged person.

"Rex, can I ask you a question?"

He anticipated what she wanted to know. "Yeah, I've never slept with a woman." He kept his eyes on her dilated blue ones and took a deep breath.

"No, silly. Everyone knows that." She stared at her breasts. "You think these are okay? Layla makes them feel inferior. She calls her girls Pride and Joy. Mine don't have names."

He stole a quick look. "How about Pretty and Perky?"

"You are so sweet! Want to touch them?"

"I shouldn't."

"It's okay because I'm not."

"Not what?"

"A virgin. Didn't you ask me that? I bloomed late though. Never slept with a guy until I went to college. Thought I loved him. Thought he loved me—until I found him in bed with Layla. Layla has really big boobs. Men like that."

"Remember when you said some women weren't all that impressed by fancy cars? They just want to get home safe and be treated with respect."

"Nope." Tricia tweaked her pale brown nipples and

watched them peak with great interest.

Rex swallowed. "Well, not all guys are interested in breasts big enough to smother them in their sleep. Some men can see beyond the flesh to a loving heart. That's what really counts."

"My mother has no breasts. Lost them both to cancer. She says it's no big deal at her age. I'm afraid."

"Of losing yours?"

"Of losing my mother." Two tears formed in the pools of her deep blue eyes and wandered down Tricia's face.

"See, that's what I mean by a loving heart." He should go over there and comfort her, but if he sat on that bed, put his arms around her, held her close, those naked breasts pressing against his chest....

Tricia yawned. "Maybe I am tired."

"Right. Lie down. Go to sleep." Rex turned toward the computer again. How long did the effect of the drug last? Eight to twelve hours, up to thirty-six when mixed with alcohol. Dear God in heaven, help me through this night.

"Rex, why don't you ever shave?" Trish asked in a voice both curious and drowsy.

"Okay. You told me a secret so I'll tell you one. I have sensitive skin. My mom said I was a rashy infant. And when the facial hair is off, I have sort of a baby face. I need to look tough to play in the NFL."

"Oh, I think it's sexy."

"That's not one of the reasons I don't shave often."

"Sure." She blinked her eyes heavily.

Go to sleep. Go to sleep. Go to sleep. Rex willed it. There, she finally rested. He gently lifted her limp wrist and took her pulse. Seemed normal. Carefully, very carefully, he drew her dress over her naked breasts, taking care not to touch. Whether they went back where they were supposed to go, he had no idea. Finding a spare blanket in the closet, he covered her tenderly. Smoothing Tricia's long bangs aside, he enjoyed the silky slide of her hair beneath his fingers. The Bible was right about many things, and the temptation of a woman's loose tresses was obviously one of them. A kiss on the forehead wouldn't awaken her he hoped, but a kiss on the lips might. He leaned over Tricia.

A phone rang deep inside of the large, black bag Trish often wore across her chest. He delved frantically into its depths and fished out the cell. Layla's name showed on the I.D. Rex pressed the button and said quickly, "She's asleep. I think she'll be okay."

"Good, I guess. What I really wanted to know is if you are coming back to our party."

"No, thanks. I should watch her through the night."

"Oh, for Christ's sake!"

"Exactly." He disconnected and turned off the phone. A moment later, the room phone sounded. Before Layla could say a word, he depressed the button and left the receiver off the hook. Surely watched over by an angel tonight, Tricia slept on in safety with her dark hair spread on the pillow.

Chapter Thirteen

Rex tried to stay awake by playing computer games. Every half hour or so, he'd check Tricia's breathing and pulse. A couple of times, he laid his lips on her forehead to check for fever as his mother used to do when he was small, though fever wasn't one of the symptoms of ruffie poisoning. Around three a.m., he stretched out in the upholstered chair near the bed and put his feet up on a matching hassock. Didn't mean to sleep, but he did. When he woke, he realized he'd missed the team meeting.

Taking Tricia's cell into the bathroom and shutting the door, Rex called the Sinners' office to explain he sat with a sick friend. He only wanted to leave a message. They put Coach on the line regardless.

"That what they call a bad combination of booze and broads these days, Worthy? No need to explain. You earned a celebration. I'll wave the fine this time. Don't miss practice tomorrow, you hear me now? Joe's left side is a deep shade of purple and pretty stiff. We might have to use you again come Sunday. Depends on how he does."

"That would be great! I mean, I hope Joe feels better soon."

"Your *friend,* too. Good to see you loosen up a little, boy. See you early tomorrow."

"Yes, sir."

A fist pounded on the bathroom door. "Let me in, let me in quick!"

"Not locked."

Tricia hit the door running. "Out, out!"

Giving her privacy, Rex backed away. He stayed close enough to hear the noise of retching finally followed by the trickle of pee. Good, no urinary retention, but definitely a stomach disturbance. Tricia opened the door and stumbled past him. She rooted in her black handbag and came up with a toothbrush still in its wrapper, a travel-sized toothpaste, and a hairbrush. Walking past Rex as if he weren't there, she took possession of the bathroom again. He waited patiently.

Trish emerged a trifle pale and shaky but with her face washed and hair groomed. "I'm sorry about all this, but what exactly are you doing here, Rex? In fact, where are we?"

"Still at the Windsor Court a few floors down from Layla's suite."

"I seem to recall that she got me another room. When are we?"

"Monday around noon. Could have been worse. The effects of a ruffie mixed with alcohol can last thirty-six hours."

"Thanks for that enlightening information. You haven't said why you are here." She sat down on the still nicely made up bed with a dent in the middle and a rumpled blanket tossed to one side.

"When the drug in the champagne took effect, I carried you here and spent the night watching over you."

"Is that all you did?"

127

"Scout's honor." Well, he had lusted in his heart but didn't think that needed saying.

"You are the only guy speaking that oath I would believe. Okay, so nothing happened."

Wanting to be as truthful as possible, Rex pondered his words for a moment. "You were kind of talkative. I want you to know it's all right about that guy in college. I mean you thought you loved him. If you pray on it, God will forgive you for sleeping with him before marriage."

"You asked me if I was a virgin while I was drugged? I thought I made it clear my sex life is none of your business. Why are you so obsessed with my virginity anyhow? And you did take advantage of me even if it wasn't physical!" She came off the bed like a trash-talking WWF wrestler and got in his face.

Rex took a few steps back and held up his hands. "No, it wasn't like that. You volunteered the information about that fellow you dated who slept with Layla. Like I said, you were deceived, and God can forgive that."

"Look, I made a big mistake with Boyce, and then I made a few more mistakes trying to prove I could attract other men. All I proved was I don't really enjoy sex without an emotional connection to the guy. Layla can do it anytime, anywhere, just for fun. I'm not made that way. I learned something about myself. But I am certainly not going to ask God's forgiveness for errors made growing up. I hurt no one but myself." Registering the utter desolation on his face, she stopped talking.

"You slept with more than one man."

"Yes, Rex. Grow up. I'm twenty-four. So are you.

By this age, most women have had more than one partner. In fact, I think a man should know what he's doing before marrying so he doesn't screw up the wedding night." She watched his expression turn to pain like a boxer hit below the belt and, still angry, she did not care.

"I've never been promiscuous like Layla, but if you are searching for a virgin—I'm—not—her." Tricia poked the hard wall of his chest three times with her finger as if pushing her statement into his heart. "You found out what you wanted to know, so get out of here." She went to the door and opened it wide. "Out!"

He could be thankful she didn't recall he'd christened her breasts Pretty and Perky. No telling what she would have done then, probably more than throw him out. He made one last effort. "Are you sure you're going to be okay? I wrote my private number down on the notepad by the computer if you need me."

"I don't need you. I can take care of myself. Out!"

Rex stepped over the threshold, and she slammed the door hard. The same family encountered last evening straggled along the hallway fresh from a swim in the rooftop pool. The boy wore a striped inflatable swim ring around his waist, and his sister had floaties on her arms. She stopped to point at Rex. "See, Mommy, the prince is still here."

Her mother, a chic semi-transparent cover-up over her bikini, answered harshly, "That is no prince, honey. What you see is a holier-than-thou hypocrite."

"He doesn't look like a hippopotamus."

Rex gave the child a feeble smile. "I swear I didn't even loosen my tie." He hadn't, and the silk noose around his neck had strangled him all night as he struggled with impure thoughts about Trish.

"Mommy, hippos don't wear ties. I think he is still a prince, maybe in disguise, because he doesn't have a crown."

"Come along and don't bother the man." The mother herded her children before her as if he had a contagion.

The father stayed back. He sucked in the gut that hung over the top of his trunks. "Sorry about that. Women. Nice touchdown yesterday. I mean a man should be able to celebrate. Great meeting you, Rex." He hurried after his wife impatiently tapping her toe outside their door where the rest of the family had come to shore like the Swiss Family Robinson.

Rex moved quickly to the elevator. He had one place he needed to go before returning to his condo to catch up on his sleep. He prayed he would not dream of Tricia Welles.

****

Tricia leaned against the closed door. So, now Rex Worthy knew she wasn't good enough or pure enough for him and unrepentant besides. Nothing more to do than go up to the suite and face the music, pay the piper, whatever. She slid her suitcase off the rack and slung the black bag over its handle.

After disconnecting and closing her laptop, her fingers lingered over the notepad. Finally, she tucked it into a compartment of her handbag and zipped that pocket shut. Taking a big breath, she started for the suite where Layla lurked.

Upon arrival, she noted the closed bedroom door. Lucky break, no one dared bother Layla in her lair. All that remained of the buffet were a tray of empty oyster shells, some stalks of limp asparagus, and a few slices of fancy breads gone dry in their basket. Layla had either called in another man or gone on an eating binge to console herself. Tricia considered making toast with the bread and brewing a cup of tea from the selection of bags arrayed next to the coffeemaker. She still felt wrung out despite the long sleep watched over by Rex. Okay, she'd make a prudent breakfast and gain some strength before Layla confronted her.

Just as she finished her last bite of dry toast, the door to the suite opened, and Layla burst forth. "I thought I'd find you here dining off my leavings when I couldn't reach you in the room downstairs—or Rex either. I know what you did Patsy."

"I must have picked up the wrong glass last evening and passed out. Sorry."

Layla moved close enough to sink her nails, still painted Sinners' red, into her PA's arm. "How stupid do you think I am? You did that on purpose because you wanted Rex for yourself. Passed out? Hell, you were plenty lively when he carried you away. How was he by the way? Bumbling, too quick, or did he have stamina because of all the football training? I'll bet I had a better time with Lee."

"Lee?"

"Lilah Divine. After the two of you ran out on me, I took him up on his offer to see his show. A very flattering portrayal. He did several scenes from my movies and added in a few songs. Afterwards, we came back here and finished off the goodies, then went to his place. An interesting experience and fairly satisfying. I'll bet you can't say the same."

"No, because I remember nothing about last night.

Evidently, I grew talkative and I revealed a few things he didn't need to know."

Layla brightened. "About your failed acting career?"

"No, about Boyce."

"You, me, and Boyce."

"There was me and Boyce, and you and Boyce, but no you, me and Boyce ever."

"Honey, I did you a favor. In bed, he was at best mediocre."

"Believe it or not, I didn't fall in love with the man for his sexual skills. I thought he cared about saving the world, making it a better place. We were going to do that together." Tricia tried to shake loose of Layla's grasp and failed.

"Oh dearie, you know he's running a medical marijuana place in Colorado now. That's how he plans to save the world—by getting everyone mellow. Like I said, *big* favor."

"You keep in touch?"

"What can I say? He's a rabid fan and still adores me. He sends me some prime weed every now and again."

"Okay, Layla, you did me a favor. I'll tell you what you really want to know. According to Rex, nothing happened between us last night. He's a decent guy and wouldn't take advantage of a drugged woman. To say the least, my sexual status disappointed him. He left when I asked him to go."

Layla finally removed her claws leaving smalls dents behind in Tricia's skin. "Indeed. He's still a virgin then and such an innocent. Who else would bring a woman like me pink rosebuds? I'm scarlet roses or hot orange Tropicanas, but maybe they weren't intended for me."

"You know they weren't. You phrased your note to make Rex believe I'd asked him out."

"You read my private letter to Rex, stole him away in the night. How am I going to punish you, Patsy?" Layla closed her violet eyes as if in deep contemplation, then opened them to stare hard at Trish like a Siamese cat stalking a canary that had imprudently flown free of its cage.

"I should fire you outright for betraying my trust. However, I am a woman of compassion. Only this morning I called that fancy cancer care place in Iowa where you have your mother stowed on my dollars. Terribly sorry to learn she is in the ICU again with serious complications from her second round of chemo. Of course, they wouldn't let me talk to her. Only the daughter who neglected to think of her today could do that.

How upset she would be to learn you'd lost your high-paying job. By next week, your mama will be carted off to some state hospital to die among the poor."

"We'll somehow manage without your money."

Layla blinked slowly, again the cat toying with her prey. "You needn't—if nothing happened between you and Rex."

"He gave me his Scout's Honor. I'd say he's completely over me if he ever had any interest."

"Good, very good."

Tricia half-expected her boss to rub her hands together like an old-fashioned villain. She waited for the next nail in her coffin to be pounded home.

"Figure out a way to bring Rex Worthy to me on a

platter, and your mama won't have to make a change of address any time soon."

Layla threaded her fingers together making them into a small trap that closed with a clap of her hands.

Chapter Fourteen

Grateful the Sinners had no practice today, only the team meeting over and done with, Joe settled next to Nell for a little afternoon delight in the huge, round bed of his bachelor days. They might even sleep for a while afterwards. She'd gone for a checkup with Dr. Stewart while in New Orleans, no problems, all progressing normally. Nell emphatically did not want to know the sex of the twins, but he'd taken a peek into Madame Leleux's chest and figured he knew who was coming to join the family.

His empurpled side hurt like the devil keeping him up at night, and he hated taking painkillers. Oh, he'd tape up and do what he was told on game day, but for now wanted to tough it out. At the moment, he took things slow, just smoothing Nell's rounded belly and dropping light kisses on her neck. She wore nothing but the locket containing his severed curl. He did love the horny stage of a pregnancy, but that last trimester, always a bitch. Nell moaned softly ready to go on to stage two of the seduction.

The telephone by the bed rang. "Leave it," Joe said.

"Could be a problem with one of the children." She picked up. "For you. Gregory, the doorman."

Joe rolled over to take the call and swore briefly, having forgotten about his bruises while anticipating sex. "Yeah."

"Mr. Rex Worthy to see, sir. Shall I send him up?"

How he wanted to say no, but being the quarterback and team captain came with certain responsibilities, like it or not. "I guess." He hung up and told Nell about their unexpected visitor.

"Really? He's never come here before." Nell sat up and began dressing.

Joe pulled up his jeans, sans underwear, and threw on a Sinners' hoodie. No sense letting the competition see how bad his injury was. Next thing you knew, the kid would expect to play in every game. Sure, sure, Worthy had done a nice job on the touchdown, a gutsy move and one Joe would not have attempted, but who'd set him up for that last play? Maybe he'd come by to say thanks.

Joe opened the door when the bell rang to find Rex Worthy dressed like a man on his way to church, white shirt, tie, and slightly rumpled blue suit. "Come on in then. You missed team meeting. A quarterback should never miss team meeting—unless his wife is giving birth or something."

"Yeah, I know. I sat up all night with a sick friend."

Joe merely raised his eyebrows. He'd used that a time or two in his days as a backup quarterback and in reality with Connor Riley. He didn't buy that virgin guy crap either. The man had to have done something with a woman sometime if he wasn't queer. "So what do you want?"

Nell hurried up full of lively curiosity and much better manners. "Sit down, Rex. Would you like some coffee?" The three of them settled at the breakfast bar, the two men with Nell between them like a referee.

"I'd better not, Miss Nell. I need to get some sleep soon in order to be ready for practice tomorrow, but something is on my mind. I thought Joe could help me with some advice."

"Just Nell. I always have to convince the new players I'm not as old as their mothers. How about a glass of milk, warm or cold?"

"No, thanks, but maybe you could help me out, too. A woman's opinion on this would be mighty valuable."

"I think I understand. You were with a woman last night and botched it. Not the girl with the orange hair and nipple rings?" Joe said with a great deal of satisfaction in his voice.

"Not her!"

The man's horror seemed genuine. Joe grinned, enjoying the reaction. "Then that Patsy-Tricia girl. I saw her hand you a note. Or was she only shilling for Layla Devlin?"

"For Layla, but I thought I went to meet Tricia."

"Ah," Nell said. "Beauty and the Beast. By beast, I mean Layla."

"Yes, ma'am. Layla tried to ruffie me, but Tricia drank my champagne to save me. I couldn't do anything else but stay with her all night and make sure she didn't hurt herself."

"Yes, you did the right thing, Rex. What else happened?" Nell leaned forward over her belly as if watching a soap opera in progress.

"Nothing physical, God's truth, but Tricia talked a lot and maybe said things she didn't want me to know. This morning when I told her the Lord would forgive her for her trespasses, like sleeping with a man before marriage for example, she blew up at me. She said a woman wanted an experienced man to marry, one who knew what he was doing in bed. Should I believe that?"

"Yes," said Joe immediately.

"No," Nell replied at the same time.

Rex looked up at Joe and down at Nell. "I'm confused."

"I'll say you are. First, never mention God the morning after—or forgiveness," Joe advised.

Nell broke in. "Are you attracted to Tricia? Do you care about her?"

"Yes, ma'am, but she made if fairly clear she only wanted an experienced man. But then, I thought I only wanted a virgin. Should I get some experience or what?"

"Definitely," Joe advised. "New Orleans still has plenty of houses where the girls can teach you all you should know and then some. That might have to wait until we get back from our three week road trip, or maybe we could find a classy bordello in Dallas. I'd only go along to make sure they treated you right."

Nell put up her arm and clapped a hand over her husband's mouth. "Don't listen to him, Rex. No bordellos for either of you. What you do is give Tricia a little time to cool off. Then, tell her you want to get that experience, but only with her. She'll be your first. A woman cannot resist that."

"My first and only if I marry her. I mean, she's just right for me mostly. She puts up with Layla for the sake of her sick mother. Now, that's a loving heart."

"Has Tricia asked you for money?" Joe asked.

"He's not that green, Joe," Nell said, slapping her husband's knee. "Don't be so cynical."

"Oh, I'd give her money if she asked, but she hasn't. Her mom has cancer."

"Yeah, that's what all the working girls say." Joe got another glare from his wife.

"Well, I believe you are on the right track. Take it slow. Really get to know each other first," Nell said.

"*Mais,* yeah, boy. Don't go rushing into marriage and kids and all dat," Joe said, his Cajun showing.

Nell turned on her stool to face her husband. "Are you unhappy about something, Joe?"

"Having our afternoon interrupted."

"Sorry, really sorry. I should go." Rex stood up wearing his discomfort like a hair shirt.

Nell hopped down from her stool and put a hand on his arm. "Think about this carefully for the next couple of weeks. While you are certainly old-fashioned, you shouldn't do anything that doesn't feel right to you."

"Thanks, Nell. Sorry for disturbing your day."

"Oh, you didn't interrupt anything important. I'm just spending a little time with Joe before the team goes on the road. I really have to get back to the children by tonight." She walked their guest to the door and saw him out.

The second the door closed, she turned to her husband. "Now we have our answer why he didn't find any of our young ladies of interest. He's in love with Tricia."

"Maybe in lust, and don't tell me he's incapable of that, but she no longer meets his criteria—not a virgin. She burst his balloon last night. You caught that, right?"

"I did, and he bungled it with her but can overcome it. Now where were we?"

"Not doing anything important evidently." Joe looked as sulky as undersized Trinity when told he was too small to do something he really wanted.

Nell came very close and fingered the cowlick where his curl had once been. "By the time you get back to New Orleans, this will be grown out again." She fished her locket from its place over her heart and kissed it, then his lips. "Nothing is more important right this minute than our being together. I only wanted to put Rex at ease."

"How about me?"

"Lead the way."

Chapter Fifteen

Tricia stalled—and lied. First, she told Layla she had no way to get in touch with Rex. Since they'd had a fight, he would have to call her when he got over himself, which might never happen. That excuse did not wash with Layla, but Trish managed to delay any action until the team left for a long road trip, three away games in a row, putting Rex safely out of reach for a while. She needed time to think.

The Sinners were gone, but that didn't prevent disaster from striking in the gossip magazines. Layla snatched the tabloid headlines again. Under a full-length photo of the actress in the billowing caftan that made her ass appear tremendous the caption read, *Layla Packs on Pounds Pining for Worthy*. There followed a report of beignet runs and a huge feast sent to her suite. "Did she gorge all this food alone after being rejected by the supposedly saintly quarterback?" the article speculated.

Worse, the rag had paired that story with another, one Tricia didn't recall. Still, there she was in a photo placed just under Layla's big butt story waving happily at someone's camera phone as Rex held her in his arms awaiting an elevator. *Rex prefers PA. Spends night in her room. Did they or didn't they?* Testimony supplied by lobby lurkers verified the truth of the picture. They had seen Rex Worthy with a drunken woman in his arms obviously going up to a room. "But what happened after that?" the gossip reporter inquired breathlessly.

Mrs. Luanne Davis of San Antonio, Texas, answered her question. "I saw with my own eyes Rex Worthy entering a hotel room with a drunken woman. I have no idea who she is, but he took advantage of her right in front of my children, practically tackled her on a king-sized bed. No case of mistaken identity I assure you. I watched that boy play footfall his whole time at A & M. The next morning he left the room at nearly noon with her screaming at him to get out. He said right to my face he'd never loosened so much as his tie. He certainly had on the same clothes, but I say you can have sex with a necktie on or shower and get dressed again in the morning. I thought of Rex as a good Christian gentleman, one of the few left on this earth. It breaks my heart to see how far he has fallen from his values since becoming an NFL player."

The reporter picked up where Luanne left off. "We have no way of knowing what went on behind closed doors as the country song says. Other informants claim the bed and shower remained unused. As for the young lady in question, we have verified her identity as that of Patricia Welles, personal assistant to Layla Devlin, an actress known for her steamy roles but obviously unable to attract Rex. What really went on Sunday night—Bible study or debauchery—only God knows."

Layla had strolled out for her own beignets Friday morning. She returned with a double order. Judging by the powdered sugar on her upper lip she'd eaten more of the donuts on the spot before coming back to the suite with the scandal magazine tucked under her arm.

She scarfed down beignets between rants. Waving the paper in Tricia's face, she demanded, "Do I look fat to you?"

"No, Layla. You are as spectacular as ever." If the entire tissue of her life weren't made of lies right now, Tricia could have mentioned the strained seams of her boss's short shorts and the very slight puff of extra flesh above the wide cinch belt she wore with them. A striped top practically shrink-wrapped over her breasts did little to hide the small defect, but most men would be staring at Layla's long legs or deep cleavage depending on their tastes. Tricia didn't know if the extra weight acquired came from excessive consumption of New Orleans cuisine or the number of sweet cocktails the actress chugged down nightly in the clubs.

Slightly appeased, Layla offered the bag with one beignet left in it to Tricia. "No, thanks, I had some breakfast while you were gone." Beignets made her think of Rex. *Our love can never be, never be, never be.*

Layla chucked the scandal sheet into the waste can by the desk and finished the last donut. She dusted her hands of powdered sugar and demanded another inspection with her arms held out wide. "Anyone can tell I'm not fat, only voluptuous. I mean, I've been to all the hot spots where people see me for themselves. How could they print those lie about me?"

Tricia plucked the paper from the basket and studied the photo of her in the quarterback's arms. She did look drunk—and very elated. "The reporters are only speculating. They say so if you read the whole article. You aren't upset about what they said about me and Rex?"

"Only the part about him preferring you to me. Not having any experience, he doesn't know what he is missing. I suspect all this intimidates him more than your meager offerings." Layla patted Pride and Joy.

"I don't know. Mine are pretty and perky." Why had she said that? Competing with Layla in any way usually brought reprisals.

Her boss laughed so hard she had to loosen the belt cutting into her belly. "Thanks for taking my mind off this stuff with a joke. I'm going up to the pool to sunbathe. Put a suit on, and we'll see who looks best in a bikini."

"You'll win, Layla. You always do."

"Damn right."

No matter, Tricia still had to put on a bathing suit and accompany her. She'd have to fetch drinks and rub on suntan lotion. With the paper still clutched in her hand, she went to change. Once in the privacy of her room, Trisha used a scissors from her bag to cut out the picture of her and Rex and buried it deep in her black bag next to the notepad with his phone number. She had no memory of the event, but now she had a souvenir to cherish.

****

Rex Worthy trotted out onto the field at Cowboys Stadium, did his warm-up, then dropped to his knees for his usual prayer. A few boos sounded from the stands, and he suspected he knew what those were about, but he shut the noise out of his mind. As usual, he asked for the safety of all the players on both teams and added a few words for the protection of Tricia back in New Orleans and at the mercy of Layla Devlin. Taking his seat on the bench, he continued to think about the woman he'd left behind to deal with the scandal in that trashy magazine, the one a teammate taped to his locker.

Surprisingly, Joe tore it down and held the paper high. In a voice the quarterback used for audibles or to quell his horde of noisy children, he said, "We don't do this to one of our own before a game. We all have to deal with this kind of shit from time to time. Pray you aren't next." He clapped Rex hard on the back. "Get your head together. You might have to go in for me."

That last remark cheered Rex no end as did a comment from Howdy McCoy that he believed the backup quarterback only meant to help a woman in trouble. Even Adam Malala, known for doing his intimidating war dance before a game, offered to pray with him afterward if he felt the need. The rookie wide receiver and new running back went shamefaced into the tunnel. Rex would bet, if he were a betting man, that those two had done a lot more with Katya and Tatiana after the barbecue than see them safely home. He needed to get in touch with Trish later, make sure Layla hadn't hurt her in some way out of jealousy. Usually, he had lots of time to let his mind wander when bench-warming. But now, he had to get his head in the game as Joe suggested.

Already as the first few plays went off, he could tell Joe had a problem with that sore side. His passes fired off short and abrupt as he worked the team past the fifty-yard line. One try for a long spiral fizzled short of its goal and fortunately did not lead to an interception. The Cowboys noticed, too. They sent their roughest tackles to attack Joe on his weak side. So far, the Sinners' offense protected him well. As if to make up for his prank on Rex, their new running back, Jakarta Jones, carried the ball into the end zone with speed and flair after a handoff from Joe. Cowboys scored one, but before the half, Howdy McCoy kicked a field goal through the uprights that put the Sinners up by three.

Late in the third quarter as the linemen tired, Joe took a sack. He finished out the time, but failed to come up with a touchdown. The Cowboys put one of their own on the board making the score, fourteen-ten. As the teams changed sides, Joe had a few words with the coach. Must have been, "Send Worthy into the game" because Rex got the nod to get out on the field.

Young, eager, strong, and feeling every bit of it, he chose to run the ball himself on the first play. Straight-arming and elbowing, he moved the ball forty yards before being bought down. A sharp, choppy pass to his tight end advanced the team another twenty. His try at a long pass failed worse than Joe's prior attempt, but one of his teammates covered the ball and prevented a turnover. A pass-off to the running back got them close to the goal. So much for variety. When Rex saw a hole, he tucked the ball, charged through it for the touchdown, and gave the glory to God. Reliable Howdy made the extra point. The Sinners defense held the Cowboys for the remainder of the game, and the team triumphed by three points.

Back in the locker room, Jakarta Jones and Eric Blixen, the new wide receiver, groused a little about Rex hogging all the glory, but still asked him if he wanted to step out with them that evening. Rex looked at Joe who shook his head. "Not tonight. Howdy, Adam, and me are going to have a few brews and play some darts. You stick with us. I need to tell you what you did wrong today."

"But I made my second touchdown."

"Yeah, keep running those balls and taking those hits and see how long you last as a quarterback. Not to mention, you aren't a one man team. You still have lots to learn about many things, but Nell was probably right about one of them."

Rex preferred this kind of evening anyhow, a couple of beers, a platter of wings, a competitive game of darts, and a return to the hotel around eleven. Sure, Joe mentored him most of the time, but the information would help his game. The bit of advice he took most to heart—you are the quarterback, so don't let guys like Jones and Blixen disrespect you.

Back in his hotel room where his roommate, an older reserve quarterback who never got to play, hadn't returned from celebrating the victory, Rex debated whether to call Tricia at the Windsor Court. He might get Layla instead, but no, always the star, she wouldn't answer her own phone. He thought it might be too late at night, but the idea of Tricia dealing with the scandal alone ate at him. Finally, he rang their suite. The bell sounded over and over. No one answered.

In the silence after he hung up, Rex considered turning to prayer, but another notion almost as good came to mind. He didn't go in for poetry much, but his mother once gave him a volume of inspirational verses to guide his life. He'd liked one meditation by a man named John Donne enough to commit it to memory since this wasn't the sort of book he could take a chance on packing for a Sinners' road trip. He took enough ribbing over his well-worn Bible. It began, "No man is an island" and ended with "send not to know for whom the bell tolls, it tolls for thee."

He recited it aloud, keeping Tricia in his mind, before turning to his bed.

Chapter Sixteen

The Sinners planned to head for the west coast in the morning without returning to New Orleans. Coach wanted them adjusted to the time change and the playing field by the time they took on the Seahawks the following Sunday. Rex slept poorly the night before, waking when his roommate stumbled in after partying hearty, then worrying about Tricia. Once he got back to sleep, he experienced an embarrassing wet dream about her just before dawn that went unnoticed by his passed-out teammate. A quick flick of the covers over the damp spot hid his shame. He arose at six a.m. to take a cold shower and annoy the guy in the other bed with the noise, read his Bible quietly for a while before going down to an early breakfast. Most of the team stayed abed. He tried to reach Trish again.

This time someone picked up the phone on the first ring. "Layla Devlin's suite, how may I help you?" Tricia's voice sounded tired but otherwise okay.

"It's Rex. About that stuff in the papers."

"Don't worry about it. Layla was more concerned about her butt looking too big. When I said you swore nothing happened between us, she believed me—or rather you."

Tricia's naked breasts, the ones that haunted his dreams, jiggled into his mind. Perky and Pretty. Good thing he'd had some relief earlier or the waiter would be wondering what went on under the breakfast napkin covering his lap.

"That's good." He searched for more words. "Did you see the game yesterday?"

"Oh, yes. Congratulations on another touchdown. Very impressive. Layla dragged me to a sports bar to watch. The celebration went on well into the night. She's sleeping in right now. I'm making coffee and ordering the usual Virgin Marys with hot sauce she needs after drinking like that." In the background, hot water burbled in the pot.

"I'm glad I don't have your job."

"Or I yours. Sorry they booed you while you prayed. That woman from San Antonio has some nerve talking about you like that when she has no idea what happened. Of course, I don't either."

"Doesn't matter to me. If I know I did the right thing in my heart, I'm good. It's you I worry about. Your reputation is ruined now. People will believe you are a fallen woman. If you want to get married, just say the word." Laughter trilled in his ear. The waiter stood at his shoulder with the platter holding his overstuffed omelet, a side of sausages, and a heap of toast. He motioned for the man to set it down and go away.

"Rex, I fell a long time ago. Guess I told you that. Anyhow, believe it or not, a girl no longer has to marry a man if she's seen going into a hotel room with him. Put your mind at ease. So, how did you spend your victory night in Dallas?"

Reciting poetry and having a wet dream about you. "With Joe, Howdy, and Adam playing darts and eating chicken wings."

"Sounds pretty tame."

"I didn't get any of that experience you want in a man, if that's what you mean." Should he ask her now to show him as Nell suggested? No, better to say something like that face to face. Rex took a big gulp of orange juice. On the other end of the line, Tricia stayed quiet for a moment.

"Layla is still up for teaching you all she knows, which is quite a bit. You should take her up on the offer."

Suddenly, his massive breakfast had no savor. The best he could answer was, "I don't think she's my type."

"She's every man's type. Gotta go. The Virgin Marys are here, and I don't want room service to wake the sleeping demon. Thanks for your concern, Rex, but I'm fine, really."

He didn't think so. Her voice wobbled a little under a false cheerfulness, but she'd disconnected. Across the hotel's restaurant, Joe, Howdy, and Adam entered appearing well-rested and hungry. A few bleary-eyed Sinners straggled in after them. Most hit the buffet line, but the three older men came to sit with him.

"Joe, I think I just proposed to Tricia, and she told me to go sleep with Layla," Rex said miserably.

His team captain motioned the waiter over and indicated he needed coffee. The waiter poured, and Joe remarked, "Weak" as he tasted it. "Frankly, I can't begin to deal with a statement like that before I have a couple of cups, maybe more considering the brew. Don't they know about dark roast in Dallas?"

Howdy grinned, boyish as ever with his freckles. "It seems to me a guy either proposed or he didn't. Like a woman can't be just a little pregnant."

Adam disagreed after he gave his order for three poached eggs on a bed corned beef hash. "In the islands once your family settles on a bride, you can be engaged without knowing exactly how that happened, but in this case I don't think she took you seriously, my brother."

"She surely did not. Trish said if a couple spent a night in a hotel room together, they didn't have to get married anymore."

Joe sputtered into his cup of weak coffee. Once he could breathe again, he replied, "Remember what Nell said about taking this slow and steady. Too soon for a proposal, man. Think about dancing in the pocket looking for a target for your pass. Don't rush it."

"Slow and steady works," Howdy agreed.

Jones and Blixen, who roomed together, sauntered into the restaurant and swung by Rex's table. Blixen gave him a sharp slap on the back. "You missed some prime Texas ass last night while you were out with the old, married guys. I tell you these cowgirls like riding more than mechanical bulls."

Joe set his cup down with a decisive click. "You know I often have a bunch of receivers to choose from when I toss the ball. In my old age, I just might forget about some of the new ones."

"Sorry. Didn't mean to diss you, Joe," Blixen backpedaled.

"Get some breakfast. The bus for the airport will be here in an hour." Joe dismissed them. As the young players moved away, he said to Rex, "And that is how you keep their respect."

****

Tricia sat in the kitchen area of the suite with her face buried in her hands. She couldn't offer Rex her long gone virginity, and she suspected with his high morals he scorned liars as well. Merely suggesting he learn about sex from Layla nauseated her. What would she do when Rex returned to New Orleans, and she had to make good on her promise to deliver him into Layla's clutches?

She took advantage of the momentary quiet to phone the woman she did all this for, her mother. The answering voice sound dry and weak. "Hey, my baby,"

"How are you doing?"

"Complications and more complications. Now it's blood clots in my legs. Doesn't hurt but I have to lay still here with those awful white stockings on my legs until the Coumadin takes care of them. I never thought I'd miss cooking big meals for harvest hands, but seems like fun compared to this. Enough about me. Tell me all about your glamorous life with Layla. I'm so glad the two of you stayed friends after college and are still together looking out for each other."

As always, her mother deflected the conversation away from her health. Tricia scrambled for some cheery tale she could conjure for the sick woman's entertainment. Only one came to mind. "We met some of the Sinners players the other week and went to a barbecue at Joe Dean Billodeaux ranch. Dozens of children running around and lots of good but plain food, not quite what you'd expect."

"But you had a good time."

"I guess so. We had to cut our stay short." Tricia smiled, recalling Layla covered in manure. She revamped the story minus Rex. Hearing her mother laugh—worth all she put up with from Layla, but Mom stayed on point when it came to her daughter and men.

"You didn't meet these Sinners in a bar, did you?"

Mothers always knew. "Not exactly. We went to one of their practices and then out later to a club. Layla knew Joe from making *Savaged!,* but one of his friends introduced us to some of the others. Don't worry. When I go out with Layla, I am always the designated driver." And flunky. "One of the guys was Rex Worthy."

She tried to suppress any special interest in her voice, but her tone must have changed involuntarily. For certain, her mother would not have seen the gossip magazine because Dad would never bring upsetting news to the hospital. Besides, he paid no attention to such stuff, only reading headline articles in the regular newspapers and the sports page mostly. Chances are he did not know about the scandal either.

"The young man who prays so much? Ordinarily, I'd say to watch out for football players, high school, college, or pro, but he seems very nice. Are you interested in him?"

"No, no, but Layla is. He is a good man, kind and trustworthy."

"Now that would be an odd combination, him and Layla. She was none too religious when we all went to the Methodist church. I doubt she is any better than she should be now. I mustn't say that. Layla took the time to call me the other day and inquire about my health. You wouldn't expect a big star like she's become to do that, now would you?"

"Layla is full of surprises." Mostly bad ones.

"You think he will marry Layla? Imagine, I might be the first to know."

"Doubt it. Layla often says she's not the marrying kind." She'll only ruin Rex and toss him aside, words

Tricia could not say to a very sick woman.

"But is he?"

"Definitely."

"Maybe he'll see past her star and notice the one I brought into the world."

"Only my mother would say that about me." And that was why Tricia would do anything for her.

"Oh, no, here come the needles and meds again. I have to go, but don't let Layla or anyone else say you couldn't get a man like Rex Worthy."

Too late for that now, way too late.

****

At the airport, Rex called home. No one would rag him about that. Lots of team members were close to their mothers, especially Jakarta Jones who had grown up without a father in the picture. His own mother answered immediately, one of the advantages of the caller I.D. he'd gotten for them to sift out reporters and cranks.

"Honey Lamb, how you doing? You did so good on Sunday, we're right proud of you, and you gave the credit to God, too."

Ten years under the African sun had not taken the sheen off her Texas twang one tiny bit. To Sue Grace Worthy everyone deserved to be called honey something. His sister grew up as Honeybee. His father answered to Honeydew and returned the favor by referring to his wife as Honeybunch. At least, she'd stopped calling her son Honey Lamb in front of his friends when Rex begged her to desist during his high school years. Today though, the fond nickname soothed his soul.

"I'm glad you're still proud of me. Did you by any

chance see my picture in the paper lately?"

After a request to put the call on speaker-phone by his father, the reverend answered. "We certainly did. The sports page had a wonderful shot of you completing that touchdown with your hand raised to heaven."

"Nowhere else?"

"If you mean that scandal sheet, Mrs. Murray had the nerve to bring it to church and shove it right in my face during the social hour. Ruined my appetite for the cake," his mother declared. "I told her I simply knew you were helping that poor girl get safely back to her room. That is what you were doing, right?"

"Yes!"

"I told you so, Honeydew. Your father said boys will be boys, and you would outgrown lust and repent of it, but I said my boy has nothing to repent."

He surely had not outgrown lust yet, but no need to tell his mother. "Say, Mom, do you remember you once told me when I met the right girl, I'd recognize her as the one?"

"Yes." That one little word came back to him full of hope and excitement.

"Well, what if you meet her, and she doesn't recognize *you*?"

His mom was on that like a speckled hen on a June bug. Her disappointment registered immediately. "Would this be the young lady in the picture?"

"Yes, but she's better than that. I mean she drank a Mickey intended for me on purpose. I had to watch over her."

"Son, did you spend the night with her?" his father asked in that measured, neutral preacher's way of his.

Rex could imagine him clearly, the kitchen light shining down on his bald head, accenting his hollowed cheeks and yellow-toned skin. Africa had sucked the life out of his dad, forced to give up his mission because of ill health. About now, the reverend would be cleaning his glasses as he considered his next words. Rex felt a pang of guilt because he'd always been glad he took after his mother's big, round-headed German side of the family who kept all their hair into old age.

"Now Elton, he already said he didn't," interjected the mother who believed she'd raised the perfect son.

"I meant I saw her safely to her room—and I stayed the night watching over her, but nothing carnal happened." Except for staring at her naked breasts and being unable to forget them. "She wasn't too grateful in the morning."

His mom, always ready to play defense when it came to her children, groped for a mild pejorative. "Why that—that hussy!"

"Sue Grace, we do not know this girl and cannot judge her."

"Really, she's a great person. If you knew what Tricia endures from her boss in order to get her mother top cancer care, you'd admire her. She isn't exactly the kind of girl I thought I'd fall for, but you'd love her, honest."

"I believe Rex and I need to have a father-son talk. Would you go in the other room, Honeybunch, and shut the door?"

His mother left, unwillingly judging by her heavy tread followed by a slam. No frail bluebonnet, his mom outweighed his dad by quite a bit. Her German genes, she said, but a fondness for those social hour cakes figured in there somewhere.

"Now, tell me what's wrong with Tricia."

"It's just that she's not a virgin, and she's been with more than one guy." Rex scanned the waiting area, but most of his teammates were plugged into their iPods or deeply immersed in their own calls since their flight had been delayed until late afternoon. Joe appeared to be talking to each of his kids one at a time and would be on the phone until the flight boarded most likely.

"Neither was I when I married your mother."

"Dad, you're the holiest man I know!"

"I wasn't hatched under God's right wing, Rex. I grew up in west Texas groping girls in the back of pickup trucks on Sunday nights. I came to Jesus after my stint in the military, met my Honeybunch at Texas Bible College, and that was it for me."

"So you were experienced before you got married. Was Mom?"

"I never asked. She took me as is, defied those racist parents of hers to embrace my dream of going to Africa as a missionary. All that mattered was our future together."

"Because God would forgive her trespasses if she asked."

"Of course, but that would be between her and God. It isn't wise to press an issue like this with a woman."

"Seems like I've already been unwise. Mom always said I should save myself for my bride, and the woman I chose should do the same for me."

"You have a great mother, but sometimes I think she's overprotective. Despite your size now, you were a sickly child in your earliest years. She feared to lose you. When Honeybee came along, she loosened her grip a little, but she still wants what is best for you. A virgin bride would be wonderful, but in this day and age, not too realistic. I'd overlook Tricia's past if you truly care for her. Forgive and forget."

"I'm glad we talked. Let me say good-bye to Mom. Our charter finally is being called." His mother spent her last few seconds of the call warning him about bad women. She meant Tricia, but Rex knew the term applied much better to Layla Devlin.

Chapter Seventeen

Layla dragged Tricia to a sports bar for the next two Sundays to watch the Sinners games along with other ardent fans. With wing sauce dribbling from her plush lower lip, the actress screamed with delight when Rex went in during the fourth quarter of the Seahawks game to give the obviously fatigued Joe Dean a break. The regulars stared at her and mumbled under their breath about Worthy's not being able to throw a pass. Eighty percent of them wore Billodeaux's number 7 jersey. Rex did not make a touchdown this time around but managed to run a lot of time off the clock moving the ball slowly down the field. Despite this, the Sinners lost on a last minute field goal made just under the wire by their opponents. The defense had to take the blame for this one.

Feeling better and not giving Rex a chance, Joe Dean played the entirety of the Cardinals game the following week and brought off a stunning victory based on four of his long passes. Layla pouted and loudly voiced her opinion about not putting in Worthy. A man with the build of a dockworker told her to shut her yap. After emptying a pitcher of margaritas on the guy's head, Layla pitched chicken bones from their platter at the TV. Asked to leave, they'd have to find another bar when the team left New Orleans again.

Other than that, Tricia finally located a furnished

rental condo on Decatur Street that met Layla's specifications. They moved in, and she got a small respite as the star amused herself with Lilah Divine who took Layla to the best restaurants and most interesting dives in the city. Time off to visit the art museum, the aquarium, the zoo in the afternoons before the transvestite needed to go to work, what luxury. Now, if she could only stop envisioning going to those places with Rex. Probably not the art museum, but she'd bet he liked animals. This had to stop. She needed to think of him as Layla's man, hands off!

When the team returned to New Orleans, Layla insisted on being front and center at the airport. Wearing the jersey that appeared to grow tighter each week, the actress rushed the security line and shrieked her favorite player's name over and over. A hunted expression on his broad face, Rex passed quickly, flicking a brief wave their way and boarding the bus without pausing for so much as an autograph or a fist bump. Layla did the whole "Do you know who I am?" bit with the officers before being escorted to a cab. If they didn't, the paparazzi sure did. There would be pictures within the next week, Tricia knew.

Lilah whose real name was Lee kept his idol supplied with various drugs. Although Tricia flushed what she could find, the amount and variety seemed endless. She and Layla had been around this particular street corner before after the first big hit movie. Conceiving a passion for the co-star, a married man but willing enough to sleep with Layla while they filmed to enhance their love scenes, Layla stalked him afterwards. There followed a restraining order, a weight gain of fifty pounds, and indiscriminate drug use until she had to gain control before her next movie or lose her contract.

Layla stabilized, stating her career meant more than any man. Her mentor and sometimes lover, Micah Stanley, quietly thanked Tricia for hanging in there to prevent worse damage by presenting the PA with an eco-friendly Prius, and Layla with a Jaguar for shaping up. Now, having been rejected by Brandon, Joe, and Rex, matters with Layla would only grow worse if the actress didn't get what she wanted. How Tricia wished she could get in that car currently parked at Layla's mansion in L.A. and return to Iowa instead of doing this all over again, more awful than before because a decent man was involved.

She didn't expect to hear from Rex after the scene at the airport. Let that be his hint to stay away from both of them. If he didn't get in touch, they were safe. But, she'd given into the temptation to program his private number into her phone, not under his real name of course. That courted disaster. She chose King Oliver after an old New Orleans jazzman and a signature ringtone of a song called *Sweet Like This*. Layla might be enjoying all the vices New Orleans could offer her on a golden platter, but Tricia used her free time learning the history of the city and gradually becoming more comfortable with it.

The notes of *Sweet Like This* burst from her phone late on Monday night while Tricia holed up in her new bedroom on the other side of the condo from the one where Layla entertained Lee, who consoled her after the dreadfully humiliating airport debacle as the actress referred to it. "They didn't know who I was," she told the transvestite mournfully.

"Then shame on them Lay-Lay. Let Lee-Lee make you feel all better because you are a diva, and I discovered you first. No other tranny is doing Layla Devlin in the entire city."

With a full kitchen and a spacious living room having a great view of the Mississippi between them, and the television turned on, Tricia couldn't hear their weird coupling or whatever else they were doing. No wonder airport security hadn't recognized the movie star with her unkempt hair resembling Medusa's snakes in the high humidity and the added fifteen pounds. Good thing no mug shots were taken.

"Hey, it's Rex. Sorry for calling so late. Is Layla asleep?"

"No, but she's occupied. What did you want?" If he said you, she'd be done for.

"I've been thinking about your situation."

"Not your problem, Rex." She wanted to mean that.

"When you see a person struggling, you should try to help. No man or woman is an island. At least they shouldn't be. I got this two million dollar signing bonus and used it to set up the Worthy Foundation. Right now most of the money is tied up in growth stocks, but if Joe does retire, I'll make a lot more. We held back some to assist the needy immediately. Maybe my charity could pay your mother's medical bills. You could quit Layla and—"

"You think I'm a charity case! I have a horrible job working for a terrible woman, but I can take care of my mother without your assistance." Anger helped keep her on track to do what she had to do.

"Well then, you could marry me, and my money

would be your money."

"You believe I'm the kind of woman who would marry a man for his money. That's as insulting as needing your handouts."

"No, I didn't mean that. I thought maybe you liked me enough to consider it."

"Are we back to you feeling obligated to marry me because of one night where nothing happened and a ridiculous newspaper article?" Rex, Rex, Rex, too good for his own good.

"I only want to help you. Tell me how." He begged for it.

"You can get Layla off my back by going to her and getting that experience you so sorely lack." There, said and done, but how would he respond?

The pause on the other end of the conversation stretched to such length, Tricia thought he'd disconnected. She almost prayed he had.

His deep voice came back with a gruff edge to it. "If that's the only way I can help you, I'll do it."

"Good. We have a condo now. I'll give you directions. When can you come over here?" Keep it brisk and businesslike. Do not whimper.

"Big game this Sunday, the Falcons. Practice will be tough. Maybe next Monday night when that's over with. Is seven too early?"

"Like I said before, people can have sex anytime, anywhere. I'll put you on Layla's calendar. Don't worry, it won't hurt." Only me, I'll hurt. "Sleep well, Rex."

"You, too, Trish."

****

Rex Worthy didn't sleep well for the rest of the

week. He had so many wet dreams he changed and washed his own sheets to avoid any questioning looks from his cleaning lady. By day, he dreaded his appointment with Layla and by night when deep asleep, he desired Tricia. Sluggish during practice, Coach reamed him out on a daily basis. He didn't believe he'd play on Sunday, partly because of his recent performance and more because Joe would want to keep the intense rivalry with the Falcons in his own competent hands.

Whether the flattening level of crowd noise in the Dome affected their rivals or Lady Luck had momentarily deserted them, the Falcons could do no right on Sunday afternoon. Adam Malala intercepted one ball and popped out another for a crucial fumble. Joe played like he had ten more good years in him, connecting pass after pass and driving up the score to the roar of the fans. By the end of third quarter, the game was over by any standard.

Coach motioned Rex to go in and run down the clock. "You don't need to do anything, but keep the ball as long as you can. It's good practice."

He started out obeying those instructions, mostly letting the backs run the ball for short distances just enough to achieve the first downs by inches, but the Falcons made a goal line stand and blocked Rex's short pass into the end zone. Two more failures to score followed, and Howdy McCoy came out to make a field goal with his usual ease. Rex headed back to the bench and let the defense do its job.

Joe Dean sat next to him and said, "No big deal this time, but you need to get women out of your head," as if the quarterback read minds. The only problem, now he'd planted the thought of Monday evening and Layla in the forefront of Rex's brain instead of buried in the back where she belonged. The game paused as the medics came out on the field to remove a Falcon's receiver with a possible broken leg. An idea formed.

The big men of the defense polished off the rattled Falcons after four pitiful possessions. Rex went out again, same instructions, but he could not bring himself to follow them. He hugged the ball close and ran it three times in a row making good progress down the field but taking hard hits that brought him crashing to the ground and had the coach screaming in his ear. Each time, he got up and ran the ball again. As the end zone loomed ahead, he slowed enough to allow the opponent's most aggressive tackle to bring him down by the ankle as he stretched his arms across the goal line. Touchdown! With the air knocked out of him and pain attacking his lower leg, Rex hardly had enough presence of mind to raise that hand to God.

Two trainers helped him limp off the field. X-rays and ice followed. Nothing broken but his eardrums as Coach Buck lit into him. "What the fuck were you thinking? Practice your passing, I told you. Now you got a sprain bad enough to keep you out of the next couple of games. You coulda broken that leg and ended your season, shit for brains."

He'd hoped for exactly that. A man with a cast on his leg could hardly be expected to perform in bed. If his season ended today, maybe Layla would move on, but evidently God did not see fit to give him an easy way out. As it was, he'd had to endure her parading around wearing his number in her luxury box along with that transvestite who found it cute to dress exactly the same right down to big, false boobs. The camera followed them pressed against the windows of the suite nearly as often as they did the plays, or so it seemed to Rex. Right now, the lens caught Layla weeping hysterically over his injury in the arms of her double. Gave him the willies.

After the game, he limped into his condo with a tightly taped ankle and a bottle of painkillers, the Monday night date still on as far as he knew. Rex thought about calling Tricia to see if he could get a reprieve, but remembered how badly their last conversation went. He'd never gotten a chance to say he'd rather be with her, let her teach him and train him to please her. Instead, he'd promised to go to Layla, the worst mistake of his life.

Chapter Eighteen

Rex got through the team meeting on Monday fairly well despite having his stupid last plays dissected over and over. "You don't take unnecessary risks like this unless you want a short career. Sure, play hard, but don't play dumb," Coach Buck repeated, running the sequence one more time.

He stayed at the training facility all afternoon doing some weight lifting since he had to stay off the ankle. Waving a trainer away, Joe sidled over to spot for him. Rex knew he could press more than old Daddy Joe, not that it mattered when you had an arm like Billodeaux. He prepared for a lecture as perspiration dribbled down his forehead and stung his eyes. Joe tossed him a sweatband and a towel during a short break. Almost casually, the great quarterback brought up a different subject.

"You tell Tricia how you *feel* yet? I can tell it's eating at you." Joe said "feel" as if as the word spoken to another man caught in the back of his throat and needed to be expectorated. "Sorry, I sounded like Dr. Mind Fuck there. I mean how's it going with Trish. You two get it on yet?"

"No."

"I could tell. You sure aren't any more relaxed."

"When I called, she made me promise to go with Layla."

"You're shittin' me! Maybe she doesn't return your interest after all."

"I don't know. I think Layla forced her into this."

Joe considered this statement while stroking his newly regrown forehead curl like a pet he'd lost and found again. "Layla can be pretty persistent. I've seen her goods, all of them. It's not a shabby offering. She's used to more experienced men. My guess is her infatuation won't last long, and you'll be free to go with Tricia. On the other hand, she might make Tricia off-limits because she's that kind of bitch."

"That's your advice—sleep with Layla and hope she lets me see Tricia later."

"Since Tricia won't have anything to do with you otherwise, yes. I imagine Layla will make the experience very pleasurable. Wish I had some other idea to offer. Let me know how it goes, particularly if it's going to affect your game." Joe stood and beckoned the trainer back into position. "Don't let him hurt himself, you hear."

Rex worked on his muscles until the trainer forced him to quit. He wanted to be exhausted this evening, too tired to arouse by any means. He shouldn't shower. Body odor might repel Layla. He bathed anyhow because Tricia might be around. Shaving, forget about it—and no lime aftershave this time.

Later, when he ripped through his closet considering what to wear, he finally settled on plain khakis, a deep green dress shirt with plenty of buttons down the front and two on each cuff, a hassle to take off. Remembering his sister said this particular shirt make his hazel eyes look greener and lots more attractive, he considered discarding it, but then it *was* a pain to unbutton. Same with the shoes, brown oxfords with tight laces he could untie slowly worn with long socks that wouldn't come off easily. He considered adding a sweater over the top, but October in Louisiana remained steamy, and he'd already put on an undershirt with his snug boxer-briefs. He tied all this together with a stiff leather belt harder to unbuckle than the one he'd worn the night Layla tried to molest him in the cab.

The virgin had girded his loins as well as he was able. Rex said a quick prayer for deliverance from his fate, took a deep breath, walked out his door and toward Layla's new lair. A little more exercise couldn't hurt even if his ankle did. He took a couple of pain pills he'd stowed in his pants pocket, but didn't pause to pick up flowers on the way.

He arrived a trifle late and rapped on the condo door wondering if Tricia would let him in. She'd texted him a reminder of his appointment on his cell phone earlier in the day. A call to her went to voice mail, and he did not leave a message. Neither woman answered his knock. The creature known as Lilah Divine, but dressed as a man for a change, waved him inside. Rex had only a moment to observe that Lilah, a male so nondescript he would have made a great spy, appeared much more attractive as a woman. Maybe that's why he did his act. God loves all creatures, Rex reminded himself.

"Layla awaits you in her boudoir," the transvestite said grandly, pointing in the proper direction. "You are in for a treat. We've been getting ready all afternoon. Don't mind me. I'm just leaving."

"Where's Tricia?"

"In her room way over there with her headphones

on, I imagine. That's where she usually goes when I'm around to take care of Layla for her. Not that I mind. Ta ta." Although wearing trousers and running shoes, the tranny swept from the condo as if gowned in satin and six-inch heels.

Turning his eyes away from Tricia's bedroom, Rex took another deep breath and forced himself to walk in the opposite direction. He rapped lightly on the indicated door.

"Come in dear Rex. I've been waiting." No Southern accent now but a throaty purr.

Layla Devlin stunned him, absolutely stunned him. Rex stood just inside the doorway, yet almost at the foot of a king-sized bed with an ornate brass bedstead arrayed with icy blue satin sheets but no bedspread to get in the way. That lay crumpled on the floor. Layla reclined like a nude centerpiece amid a mound of lacy cushions with peach-colored walls for her background. She bore no resemblance at all to the snaky-locked Medusa at the airport. Her blonde tresses cascaded in smooth waves down her shoulders and across her chest. Other than that, Rex could swear on a stack of Bibles she hadn't another hair on her body.

"Look all you want, baby," Layla encouraged. "That will get us both started."

His eyes roved over a lavish display of breasts tipped with shining nipples a peculiar shade of deep pink. There appeared to be more of her that didn't show when sausaged into tight clothes. Her navel sank deep into the soft dough of her belly as if someone had tested her for doneness at that spot. He blinked twice when he got to her naked pubis. Did it glitter beneath the light cast by a modern brass chandelier? He knew his mouth hung open and couldn't seem to shut it.

"All for you, darling. Cherry gloss on my tits for a whole new taste sensation and a little sparkle down below to get the fireworks started. Come lie beside me." Layla patted the space next to her.

Rex knew most men would be drooling and erect by now, but he viewed only the goddess of lust carved from a block of pure white lard. Far from exciting him, he merely felt repulsion. He didn't go beyond her dimpled thighs, but looked up again to her best feature, those lilac eyes, not lovely and provocative tonight, but hard and voracious. She did not move him at all.

Impatiently, Layla punched the mattress. "Here! We can't do more with you way over there." She pouted her lush lips, the same shade as her nipples and presumably also cherry glossed, at him and then smiled coyly. "Or perhaps we could. Would you like to watch while I play with myself?"

"No!" That brought Rex to heel. He moved to the side of the bed and lay down beside her without so much as taking off his shoes.

"Do you want Layla to undress you?"

"Uh, no. I'm fine." He licked his dry lips.

Layla answered his gesture with a pink tongue circling her own lips. She placed them hard against his and walked her hand down his body with her long, cherry-colored nails making little dents in his clothes as it went. Rubbing her palm against his crotch, she broke off the invasive kiss. "You aren't ready for me. Do you need something to help you relax?"

Rex fastened his gaze on the clear bulbs of the chandelier. "No. If I'm supposed to learn something I need to remember it in the morning." Suspecting all he would retain was shame, he closed his eyes against the little blue dots he started to see.

"That's right. Close your eyes and just feel." Her lips and hand went to work again.

Rex opened his eyes wide and turned his head to one side. He concentrated on the jolt of being tackled, the pain in his sore ankle now numbed by drugs. Numbed. Without thinking about it, he'd given himself the perfect defense against Layla. Thank you, Jesus. But if she kept him here for hours of torment, he had no backup.

"This would go better if you undressed." Layla worked at the small, annoying buttons on his shirt and revealed his pristine white undershirt. "I didn't know men wore these anymore, at least not under another shirt. No matter. It's like unwrapping a fabulous birthday gift with many layers and a great surprise at the end. I'll bet you aren't all scarred up like old Joe Dean. Here we go."

She finished with the buttons down the front and struggled with the cuffs, breaking a nail in the process. Cursing under her breath, Layla finally pushed the green shirt off his broad shoulders and pulled out the long tails. "Well, take it off. Don't make me do all the work."

Rex sat up and removed the shirt, folding in neatly into an oblong. He started to rebutton it as if returning the shirt to a display in a men's wear department.

"Oh, for heaven's sake!" Layla flung the bundle onto the floor and striped off his T-shirt in one swift movement. She shoved him down on the pillows. "That's better." Slowly, she circled each of his nipples with a fingernail. "Such great pecs, so big and firm, but you might consider waxing your chest, not that it isn't gorgeous as is. Your pecs need to get to know mine." She rubbed her breasts back and forth across his chest and stroked the bruises he'd gotten in the last game. "These kind of turn me on, my brave warrior."

Heaven had nothing to do with this. Funny, he'd always believed the torments of Hell would be fiery, but mostly, he felt chilled. She didn't arouse him, whether because of his own free will or the drugs for pain. He didn't care which.

Straddled across his thighs now, Layla unzipped his fly and ground herself against his groin with only those black boxer briefs between them. She breathed with small, gusty pants. Her head thrashed her blonde hair across his muscles. His penis made a feeble attempt to provide her with a mount, but for him, nothing much happened. Layla gasped until she came, those violet eyes all but rolling back into her head, and collapsed against his chest. Rex guessed he should have held her in his arms, but he kept them rigidly at his side. Layla cuddled close licking at his nipples until she caught her breath. Again, that chilly sensation. He shivered.

Layla chuckled. "Now you are supposed to climb on top of me. I'm all primed and ready for another, but it is nice to let a girl go first."

"Don't think I can."

"What do you mean by that? You're young and healthy. You can't be impotent." She explored inside his briefs. "Right position but wrong consistency. You'll need some handwork or maybe a BJ. Let's get the rest of your clothes off." Layla did a reverse straddle and tried to force his shoes from his feet. Rex got a premium view of the size of her butt.

"Did you glue these things on?"

"No, ma'am. They're just laced up tight."

"Like all the rest of you."

"I think it's my leg injury. I took some painkillers for it."

"Oh, my poor baby. Of course." Layla swiveled around again flailing him with her breasts as she reached for his face and stroked his stubble. She offered him a nipple to suck for comfort, rubbing it against his lips.

Rex clenched his teeth. "No! That's a lie. Okay, not a lie because I did take some pills. But Layla, I just don't want you. I think I love someone else."

She cackled like a witch in Macbeth. "This isn't about love, sweetheart. Nobody does it better than Layla Devlin. The woman you think you love is going to be a great disappointment in bed. She can't compete with me."

"She doesn't have to." Rex stood up and zipped, noticing with dismay that some glitter and the scent of Layla Devlin got on his hands. He wiped them on the satin sheets. "I'm leaving, and I won't be back." Pulling the T-shirt over his head, he shrugged into the dress shirt without bothering to button it, just pushing the long sleeves up to his elbow. He headed for the exit.

A barrage of pillows followed him. "Soft just like you! I swear you'll come back begging. You'll never get over Layla Devlin."

Chapter Nineteen

The soft thumps continued after Rex shut the door, crossed the length of the condo to the other bedroom, and walked in without knocking. Tricia sat crossed-legged on a wildly flowered spread in the middle of a queen-sized bed that made her appear to be sitting in a meadow in full bloom. She swayed to the music playing through her earbuds. Tears leaked from under her closed eyelids and stained a simple cotton knit shirt the same color as the sky the day he first saw her suffering at the practice field. She'd drawn her straight, dark brown hair back in a high ponytail, keeping it out of the way of the waterworks. Wearing cutoff jeans so old they'd turned nearly white and grown a long fringe, she'd left her feet bare.

Rex touched her shoulder. She startled, those summer sky eyes opening wide and watery. Gently, he removed the earbuds.

"What are you doing here?"

"You're crying. How come?" Rex removed a tissue from a box on her dresser and tenderly dried her face.

"Sad, sad songs. Why aren't you with Layla?"

"I'm done with her. I want you to teach me anything I need to know, anything you enjoy. Come with me." Rex stooped to hand her a pair of sandals discarded on the floor.

"Where?"

"My place."

"You know I can't do that. I'll lose my job. If you left her, Layla will be furious, I—"

"Don't care." He strapped the shoes on her feet and heaved her off the bed. "Let's go. We can walk like normal people, or I can carry you the way I did the night you took the ruffies for me, but people will notice."

"I'll walk." Tricia grabbed her large, black bag and slung it across her chest.

"Leave that."

"No, I could survive a month on the run with the contents of this bag, and I might need to."

"Don't you understand? I'll protect you. Let's move before Layla starts screaming, and you go running like always."

Rex cupped a large hand on her elbow and guided her from the apartment, down the elevator, and out onto the street coming alive as the night deepened. Jazz wailed from nightclubs, and the ladies of the evening lounged on their street corners in outfits of bright Spandex or leather that barely covered. Rex looked neither right nor left, only straight ahead. The long walk might do them both good. They skirted the casino, crossed busy, treacherous Canal Street, passed by the Windsor Court, and kept on going so fast they had no time for small talk.

"Aren't you supposed to stay off that ankle?" Tricia gasped.

"I'm feeling no pain. You want me to get a cab?"

"No, only slow down a little. I like to go running now and then, but I haven't done any wind sprints lately and I'm carrying some baggage here." She slapped a hand against the enormous bag.

"Sorry. Want me to carry that for you?"

Tricia smiled at the thought of great big Rex carrying a purse, even a large one. "No, I'm fine if we don't have to power walk."

"I just want to get down to it in a hurry."

"So romantic," she grumbled.

Still, he slowed his pace as they entered the Warehouse District. A few galleries beckoned passersby with wine, cheese, red grapes, and an opening show of promising new artists. The hulking museums of the district had gone dark for the evening. Rex stopped before one of the trendy renovated buildings and let himself into the lobby with a key. The elevator took them up just high enough to see the lights glinting off the wide river and the humped back of the Huey Long Bridge from the window the illuminating corridor. The apartment had the same view.

Attractive, Tricia observed, and probably professionally decorated. The living area surrounded her in deep brown leather and shiny dark wooden surfaces. Yes, he had the recliner essential for every man and a large flat-screen TV mounted over a black marble fireplace, never used, all enclosed by walls of hunter green. The designer had tossed a few wine-toned cushions onto a massive sofa to add more color. The dining area adjoined the space to take advantage of the view, windowless kitchen to the rear. The mantel held a few golden football trophies from Rex's college years, and the end table a worn Bible, no men's magazines, but a small volume of poetry.

"It's only two bedrooms, two baths, not a big one like Joe's. I like to have the extra room in case my parents or sister visit. They haven't come yet. My mother says I signed on to live in Gomorrah." Suddenly tense, Rex added a feeble joke. "At least it's not Sodom."

"You have a nice place, and remember, the angels did find at least one righteous man in those cities."

"Not enough to spare the places. Hey, you know your Bible."

"Hardly. I liked the more gruesome stories when I was a kid. Rain of fire, wife turned to salt, you know."

"Want to sit down?"

"Sure. You should get off that ankle, too." Tricia seated herself on the couch so wide it could have been a bed and tossed her black bag into its far corner out of the way.

"I-ah-want to shower. Is that okay with you? I mean just make yourself at home while I clean up."

She could have offered to shower with him, but he seemed spooked enough already simply having her here. "You look clean enough to me."

"Believe me, I'm not. I won't take too long."

He entered the first room off a short hall, shut the door, and she swore he locked it as if she might run in there and catch him naked. Tricia took her bag to the other bathroom and unzipped the pocket holding the drops to take the redness from her eyes and found enough cosmetics to repair her light makeup. Taking down her ponytail, she brushed her dark hair to a nice sheen.

Looking in the full-length mirror on the back of the door, she regarded her sorry outfit not exactly geared for seduction. She supposed she could take off her clothes and spread herself out on the deep sofa, but she wasn't Layla and didn't desire to be. How far had they gotten before Rex walked out? In the end, she only removed her sandals and enjoyed the feel of Rex's plush burgundy-colored carpet, thick and soft enough to serve as a mattress, as she returned to the living room. Behind his closed door, water drummed hard in a shower.

Tricia put her purse back in the corner and settled on the sofa with his book of poetry, a pleasant discovery, but no surprise that the poems were inspirational. The leaves fell open naturally to John Donne's *Meditation 17*, the "no man is an island" poem. That explained his odd comment when he'd tried to make her an object of his charity. She wondered if he knew Donne had written love poems, sometimes erotic, before finding God. She doubted it. The rain of water in the shower stopped. Now, she got to be the one to feel tense. What next? How to begin?

Rex toweled off with one of those super-sized bath sheets the interior designer had gotten for him. Big towels for a big man, she'd said with a suggestive gleam in her eyes and a pretty head cocked to one side as if issuing an invitation. He liked the towels but didn't take her up on the implied offer. He knew now he'd waited for Tricia. Wrapping the bath sheet around his middle, it came down well below his knees like one of Adam Malala's lava-lavas.

He considered his face in the bathroom mirror and decided to shave. He didn't want to chafe her skin and would have to take his chances that she might laugh at his round visage kind of pink from the scalding hot shower. Rex scraped away the stubble and patted on the lime aftershave he hadn't worn for Layla. Brushing back his wet hair, he debated getting dressed again. His clothes lay in a heap by the hamper. Gingerly, he picked up his briefs defiled by Layla's slime and a scrim of glitter and deposited them in one of the plastic bags his cleaning lady kept under the sink for trash collection. He knotted the bag tight and placed it in the waste can. The rest of his clothes made it into the hamper for a thorough washing before he wore them again. Taking another deep breath, he went to the living room wearing only the bath sheet.

Tricia, reading his poetry book, looked up. "This okay or should I get dressed?" he said.

She took a moment to answer. All that fine male flesh on display, even a bit bruised, would stir any woman's juices. Thick neck, wide shoulders, hard pumped pecs, a coating of light brown hair spread across them and arrowing into the towel. Below it, well-defined calves, an ankle in a tight wrap, and feet big enough to carry a man far. "Not if you're comfortable. You should put that foot up though," she finally managed to say.

Rex took a seat on the edge of the recliner but did not recline. "See, I took some painkillers for my injury. Maybe that's why things didn't go well with Layla, that and my not wanting what she had to offer. We should probably wait for them to wear off a little. Maybe talk a little first."

"Okay." Tricia noticed a new detail. "You shaved for me."

Already pink from the shower, Rex grew redder. "Yeah. I didn't want my beard to hurt you."

"So why is it you don't shave often?"

"I already told you this." He gestured to his face.

181

"Sensitive skin, round baby face, need to look tougher for the NFL."

"Sorry, I don't remember. Thank you. That's very considerate. And I don't think you look like a baby." Maybe an "oh, baby", but definitely not an infant. Tricia set aside the book of poetry and curled up on the end of the sofa nearest to his chair. "Maybe we should find out what you do and don't know. Have you kissed, petted, beat off, had a BJ?"

His complexion headed toward the hue of boiled crawfish. "Kissing, sure. I had a religious girlfriend from my father's church in high school and one in college for a while that I met on Christian Mingle. Petting only above the clothes. No BJ's from either. As for the other thing, sometimes it just happens. I had a really bad case of self-pleasuring in middle school, but you know, Leviticus 15:16."

"I'm not familiar with that particular Bible verse."

"Basically, it says if you spill your seed you should wash up and keep your hands to yourself for a day or two. My dad gave me the same advice."

"He wasn't against that altogether?"

"No, really, he's a pretty understanding guy, I guess because he is a guy. I found out recently my father had a whole different life before he become a missionary. My mother is all about purity. She made me wash my own sheets because she wasn't touching them."

Tricia seemed to remember her mother's mild complaints about how often she had to change her boys' bedding, but she'd never shamed them by saying why. Poor Rex. "Why don't we start with kissing? You want to come here or should I go over there?"

"You could sit on my lap."

"Now that's an old line if I ever heard one."

But, she went and settled herself on his sturdy thighs enrobed in the thick towel. He positioned the chair to a reclining position and put his feet up. Tricia stretched out along his length and framed his face with her hands. Rex closed his eyes. His lips were heavy but soft beneath hers. He took his time exploring their boundaries with his tongue before teasing her mouth open and going in shallow at first, then deeper, definitely mimicking the act of love. Surprising. When they came up for air, Tricia pushed against his chest said, "I'd say you passed Kissing 101 and went on to the accelerated group."

"Well, when Chastity told me kissing was the gateway to sex and we weren't going through that gate, I got fairly good at what we could do. May I touch your breasts?"

"Don't ask, Rex, just do. If I don't want you to, I'll lean back. If I'm interested, I'll lean in." She leaned into those big hands that soon found their way under the plain cotton top. He had trouble with the hooks on her bra but finally got them undone.

"I want to see Pretty and Perky again," he said, rough-voiced.

"Huh?" Tricia sat up straight.

"Your breasts. I named them that when you exposed yourself to me from the neck down that night. I mean I know you were out of your mind at the time. You seemed sad that Layla's big ones had names and yours didn't so I-I should have confessed before."

Tricia took a turn at blushing. "I'm sorry I embarrassed you."

"Not so much. I mean I didn't touch them or anything, but I did pull your dress up again so you wouldn't be upset in the morning."

"Okay, now I understand why they weren't in their cups. You really want to see them again?"

He nodded. Tricia raised her arms and allowed him slip the shirt over her head and discard the dangling bra that had nothing sexy about it. She let him look. Beneath the towel, something stirred and grew more restless when he placed his hands over Pretty and Perky and started a gentle massage that encouraged her nipples to peak. How she loved that and the names he'd bestowed. Her eyes closed. She enjoyed the moment.

"I guess I'm not as numb as I thought," Rex said. "I think we should go to the bedroom now. Don't get up. I can carry you."

"Your ankle."

"Still not feeling any pain down there."

He gathered her and closed the distance to his room faster than he could run the ball for ten yards. Showing no shyness, Rex removed her sandals but hesitated when his hand came down on the zipper of her jeans. "You sure?"

"Oh, yes. Go ahead."

A man good with his hands, in seconds he had the cutoffs on the floor and began reverently removing her panties, cotton, pale blue, not bikinis or a thong, but low enough to expose her navel. She had a dark patch of hair between her thighs, probably trimmed up some for wearing a bathing suit, but he couldn't be sure. Not much experience in this area. It looked natural to him, a soft place where a man might want to rest. He lay down beside her and began to stroke that mound. She rewarded his efforts with quiet moans.

"One thing I learned from Layla. It's all about friction."

"Yes, it is, but don't ever mention another woman's name while doing someone else. Harder, deeper."

Rex complied, getting his broad finger in there, finding exactly the right spot to make her writhe.

"Quick learner," she gasped.

"Yeah, a quarterback must be able to think on his feet—or off them, I guess."

No answer to that but an arching of her back and a clamping of her thighs against his hand, keeping him in place, rocking against the pressure, until she suddenly loosened with a great sigh. "Ladies first," he said.

"And thank you for that. Your turn. I'm ready. You won't hurt me."

"Maybe a little more friction first." Rex positioned himself over her as she opened wide for him, but he placed his penis, so hard, more swollen than he imagined it had ever been before, into her cleft and rubbed it back and forth. Not slime, lubrication. He got it. Tricia started tossing her head and pressing against him again. He'd held out for twenty-four years. He could wait and give her two orgasms, maybe three once he entered. That would be good, right? He didn't have the ability to ask her right now.

In the background, music began to play, nothing romantic, some corny old song about not being able to keep 'em down on the farm after they'd seen Paree. He traveled very close to Paree right now and needed to reach his destination. Condoms! Did she have any in that black bag?

Tricia pushed her hands hard against his chest. "I have to get that."

"No! Must be Layla trying to get you back. Let it go to voice mail."

"Can't. It's my father."

She might as well have invited her parent into the bedroom. Rex rolled over onto his stomach and with an immense groan, buried his face in a pillow. Tricia, not pausing to dress, padded to the living room. He heard murmured conversation that went on for a while, then nothing. When she didn't return to the bed, he wrapped the towel around the wreckage of that magnificent erection and went to find her.

Chapter Twenty

Tricia huddled on his sofa with her knees drawn up and her face pressed against one of those little pillows he never used for anything. Her shoulders shook hard. For the second time that evening, she cried, but not in the same way as before. Last time sadness—this time grief?

Rex looked around for that plaid blanket his decorator called a throw and claimed it matched his colors. He found it folded on the lower shelf of the end table where his cleaning lady put it because the thing always slid off the back of the couch and ended up on the floor. Shaking it out, he wrapped the blanket around her nakedness and sat beside her. His arm went around her shoulders as the most natural way to offer consolation. "What happened?"

"My mother died tonight."

"While we were…" The very thought upset him.

"Earlier, probably when you were with Layla. My dad had to make some arrangements and get himself together before he could make himself call." She burrowed against his warmth and slowly stopped shaking. "He went to sit with her like he did every night for a few hours, kissed her good-bye, and got the call that she'd slipped away before he got back to the farm."

"My father said that often happens. He visits the sick and says it's like they hold on until the family leaves so as not to distress their loved ones. Or maybe being loved holds a person here on this earth. He'd say she's gone to a better place where she won't suffer anymore and someday you'll be reunited with her."

"You believe that?"

"I do." He put force behind those simple words.

"I talked to her this morning trying to take my mind off you and Layla being together. I didn't let her know how miserable I was. She thought to her last hours that I led a glamorous life. I told her earlier that I'd met you, that you were kind and trustworthy. She and Dad followed the Sinners and the Broncos since Iowa has no pro team of its own. They watched the game together yesterday. Mom said you needed to take better care of yourself on the field and to pass that along if I met you again. Then, she asked if you and Layla were still seeing each other."

"I've seen way too much of Layla, more than I wanted."

"Mom said she hoped you'd look beyond Layla and notice me because she'd like to know I'd settled with a good man before she died. Rex, she never mentioned the possibility of her death before. I think she knew the end was near."

"Sometimes folks do. I wish you could have told her I looked beyond Layla from the very first when I saw your blue eyes so filled with goodness behind her shoulders that night at Mariah's Place."

Tricia squirmed. "I'm not that good, and you didn't know anything about me then."

"You made sure Layla got home safely even though she's not a nice person."

"Rex, I'm paid to do that. Many a time I would

have liked to leave her in the gutter. What I put up with—for nothing, nothing at all."

"That's not so." He wanted to say if not for her job with Layla they would not have met. God had sent her to him, kept Mrs. Welles alive long enough for them to get to know each other. Good had come from the suffering of both mother and daughter. Not the right time or place for those words. "Your mother knew you loved her, and you saw she had the best care. That's all you could do. She would have lived for you if she'd had a choice." Rex parted her bangs with a blunt fingertip and kissed her forehead.

"Yes, she would have." Tricia forced herself to leave the comfort of Rex's arms. "I have to get back to the apartment and pack my clothes. The funeral is on Thursday. I'll try to get a flight out in the morning."

"Let me make the arrangements. I'd like to go with you, see you through this, meet your father and brothers."

Suspicion crossed her face. "Rex, I've told you before that one unconsummated night in the sack does not mean you have to explain your intentions to my dad and brothers. This isn't a good time to get involved." How would she ever be able to separate being with Rex and the day of her mother's death? She had to leave immediately. Tricia rose and swathed herself in the muted hunter's plaid of the throw.

The hurt showed momentarily on his round face as clearly as if he was an injured child, but he clenched his jaw and stood up, too. "I want to do something to help. I'd do that for anyone."

"Fine." Tricia removed a credit card from a slot in her purse. "Make flight reservations for me, then. New

Orleans to Dallas to Des Moines. My father will pick me up there. Get the best deal you can because I won't be working for Layla Devlin much longer. Call me in the morning and let me know what time and airline. And, please call a cab for me now. You shouldn't be doing so much walking." Dealing with airlines would be certain to take his mind off of sex and what hadn't happened. She went into his room, turned the lock, and dressed.

With reluctance, Rex summoned a cab. She came out quickly, not much to put on, and picked up her bag. "I'll wait in the lobby with you."

"Don't." She allowed herself to have one last brief kiss from those warm lips. "Rex, I want you to know you'll make someone a wonderful lover. You are gentle, considerate, a great kisser—and have more control and stamina than any other man I've know." She noticed the wince as if she'd pinched him hard in the wrong place. "Sorry, I broke my own rule about mentioning others. I guess that tells you to hold out for better."

He didn't acknowledge that statement in any way, but simply walked her as far as the elevator and watched the doors close behind her. Tricia forgot one of his good qualities, he thought. Maybe she wasn't aware of it yet. He always figured if someone challenged his Christianity he'd be willing to go into the fiery furnace or the lion's den for his faith. When he believed, he believed deeply, and he believed he and Trish were met to be together. Call it stubbornness or persistence, some day they would finish what they started here tonight, and she'd see the light.

****

When Tricia opened the door to the apartment, she found Layla possessing the turquoise leather sofa like Sheba, Queen of the Jungle. Their condo decorator had gone wild with tropical colors: red, azure, yellows, greens, and peach. She wore a naughty nightie in a semi-transparent leopard print that showed off the black panties and overstuffed bra beneath. Must have been a gift from Lee because Layla rarely bothered to buy such items. She slept in the nude and firmly believed in getting right down to business when it came to sex. Lingerie only got in the way and didn't stay on long enough to make an impact.

"Oh, it's only you. Where have you been, Patsy?" She licked the orange off her fingers from the consoling bag of cheese curls by her side.

"Out," Tricia replied tersely. No more need for lies or diplomacy.

"Out trying to get over Rex Worthy? I know you want him. Can't have him. Don't waste another thought on the man. If he couldn't get it up for Layla Devlin, he won't be able to for anyone."

"Maybe his injury…" Tricia started to say. What, was she actually trying to make excuses for Rex so Layla would take him back? She clamped her mouth shut.

"Yes, his injury. He said he'd taken painkillers, but I wonder if the injury isn't in his mind or somewhere lower. Never seen a man so stiff and I am not talking about his dick. I thought maybe he'd come crawling back tonight, but no, only you."

How Tricia wanted to boast that she'd overcome both painkillers and any reservations Rex might have about pre-marital sex, but she hugged that secret to herself. "I'll be leaving tomorrow. My mother passed away this evening. The funeral is on Thursday."

"My condolences," Layla said with a hand wave as casual as if she flipped Tricia the bird. "Buy a nice big wreath when you get back to Iowa and put my name on it. You'll be back by the weekend of course."

"I won't be back. I quit."

"Come on, Patsy. Most employers only allow a couple of days for a funeral. I'm letting you have nearly a whole week."

"Layla, I've put up with your crap for four years, longer if you include rooming with you and letting you steal my boyfriend."

"Letting! He came running when I crooked a little finger." Layla demonstrated how easy that had been by bending her pinkie.

"Exactly. I've fetched and carried and probably saved your life a few times. Not anymore. My father and brothers need me in Iowa. I'll take everything I brought here and arrange to have my things sent from Los Angeles. As of tomorrow, you'll have to find another Patsy—and if you ever call me that again, I won't answer. It's Tricia or nothing."

"I'll double your already generous salary—no, triple it. Don't leave me here all alone."

"Good night and good luck, Layla." Tricia entered her bedroom, locked the door, and began packing. She'd acquired only a few pieces of clothing since coming to New Orleans. Everything would fit nicely in the large suitcase she took along when Layla conceived the idea of seducing Rex Worthy. Thinking his name made her heart clench a little. He'd move on and complete his lessons with someone else, or not, if he decided to wait for marriage after all. She'd provided an alternative to Layla that he found more palatable, that was all. Duty summoned her to Iowa.

Layla must have wrenched herself from the couch. She knocked hard on the door. "Come out, Pat—Tricia. Let's discuss this some more. You can't be serious about staying in Iowa."

"I'll see you in the morning, Layla, just to say good-bye." She carefully folded her black dress, which would do for the funeral with the addition of a jacket.

"No severance pay for you!"

"Didn't expect any."

"Bitch, cunt, whore, slut!" Layla shouted, accenting each word with a blow to the door. Tricia shook her head. The words applied to her former boss far more than to her. She almost felt sorry for the woman, but not enough to stay.

Chapter Twenty-One

Tricia didn't say good-bye to Layla in the morning. The star had gone out, probably for a bag of beignets. Rex called and gave her the name of the airline and the time of the early afternoon flight. He didn't argue about coming along, didn't even say he'd miss her. Good, she'd gotten through to him. One almost fantastic evening spent together did not mean wedding bells rang for both of them. She relayed the information to her father and turned off her phone to stop the incessant calls Layla began making from Café du Monde.

Still, Tricia wasn't surprised to see Rex, red Sinners cap on his head, black T-shirt and jeans both well filled out, stubble growing back, waiting near the counter when she went to claim her ticket. He held out her credit card. "I had to return this."

"Thanks. You did use it to pay for my ticket, right?"

"Sure. I know you can pay your own way." Thanks to a late night call to Nell Billodeaux, he got that right. "Don't belittle an independent woman by assuming she can't take care of herself," Joe's wife said. "After having to put up with Layla, she'll want to go her own way."

Tricia eyes focused on a carry-on bag at his feet. "Going somewhere?"

"Iowa. I want to pay my respects." He noticed she

still clung to her big black bag.

"Won't Coach Buck be upset if you don't make practice?"

"I went in to have my ankle retaped and told him the mother of a friend of mine had died. I wanted to go to the funeral. Since I can't run anyhow, he said to go but be back by Sunday for the game. I guess he's worried the bench will get cold without my behind warming it." Not to mention Joe chiming in with, "No problem, I can handle the Bucs at home without Rex if he doesn't get back in time." Now that stung a little.

After Rex got his permission to be absent, Joe hung around out of curiosity. "Did you and Tricia get down to it?"

"Almost. Then, she got word her mother died."

"Bad deal. That's one I never had to face. Lots of interruptions with ten kids in the house, but death makes that look simple. Nell would say just be there for her, don't push."

That's exactly what Nell had said nearly word for word. Rex would be there for Tricia. "Let's get your bag checked and walk down to the gate together."

The stuffed suitcase came in overweight. Rex let Tricia offer her credit card to cover the cost. She'd be upset enough when they boarded the plane. "Want to get some lunch? No food service on this flight and it's your last chance for some Louisiana cooking. Not much time to make the connection to Des Moines in Dallas either."

"I don't have any appetite today." Then, she looked at Rex and could tell he was hungry. "Sure, a little something. My treat." He didn't argue with her.

They settled at a restaurant offering New Orleans

cuisine cafeteria style. Tricia selected a comforting bowl of gumbo and an iced tea. Rex got a sausage po-boy and a large soft drink. She eyed his tray and his size. "You're holding back. Please get enough to eat. Who knows if Dad has any food in the house?"

Good, she assumed he'd be staying with her family. Happy, Rex added a generous side of jambalaya, some slaw, an apple, and a piece of pecan pie. He offered to share the last as they finished eating, and she opened her mouth like a nestling bird to accept a taste from his fork. Suppressing an urge to take care of her, to insist she eat more, he simply said, "We'd better get to our gate." He braced for what came next.

They arrived in the middle of first class boarding. "That's us. We better move." He held out the tickets he'd kept for both of them.

"You got me a first class ticket!"

"I'll bet you and Layla always went first class."

"Yes, but I'm not with Layla anymore. I quit last night. I must watch my money."

"Well, I need leg room. I got you a regular ticket and asked for an upgrade. They weren't full, so now we get to sit together. Not a bad deal, right?"

"Remains to be seen." She went ahead, giving him the cold shoulder all the way to Dallas, staring out the window from the seat he let her have while he stretched his injured leg in the aisle. Tricia thawed a bit as they raced to catch their connection and hailed a wheelchair for him when he began to limp a little on the bad ankle. Embarrassing because his problem didn't show, the situation evidently gave her some sort of satisfaction as she trotted alongside of the big and outwardly healthy invalid. No first class into Des Moines, so no argument.

Mr. Welles, a solid silo of a man wearing a faded blue feed store cap the same color as his eyes, waited outside their gate with his three husky sons hulking behind him like an opposing team's linemen. The middle man ruined the effect by offering Rex a mellow smile. Tricia introduced them. "My father, Cyrus Welles, and my brothers." Her father stuck out a callused hand and with no awe in his voice said, "Pleased to meet any friend of Tricia's. Call me Cy. My wife spoke of you before she passed."

"You knew I was coming?" Because Tricia didn't until they met at the airport, and she'd kept her phone off to block incessant calls from Layla.

"I figured if you were any kind of a man, you wouldn't let my baby girl travel alone at a time like this. My boys, Cody, Carson, and Colt."

Each offered an explanation of their names as they shook hands. "After Buffalo Bill." "After Kit Carson." "After the gun and the guy who made it," the last son said. Despite his size, a few pimples and an awkward manner marked Colt as a teenager. The other two Rex estimated to be college age, if they went to college, making Tricia the eldest. She added, "Patricia after my grandmother, thank heaven. Dad wanted to name me Calamity Jane."

"Or Annie Oakley. Your mother would have none of it." A small, pained smile creased a face that had seen plenty of hot summer suns in its time judging by the deep wrinkles around the eyes and mouth. "We'd better get your bags and move if we want to be home before dark."

Cy Welles led the way to the luggage carousel and handed Tricia's large bag to Cody. Rex scooped up a small, slim suitcase made of some silver high impact material. Colt raced toward the parking garage calling, "Shotgun!"

"No, sir, young man. Your sister gets the shotgun seat. You go in the truck bed with the rest of the baggage. Rex rides with Cody and Carson. Mind your manners," Cy commanded.

All obeyed him without any backtalk. Far from new, the truck did have a double cab. Rex waited to help Tricia into the front seat and got a nod of approval from her father. Then, he crammed into the back with her brothers. Carson smelled a little like an old college roommate who always kidded him about being so straight. Not a comfortable fit, but he felt like part of the family. Having brothers would be great. He got along with his sister, Honeybee, but she did have a sting to her sometimes.

"It's about a twenty minute drive once we clear the city," Tricia informed him. "I hope you're not too crushed back there."

"I'm fine."

Other than that, no one seemed inclined toward conversation. Rex studied the countryside as dusk descended like a flock of crows over the harvested fields, some with their stubble already plowed under in preparation for the next crop. The last of the light glinted off a pumpkin patch or two adding some color to the landscape. Huge rolls of hay wrapped in ghostly white plastic loomed near the barns. Iowa gave true meaning to the word flat. Sure, south Louisiana was flat, but bounteous trees and meandering bayous broke up the delta plain and kept the land from being monotonous.

Cy steered the truck off the interstate and onto a straight blacktop road, then turned on another. A gate left open allowed them to enter a long dirt and gravel drive leading to a square, two-story white frame house boxed in on three sides by windbreak trees. A light shone before a green painted door sheltered by a generous porch and a lamp glowed in one window with shutters of the same color on either side. As they left the truck, a chill breeze rushed across the former prairie and rattled the chains of a porch swing. Bats swooped, devouring insects drawn to the illumination of the house. The end of the long, hot summer lingered in Louisiana, but Iowa raced toward Halloween.

After tossing down the suitcases, Colt launched out of the truck bed over the tailgate. He'd had the sense to button up his denim jacket and jam a cap down on his head for the ride. Tricia, still dressed for New Orleans heat, shivered. Rex, unable to stop himself, tucked her under his arm to lend his warmth. Pleased she didn't draw away, he noticed the pack of Welles men exchanging glances. They need not worry. He intended to declare his honest intentions before going back to the Big Easy, but he did release Tricia as soon as the group reached the warmth of the house.

"You take our guest upstairs, Colt. Put him in Granny's old room and show him where to wash up. Put Tricia's bag in her room. I'll lay out some supper," Cy said.

"Let me help you with that, Dad." After draping the black bag over Colt's shoulder and smiling at his dismay, Tricia trailed her father down a hall to the rear of the house.

A staircase plain as a ladder ran along one wall to

the second floor. Family pictures decorated every foot of the journey upward. Four very small bedrooms, a bath, and two larger rooms filled the space under an attic. Colt dropped Tricia's suitcase and bag in the corner room at one end of the hall. From the quick glance Rex got, it appeared a teenage girl still lived there amid a collection of stuffed toy animals on the pink chenille bedspread and a fan of playbills tacked to the wall.

Colt showed him the guestroom, pointing out the others along the way. "Trish's room, then Cody's, the john, Carson's room, mine right across from yours. Granny died in here and sometimes her rocker just starts moving by itself. Mom said if Gran is still here, she's watching over us. And the floorboards creak in the hall just so you know." The teen waited for a reaction.

Rex nodded. He wanted to smile at the teenager's blatant moves to protect his sister, but respected the kid enough not to laugh. Colt might still be filling out, but would grow as massive as his father and older brothers fairly soon. "Tricia must look like her mother," he remarked mildly to the kid.

"Yep, spittin' image my old man would say, except for the blue eyes. Trish and me got the blue eyes from him. Cody and Carson's eyes are brown like my mom has, had." The overgrown boy struggled with that last word and turned his back on Rex. "I'm going down now. Come on whenever you want to eat."

Rex gave Colt a few minutes to contain his emotions in the bathroom. A flush signaled an all clear even if the kid hadn't used the toilet. Rex followed after to use the facilities, a plain old-fashioned commode. He washed up at a sink hung from the wall with a skirt of yellow-checked cloth hiding the pipes. A shower curtain patterned with playful rubber duckies surrounded the big claw-footed tub large enough to accommodate any member of the family, maybe two standing up. A vision of him and Tricia in there together popped into his mind shaming him. He'd better get something to eat and turn in early. Last night after she'd left his apartment hadn't been conducive to rest, more of those embarrassing dreams again. Maybe a big meal and travel exhaustion would take care of his unseemly urges tonight. With Colt across the hall, he sure hoped so.

Far from there being no food in the house, a long plank table surrounded by six sturdy chairs with rush seats revealed very little of its worn surface beneath a smorgasbord of offerings. A large ham sat in the middle like a centerpiece. Rex counted three whole roasted chickens and a paper bucket full of fried bird. Mac and cheese, that green bean casserole like his mom made at Christmas, baked beans, coleslaw, au gratin potatoes, and a salad of carrot coins and green peppers filled in the spaces between the meats. Three cakes, two pies, and a big glass bowl of banana pudding crowded the kitchen counter.

Tricia added one more crumb-topped hot dish to the array and spread her oven-mitted hands wide. "I guess we don't need to worry about starving."

"The church ladies went into action as soon as they got word of Martha's passing. They have this phone tree, you see. Even stocked the freezer with chili, beef stew and lasagna, though we still had plenty of soups and light stuff they brought for my wife." Cy cleared his throat. "What do you want to drink? There's pop, iced tea—and beer."

"Water would be fine," Rex said.

"Not a drinker then?"

Unsure how to answer, he went with the truth. "Not so much, but I do have a beer now and then."

Cy nodded, satisfied with the response. He filled a glass with water from the tap, added ice from a plastic freezer tray he banged against the sink to release the cubes, and handed it over. "That bottled stuff is going to be the death of the environment."

"Yes, sir." Rex took the glass and got another curt nod of approval.

"I had the hot dishes in the oven on low while we went to the airport but if anything is too cold, you let me know and I'll zap it in the microwave. Tricia, why don't you sit in your mom's chair?"

Slim as a champagne flute surround by beer steins, she took the suggested seat and appeared to be very uncomfortable there. Rex found himself boxed in with Cy at the head of the table and the boys surrounding him. Directly across the way, Carson, the middle boy, obviously the strong and silent type, stared at him like a red-eyed bull in a pasture of plenty.

"You want to offer a prayer for all this?" Cy asked him. "I know you got religion. Sometimes I think I'm losing mine."

"I'd be glad to do that." Rex went with a simple two-liner. His father would have gone on longer blessing all the church ladies.

"Dig in," Cy said.

Carson started shoveling food into his mouth as if he hadn't been fed for a month. The others joined in passing the dishes. Rex showed his appreciation by eating plenty, but noticed Tricia picked at her food. "This chicken is really good," he recommended. "Try some."

"Mrs. Welch brought that. She said she made her special rosemary chicken from scratch for us, didn't buy it ready-made at the supermarket like the others," Colt said, ripping a leg from the carcass.

"She lost her husband to lung cancer last year, sold the farm, and moved into town. Says she misses country life. I'll have some of that." Cy carved off part of the breast. "We saw a lot of each other at the cancer center before he died."

Cody waved the offered platter away. "Dad, she's already going after you with Mom barely cold."

Colt dropped his chicken leg. "No! She has a daughter my age, Heidi in my chem class."

"Don't you like Heidi?" his father asked.

"I do, a lot, but I don't want her for a sister. That would be gross."

"Settle down. No one can replace your mother."

Tricia pushed back her chair. "I'm really tired and not very hungry. Let me put on coffee before I go upstairs. I know you like some after dinner, Dad. I want first chance in the shower while the water is still hot." Tricia fiddled with an old percolator and plugged it in. It began burbling almost at once. "I'll come down and clean the kitchen later."

"We can manage. Get some rest. Rex will keep us company, won't you, son?" Cy bestowed a fatherly smile on their guest. The interrogation Rex expected came as soon as Tricia's footsteps faded on the stairs.

"You seem mighty close to my daughter, but she

hasn't said much about you, not even to her mother. Yet, she brought you along for the funeral."

No sense in trying to explain the barriers Layla threw in their path or that he'd invited himself to Iowa. Rex cut through to the main issue as quickly as if he saw a gap in the line allowing him to run the ball. "I want to court you daughter. I'd like to marry her if she'll have me."

"Court." Colt snickered at the old-fashioned term.

"I'll bet you want to do more than that with her if you haven't already," Cody said with a threatening edge. Carson simply lowered his head as if getting ready to charge across the table—or maybe he was nodding off.

"Boys, stop. He spoke his mind and spoke it plainly. Are you asking my permission?" Tricia's father said.

"Yes, sir."

"Well, you'd better ask Tricia. She has a mind of her own like her mama. As far as it goes, you have my blessing."

"Dad! We hardly know him," Colt said.

"He's a pro football player. Everyone knows everything about the man. Born in Texas, father is a preacher, raised in Africa, went to A&M, star quarterback, drafted by the Sinners to replace Joe Billodeaux, leads a squeaky clean life. Look it up on Google, Colt. I did."

Rex suffered a moment of panic. Had Cyrus Welles seen the photo of him carrying Trisha to her room, read the scurrilous article?

And the man didn't know everything, how he'd been shipped back to Texas at thirteen to get an

American education and stayed three years with his prejudiced maternal grandparents who despised blacks, Hispanics, Jews, Democrats, and the missionary who'd taken their daughter off to Africa. He'd prayed hard to be with his family again and removed from that hateful household so out of sync with his father's teachings to love everyone. He told his grandparents he wanted to return to Africa and help with the mission, not attend high school and college in Texas. They told him he could do that when he grew up.

Three years later, his parents and sister returned with his father too ill from a chronic tropical disease that attacked his liver to serve a big congregation. The four of them straggled from one small church to another, moving on when his medical care grew too great for modest coffers.

Had his fervent prayers to be reunited with his family caused that, Rex often wondered?

Had God balanced the scales by giving him the talent to play football on a level where he could help his parents and see his father got good health care to keep him alive until a transplant became available?

Not so different from what Tricia tried to do for her mother, only she had suffered for it while he lived an enviable life. He truly admired that trait in her. It had to be nearly unbearable taking Layla's verbal—and sometimes physical—abuse.

"Yes, sir. That's about it," Rex said. "The huckleberry pie looks great. Can I cut a slice for anybody?" Every last one of the big men nodded.

Chapter Twenty-Two

Lying in the white iron framed bed with the faded quilts at least a generation old drawn up around his neck, Rex watched the rocking chair move back and forth in the patch of moonlight coming through the window. Earlier he noticed it sat on a warped board and tended to rock when a puff of cold air found its way under the window frame. He did not believe in ghosts. People went directly to their eternal reward or punishment in his mind. If some did choose to not to enter glory, he doubted they would hurt him anyhow.

The hall floorboards creaked, too, exactly as Colt warned. First, he'd heard a light step approach the stairs and go down followed by a heavier tread maybe a half hour later. Could be Tricia had decided to get a snack or simply couldn't sleep. Maybe a brother joined her.

Rex got up and put a red flannel robe over a pair of pale yellow pajamas imprinted with little footballs. He never could decide if the gift from his mother was meant as a joke or not. Usually he slept in his underwear, shucking it off the next day for clean after he showered, but figured he needed more modest nightwear in the Welles household. These were the only PJ's he had. Slippers put on against the cold hardwood floors weren't such a bad idea either. He'd join Trish wherever she sat up and be there for her. Maybe, he could coax her to eat a piece of pie, but it would have to be apple since the men polished off the huckleberry.

The kitchen light burned. No one occupied the space. The back door, not securely latched, banged open suddenly under a fist-like blow from the wind. Rex peered into the darkness. The only light other than the glare from a tall security pole leaked from the cracks in a small building about the size of a chicken coop. Strange time of night to gather eggs. He crossed the barnyard unafraid of snakes or other creatures. On a night like this most would be lying low in their holes. The conversation coming from the henhouse had heat, however. He should have knocked, but stood there by the rickety door listening to Tricia argue with one of her brothers.

"You can be arrested for growing weed, you idiot, five years in jail for a start. What a way to make Mom proud. How could you?"

"I did it for her. She got a card for using medical marijuana to help her through the chemo. This way, I knew the product was good and free of chemicals."

"Great, you grow *organic* pot, Carson, and that makes what you did better. Mom couldn't possibly smoke this entire crop. You're using. Boyce was a pothead, and I know the signs. Are you selling it, too?"

"Jesus, sis, every cent you gave us went for Mom's care. Cody got a football scholarship to Iowa State, but I don't have his talent. Dad said I'd have to wait for college until—until Mom got well. So, yeah, I did sell the extra, but only to people I know. I saved the money to start college next year instead of God knows when. I'm already a year behind my class. Trish, I don't want to be a farmer all my life."

"Dad condoned this?"

"When I asked if I could use the old henhouse to grow organic herbs to sell, he said yes. I don't think he ever comes in here because he doesn't want to know. Look, Mom is gone. It's my last crop, I swear, but I didn't want to lose it on a cold night like this."

"How could you dishonor our mother's memory by becoming a drug dealer? All I sacrificed for this family and it wasn't enough."

"Yeah, some sacrifice living in L.A., hanging out with the rich, famous, and foxy Layla Devlin, getting paid a shit load while I shovel shit in Iowa. Poooor Tricia."

"Manure. You shovel manure on this farm!"

The sharpness of the slap caught Rex off guard. Afraid Carson might return the blow from his sister Rex stooped and entered the coop. Once inside he came to his full height within inches of long tubes of grow lights mounted on the ceiling. Where hens once brooded their eggs, raised trays of marijuana plants grew in various stages of maturity. Drying bundles of weed hung from the roof beams. Plastic tacked around the walls kept the howling cold air at bay and the heat from a couple of space heaters comfortably inside. The man knew how to grow—herbs.

Tricia in a gray robe with pink piping that almost wrapped around her twice stood confronting her middle brother with her hair disheveled around her shoulders. Hand-knit slippers of pink yarn warmed her feet, all except for one little toe that stuck out of a hole. From the way she turned her glare on Rex, he knew she wasn't happy to see him.

"Great! Marvelous! Now you know we have a drug dealer in the family."

"A medical marijuana provider," Carson countered. "Hey, it's cool, man. Marijuana is Iowa's fourth most profitable crop."

"It's not and never will be!" Tricia started to tear at the plastic sheeting keeping out the chilly air, rending holes in it with her nails. Tears ran down her cheeks and watered the serrated narrow leaves of the plants.

Carson grabbed her from behind and, lifting his struggling sister off the floor, handed her over to Rex. "Get her out of here before she ruins everything. Since you want to marry her, you won't turn me in, huh?"

Tricia went still in Rex's arms. "He knows you want to marry me?"

"All of us do. He announced it at dinner and asked for Dad's blessing," Carson said, pleased he'd found a way to deflect the attention from his misdeeds.

Tricia shook herself free of Rex's embrace. "Our relationship, such as it is, is none of their business. How could you?"

"She asked me the same thing, dude. I'd get her back to the house before she goes off again." Carson rummaged beneath the trays for a hammer, nails, and extra plastic sheeting to mend the damage.

"Let's go back to the kitchen together and talk about this," Rex suggested.

"Let's not!" Tricia threw the henhouse door open and turned briefly to shout at her brother. "I hope all your plants shrivel!" She charged off into the night with Rex following, but entered the kitchen quietly enough.

Tricia slumped at the table, head in hands. "Nothing I did mattered. If I'd come home to help Mom and keep an eye on the boys maybe Carson wouldn't be growing pot in a chicken coop."

"Everything a person does matters. Sometimes we don't know how until later. You do the best you can at the time. That's all God asks. And growing pot to help your family isn't the worst crime in the world. In Africa, people still sell extra daughters into slavery to feed the rest."

"I don't care what people in Africa do. My family is falling apart. I wasn't here to keep them together."

"The rest look like they're doing okay. Can I make you some tea or get you something to eat?" He did know how to boil water and could nuke practically anything.

"Not hungry. Tea would be nice. You just don't know, Rex."

A whistling teakettle sat on a backburner of the stove. He filled it and turned up the heat as Tricia continued talking. He didn't dare interrupt her to ask where the teabags might be, so he quietly opened cupboards until he found a box of Lipton's, some Celestial Seasonings herbal teas, and a few baggies of crumbled herbs he thought best not to investigate.

"Cody wanted to play football for one of the Big Ten teams, but he felt he had to stay close to home with Mom so ill. He's going to Iowa State just up the road. He's in his junior year and he's worried no one will draft him when he graduates. He promised our mother he'd finish college before turning pro. If he isn't noticed because of going to a smaller school, he might never get a chance at an NFL career."

Rex grabbed the kettle as soon as it let out its first screech of steam. "Sleepy Time okay?"

Tricia nodded, and he poked one of the teabags down into a mug of hot water with a spoon and set it in front of her. For good measure, he got out the bowl of banana pudding and dished some into cereal bowls for the both of them. If milk helped a person sleep, maybe milk products worked as well.

Tricia licked yellow pudding from her spoon, broke off a piece of soggy vanilla wafer, put it in her mouth, and sucked on it. She made eating this homey dessert almost erotic—on purpose, he considered. "My mom made this a lot when we were little. I wonder who sent it."

Rex lifted the bowl and read the name taped to the bottom. "Ida Lutz. I've been to enough church socials to know the ladies always want their bowls back. Look, you don't have to worry about Cody. An outstanding player on a mediocre team will be noticed. If he doesn't get taken in the draft when the time comes, I can get him a tryout with the Sinners. They think out of the box when it comes to finding new talent, scooped Jakarta Jones up from some no-account college."

Tricia still licked pudding from her spoon rather than digging into it—just to drive him crazy? "You'd do that for my brother even if I don't marry you?"

She'd hurt him again, and he let her know it by the tightness in his voice when he answered. "I'm not Layla Devlin. You don't have to promise me anything to give a good player a chance. The rest would be up to him. No matter how he feels right now, he has to play hard. What's his position?"

"Some kind of back, full, half, not sure. I was the drama major, and the boys were just starting to play when I left for college. They don't show the Cyclones' games in L.A. even if I had the time to watch them." She glanced down at her bowl surprised she'd finished the whole portion.

Rex, so earnest and good, asked, "More?"

Yes, please, she'd like more Rex Worthy, but not here and now. How could she think that only a day after her mother's death? "No. I'm finished. Cute pajamas by the way."

"Thanks." Rex declined to tell her his mother bought them. He took the bowls to the sink below a kitchen window and dropped them clattering against the old, yellowed porcelain. "Fire! In the henhouse."

"Carson!" Tricia moved to the door like a sprinter, but Rex got there first.

"No, go upstairs and wake your family. Where can I find a hose?"

"By the kitchen steps if Dad hasn't taken it in for the winter. Mom used it for her garden."

"Go, go, go!" Rex turned her back into the house.

Now he did pray to God that Carson hadn't set himself and the coop afire smoking weed in there. If so, Tricia shouldn't see it. He found the hose, turned it up to full blast and dragged its length along the yard hoping it would reach. No need to worry about Carson, he saw immediately. The idiot stood there with a gas can still in his hand watching the coop go up as if fascinated by every twist of the flames. The sweet smell of burning pot rode the wind carrying embers toward a field still covered with stubble from the corn crop beyond the windbreak.

Rex knocked the gas can from Carson's grip. "You have any burlap bags to smother the cinders?"

"Yeah, in the barn, but I made sure the wind blew away from the house before I lit the match. I'm not totally stoned, you know." Judging by how slowly he moved, Carson had indulged in one last doobie before getting out of the drug business.

Rex opened the nozzle and trained it on the small building. Reinforcements in half-buttoned jeans, flannel shirts, and unlaced boots clattered from the house. Cy grabbed some of the sacks from the heap in Carson's arms. "Cody, Colt and Tricia, go into the field and stamp out any cinders you see. I'll run another hose from the barn."

"Anyone call the fire department?" Rex asked.

"No need, we can handle this ourselves."

"What should I do, Dad?" Carson dropped the rest of the sacks to the earth.

"Stand aside." The older man hadn't missed the evidence of the empty gas can lying in the dirt.

The middle son bowed his head and did as he was told. The stream from two hoses gradually quelled the fire. As he and Cy continued to spray the rubble, Rex noticed Carson had thriftily removed the space heaters and the grow lights from the building before he torched it. He did not intend to ask what happened to the dried weed. Tricia, Cody, and Colt returned dragging their burlap bags.

"Not too much got beyond the trees," Cody reported. "We took care of what did."

"Good kids." Cy turned to Carson. "Whatever got into you, boy, setting a fire on a windy night like this?"

"Trish was right. Mom's gone. I don't need to raise herbs anymore. She wouldn't be proud of me."

"If you'd waited till morning, I would have helped you burn it down." Cy hugged his son, and the big boy buried his face in a flannel-covered shoulder and cried with sobs so deep his large frame quaked.

"It's still cold out here. We should go inside before everyone gets sick. Carson, I'm sorry I came down on you so hard." Tricia hugged her brother from the back.

"S'okay."

They walked toward the house with Rex coiling his hose as they went. Cody trudged beside him. No time like the present to make good on a promise. "Tricia tells me you're a back for the Cyclones."

"Linebacker. She doesn't know the difference between offense and defense. I don't know how you two ever got together."

"I heard that," Trish said from behind them.

"We aren't too good this year. Maybe you could come to the home game this Saturday and give us some pointers."

"Sorry, I told Coach I'd be back to ride the pine for Sunday's game. Never can tell when Daddy Joe will throw his back out. Just play your hardest no matter what the rest of the team is doing. I'll see you get a tryout with the Sinners after you graduate if no one takes you in the draft."

Colt gamboled beside the men eager to talk insider football. "Is Joe really that decrepit?"

"No. If he was, I'd be playing a lot more."

"Is that what you pray for every game when you get down on your knees, more playing time? Or do you pray for a big win?"

"No. It's only a game, Colt. I pray for the safety of all who play it and to do my best to support the team even from the bench."

"Oh," Colt replied, disappointed.

Tricia followed their conversation. She wasn't disappointed in Rex Worthy at all.

Chapter Twenty-Three

Tricia woke so much later than intended. Unburdened of some of her guilt regarding her family, she left pleasant dreams better quickly forgotten only to recall her embarrassment over Carson's activity, the fire, and Rex Worthy. Though she hated to make the pun, his general worthiness shone for anyone to see. How could she explain their entanglement with Layla and being in his bed when her mother died to anyone, certainly not her father or brothers who were rapidly taking to him?

No solving that problem lying here in bed. She should be downstairs getting breakfast for her father and the boys as her mother had done every day at the crack of dawn. Well, dawn no longer cracked. The giant yolk of the sun shone well above the horizon. Smells of cooking from the kitchen below rose, infiltrated the gaps in the flooring, and perfumed her room with the aroma of a country feast.

Tricia got out of bed wearing a flowered flannel nightgown found stored in the old chest at the foot of her bed. She tiptoed across the cold floor and got another pair of the slippers her granny knitted incessantly in her last years from the closet. The pink ones were goners, but she figured she had a lifetime supply. Tricia chose a set made of multicolored yarn and another robe, this one blue. The other, once belonging to her mother, was a comfort to wear, but it, too, suffered from dragging in the field last evening as they sought out sparks that might allow the fire to spread.

In the kitchen, her father stood at the stove cracking eggs still warm from the hens directly into a giant iron skillet, scrambling them as he went. Ham slices already browned lay on a platter. The eggs bubbled in the grease they left behind. Cy added salt and pepper, a handful of grated cheese from a plastic container before speaking to his daughter. "Do the toast, would you, honey?"

Trisha fed whole wheat slices into a four-slot toaster. "I should have been up to cook for you."

"I got pretty good at making breakfast these last four years, so good we often have it for dinner."

"Where is everyone?"

"I sent Colt and Cody off to classes and football practice. Funeral isn't until tomorrow and nothing much they can do here. No sense in wasting education like your mother did by marrying me."

"She never complained. She loved you and this farm."

"Sure. Doesn't mean she couldn't have done better. She quit college halfway through because of me. I won't have any of my boys do the same. Carson will get his chance even if he has to wait a bit. Once all the final bills are paid, we'll see where we stand."

"Let me take over making breakfast. You can see to the animals."

"Colt's 4-H pigs and the steer are already butchered and in the deep freeze. The old biddies still lay two dozen eggs a day because they like that new henhouse so well." Cy nodded at the basket of hen fruit and cracked two more into the pan. "Corn and beans are harvested, hay is in. I only have one thing to do today." He stopped talking.

Tricia took the popped slices from the toaster and fed it four more. She began buttering. "What must you do?"

"Got an order of fertilizer to pick up at the Feed and Seed—and I need to bring clothes for your mother to wear and take them over to Emig's Funeral Home. Maybe you can help me with that. Nothing fit her well at the end."

"They can—make adjustments."

"I guess. So when do you have to get back to Layla?"

"Never. I quit. I'll be here helping you as long as you need me."

Cy shoveled the eggs onto the platter with a large spatula and put it on the table. "Your mom said you'd try to do that. She told me not to let you give up your life because she can't be here to take care of things. I should—marry again soon, she said, but I can't even think of it just now."

"I don't want to return to Layla. Things weren't as good between us as I led Mom to believe. Maybe, I'll enroll in college part-time and get a teaching degree in English. I can direct high school plays like Miss Morgan. She had high hopes for me and Layla. One of us made it to the big screen."

Her father cleared Colt and Cody's dishes from the table and put down clean ones. "What about that fine young man who wants to marry you?"

"Like you, I can't think about that now. Dad, I-I

was in bed with him when you called me. Right now, I feel like I danced on my mother's grave."

There, she'd made that uncomfortable confession to her father. She and Rex must be sinking in his esteem like a hogs into a mud wallow. Tricia gave all her attention to carefully placing the toast slices individually into a rack her mother bought on a whim after watching *Upstairs, Downstairs* years ago, a touch of English elegance in the midst of Iowa. She braced for her father's reaction.

His words came out mildly with no anger, no shocked outrage. "She liked to dance, your mother, not that we did it often enough. Marty said life was love and love was life. Life goes on. She knew she was dying, honey, and kept it from you. Like two peas in a pod, you two. And believe it or not, we know what young people do—the same as us when we were your age. You didn't figure it out, why she quit college."

"Because she loved you, but you'd already inherited the farm and couldn't leave it. You needed her help to run the place." Tricia parroted back words often repeated in her childhood and never questioned. She placed the delicate, filigreed toast rack on the table by the platter and the jug of orange juice, the half-gallon of milk nearly empty.

"She was expecting you, Trish. We gave our marriage time to set, to make sure it would work before we had the boys, so you got four years on them." Cy poured a cup of coffee and hid behind its rim after he got the words out.

Tricia sat down abruptly. "I thought I was a honeymoon baby."

"We had no honeymoon to speak of except what

we could enjoy upstairs. Nothing wrong with that either. We fiddled with our anniversary date a little to keep all of you in the dark, not because we were ashamed, but we didn't want our kids to feel embarrassed. Folks forget the details after a while. It becomes old news, and no one cares as long as you live a decent life, which your mother surely did."

"I don't know what to say except thanks for not getting rid of me."

"Never entered our minds. Now, eggs are getting cold. Call Rex and that brother of yours to come eat before I throw it away."

****

Tricia helped her father pick out the casket clothes, a favorite dress Marty liked to wear to church with the shoes to match. Not knowing if they needed to, they packed underwear and nylons along with her favorite necklace and a little gold cross on a chain to place in her hands. The difficult task completed, Cy set off for town, taking Rex and Carson with him to load bags of fertilizer from the Feed and Seed on the way home.

Tricia stayed behind intending to clean the lower floor of the house and the half-bath off the laundry room plus the one upstairs until they shone. Beyond hope she could make her brothers' rooms presentable in a day, she simply shut their doors. Coats of the guests arriving after the service could be piled in her parents' always-tidy bedroom.

From the upstairs window, she thought at first a dust cloud moved down the lane, but when it thinned, she saw a caravan of church ladies charging ahead to do good and possibly bring more food, though where she'd put it, only heaven knew. They parked en masse in the front yard and rang the doorbell. Wearing jeans and an old T-shirt bearing an indelible stain, her dark hair covered by a blue bandana, Tricia welcomed them inside. Letty Welch stated they'd come to clean.

Still pretty in her mid-forties, Letty kept herself up, not a gray streak in her black hair and a trim little figure exuding energy packed into jeans and a fitted top. She assigned duties: kitchen, bathrooms, family room. "Tricia and I will do the parlor."

An old-fashioned space with a fireplace and impressive carved mantel, Tricia's grandmother had decorated the parlor with a tufted pale blue brocade settee and matching side chairs aping the style of long gone French kings. A spindly white and gold coffee table displayed a huge chunk of fool's gold obtained on a rare vacation and a lidded iridescent candy dish, currently empty. The print in a thick gilded frame over the fireplace portrayed an eighteenth-century gentleman on a bobbed-tailed horse bending to kiss the hand of a lady in a white wig and wide panniered skirts. Granny treasured this room off-limits to men, boys, and dogs, used only once a month when the Ladies Guild came for tea, and generally covered in plastic slipcovers the rest of the time.

"Not too bad in here," Letty Welch proclaimed, but we should take off the slipcovers and give the furniture and mantel a good dusting. You'll want to use the space for the guests after the funeral, maybe have a fire burning to make it more inviting and not so formal."

Tricia yearned to rebel, but her mother had said something similar a few months after Granny's passing. "Now we can redecorate, maybe make this place a little more modern."

Marty Welles admired and got along with her crusty mother-in-law, certainly a big help with the four children and not a word of censure over the hasty marriage, but move one item or suggest a change and one paid hell for it. She didn't get the chance to put her own ideas into effect, being diagnosed with advanced breast cancer within months of the old lady's passing. So, Trish helped fold the plastic covers, cleaned every curlicue with a soft brush, and lifted up the china figurines of the shepherd and shepherdess made in Japan that adorned the mantel to dust beneath them.

Letty kept up a constant chatter, mostly anecdotes about her mother's bravery and her grandmother's eccentricities. Mind elsewhere, Tricia barely answered. She could tell when the men entered the house after unloading the fertilizer in the barn. The voices of the women waxing the hall floor changed from gossipy banter to an almost cooing tone as they gathered around Cy and Carson to express their sympathy and gain an introduction to Rex. Letty declared the parlor finished and rushed to join them.

She hugged Cy a little too long in Tricia's opinion. "Anything I can do to help, anything, I'm your girl. And Trish if you need a woman to talk to, call me anytime."

The ladies drafted Rex and Carson to move the heavy sofa in the family room. Deeply embedded in the pile of the only carpet in the house, it yielded up long lost items: coins, plastic soldiers, marbles, and a five-year-old copy of *Playboy* once hastily hidden. The women laughed. Carson blushed and thumped down his end of the sofa few feet away.

Elderly Ida Lutz cupped a hand around her

wrinkled lips and said to her nearest crony, "Did you see those muscles? Don't think I'm too old to appreciate that."

She referred to Rex of course. Carson had gone soft in the last year. Tricia, standing off to one side, had been admiring the play of those same muscles stretching the black T-shirt and bunching as he lifted the heavy piece of furniture a foot higher than her brother. Rex set his end down in one careful, controlled move.

"Such a good, clean Christian boy," the pastor's wife murmured piously.

"Not a good boy anymore according to the papers at the grocery store," Ida whispered with a jerk of her head in Tricia's direction. "He hangs out with movie stars and their ilk now." Hard of hearing, Ida's whispering tended to come out loud and travel far.

Color crept up the back of Rex's neck. More concerned for him than herself, Tricia announced over the roar of the vacuum attacking the revealed carpet. "Thank you so much for your help. We can manage from here. See you at the service tomorrow."

"Now, Trish. We should offer them some refreshments. We still have three uncut cakes in the kitchen. Put on some coffee for our helpers."

Stymied by her father, she had no choice but to answer, "Certainly, cake and coffee in the kitchen."

"I'll start the coffee while the men put the furniture back in place. Looks good in here, ladies, very good. Thank you for coming," Letty offered as if she owned the house.

Her temper rising, Tricia followed Mrs. Welch while the others began packing their cleaning supplies.

She'd been bossed around by Layla for years and didn't intend to suffer the same from this—this would-be usurper of her mother's place. She placed a hand on the woman's arm as Letty filled the percolator with water.

"Look, Mrs. Welch, only last night my father said he wasn't ready to move on yet because no one can replace my mother, so save yourself the trouble." Tricia released her grip and rummaged in the utility drawer for a knife to slice the cakes.

With an amused look in her nearly black eyes, Letty turned and confronted Cy's daughter. "Individuals cannot be replaced, but others can fill the void. Cy and I saw our spouses through long illnesses. We were both faithful the whole time, but the experience gives us a lot in common. While I am ready now, I can wait a while longer. I only want to be first in line because every divorcee and widow in the county knows Cy Welles is a fine man who didn't cheat on his wife and always does the best he can. You don't let an opportunity like that slip through your fingers lightly. As for you, Trish, I wouldn't reject what you have in the other room by trying to play at being your mother. Now, cut the cakes."

Tricia looked at the bread knife in her hand, regretting it had no pointed edge. She threw it down and moved to the backdoor intending to seek the privacy of the hay barn as the women entered the kitchen. A few immediately remarked on the charred timbers of the old henhouse visible from the window over the sink. Opening the door, she allowed in a whiff of sweetish air before slamming it shut and running across the distance to the hay storage.

Inside the shelter, she leaned a cheek against one of

the large rolls of dry grasses and breathed in a comforting scent from her childhood. Where else could she go or be of use but Iowa? She needed to move her belongings from Layla's mansion in L.A. and supposed she could get an apartment and try for an acting career again. But seeing how the motion picture industry operated from its darker side, she had no taste for it anymore. Besides, Layla had the power to keep her out of any movie if she wished.

New Orleans? No place for her there unless she moved in with Rex and further destroyed his reputation. She didn't care about her own. Staying here and getting her teaching credits still seemed the most solid plan. Someone moved through the first of the fallen leaves from the windbreak, and she straightened up. Rex held out the Sinners jacket he'd worn for the feed store run and put it around her shoulders, gently lifting her hair and placing a warm kiss on the back of her neck.

"Mrs. Welch said you'd gone outside without a coat and would make yourself sick."

"Yeah, she wants to be my mama," Tricia said, refusing to face him.

"Well, I want to be your husband. Come back to New Orleans when you're ready. Let's finish what we started. I won't do it with anyone else, only you. But, I can wait a while longer."

Strange how those words sounded so sweet coming from Rex and so sour on Letty Welch's lips. Lips, Rex's descended on hers and proved again he knew all the intricacies of kissing from the soft approach to the passionate entry, not neglecting detours along her jaw line and down her neck to the very top of her breasts— but not beyond. Such a pity commercial farmers no longer stored hay in lofts or they might have completed Rex's sexual education right here—but nowhere to lie down and little privacy to be had.

Tricia raised his head from where he nibbled her collarbone and framed his face. "I am still amazed at how well you do that."

"Lots of practice and a passion for it, just like football."

"We should go back. I acted ungraciously."

"You go on. I need a minute to, ah, adjust."

Smiling, she went out into the sunshine fully noticing the gorgeous autumn day and start of color in the trees of windbreak for the first time since her homecoming. The cold breeze stung her face and neck a little where his beard had scraped, not that she'd noticed it at the time. Hope rose as high as the afternoon sun. Maybe she did have a future with Rex Worthy after all.

Chapter Twenty-Four

The agony of the funeral over, the remnants of the Welles family gathered in the family room to watch the Sinners play the Bucs on Sunday. Still, the distraction of the game and the glimpses of Rex "riding the pine" as he described bench-warming could not entirely erase the memory of Tricia's last viewing of her mother. Who was this skeletal woman with short hair so thin her scalp showed through?

Marty Welles was, had been, slightly younger than Letty Welch. Because of Layla's schedule and demands, she hadn't seen her mother in the last six months of her life. The men were prepared for the sight in the coffin, but not Tricia. She wept.

The funeral director suggested a wig might be added. Cy Welles said his wife found wigs uncomfortable and usually wore a bandana, but that wouldn't look right. In the end, they decided on a closed casket with a picture of Marty in her prime atop it. They'd leave the gold cross in her hands and the wedding band on her finger. There never had been an engagement ring. Cy insisted Tricia keep the necklace, a simple strand of good pearls he'd given his wife for their twentieth anniversary shortly after she'd been diagnosed with cancer. Though neither said it, they'd worried about reaching their twenty-fifth, he told his daughter. Now, he was glad he'd gone to the expense even with medical bills looming. "Keep it to remember her by."

Active in her church, the pastor knew Marty well and gave a moving eulogy. Other friends arose from the pews and recalled their memories, some evoking laughter. As the speakers thinned, Rex got up and walked to the pulpit, so handsome in his dark suit with his face freshly shaved that morning. He didn't seek the limelight, but spoke simply and briefly.

"I didn't know Martha "Marty" Welles, but I know her daughter, Patricia, and have met her family. If people are remembered by the good they have done, Marty Welles should be honored for the fine family she raised. Certainly, she is with God in heaven today. Amen."

After the burial in the cemetery right behind the solid, red brick church with its classic white spire, people flocked to the Welles home fully restocked by the church ladies with additional chicken salad sandwiches, relish trays, fruit compotes, fresh hot dishes, and an abundance of new desserts. Toward evening, the same ladies cleaned up and wrapped the leftovers before departing.

Rex returned to New Orleans the following morning keeping his promise to show for the game on Sunday. He kissed Tricia good-bye in the way a man who had declared his intentions felt free to do. Colt blushed, maybe a little enviously. The rest of the day, Cy and Tricia packed Marty's clothes in bags to be taken to the Salvation Army. "No sense in hanging on to good things people can use," she'd directed her husband. What jewelry she had went to Trish along with any other keepsake she wanted. How spare her mother's life had been compared to Layla's excesses.

On Saturday night, the Welles family went to Cody's home game where the eldest son played hard even though the Cyclones lost. Now, they watched another football game, comfortable with popcorn and pizza, soft drinks and beer, all of them hoping to see Rex play. The fourth quarter approached with Joe Dean Billodeaux still working his magic and the Sinners comfortably ahead.

Time for Rex to get some practice, but at the top of the fourth, an injury delayed the game. Commercials ran and commentators scrambled to fill airtime. The cameras panned the crowd picking out pretty girls waving second-line umbrellas, cute kids in oversized Number Seven jerseys, and a row of middle-aged men costumed as the Pope and offering blessings on the team. They trolled the suites hoping for a celebrity sighting and got one. Scrawled across the entire length of a set of windows, someone wrote, "Put in Worthy You Fuckin' Asshole!" Layla finished the sentence written in red lipstick and pounded on the glass to attract attention to her demand. The camera quickly veered away from the obscenity.

Rex sat with his head down and his hands between his knees, possibly praying, maybe to disappear. Coach Marty Buck's back stiffened. He took off his headphones and combed his buzz cut into spiky white bristles with his fingers. No one told him what to do, especially celebrity types who knew nothing about the game. He was famous for once saying, "I'd rather have one of my guys date a prostitute than a movie star. At least the first one knows to leave right after getting paid." He'd taken some flak for that, but didn't really care. Rex would not play today.

Carson watched the incident unfold. "Layla isn't looking too good. You think she's drunk or high, sis?"

"Probably both. Poor Rex," Tricia murmured.

"One good thing about being a humble lineman, you never get that kind of attention," Cody said.

"I'd like it," Colt insisted.

"No, you wouldn't," the others said simultaneously.

The game ended with a big victory for the Sinners. The men got up for a stretch and a bathroom break before the next match.

Tricia placed a phone call, not to Rex, but to California. Layla owned the house where she lived out there, all the furnishing right down to bathroom rug, so not much to pack, though she hated to impose on the housekeeper enjoying a break from their mutual employer.

"Hi, Juanita. It's me, Pat—Patricia. I hate to bother you on a Sunday evening, but could I ask a big favor? I'm no longer employed by Miss Devlin. Could you pack up my room, it's mostly just clothes and personal pictures. I'm getting a car service on Monday to drive the Prius to Iowa. The spare keys are in the desk drawer. Just put everything in the backseat and trunk if it's not too much trouble.

"This I already know, Miss Patsy. Miss Devlin call and say to put your stuff out for the trash, but I don't. You always nice to me. Is already packed. I watch for the car people, okay?'

"Thanks. You are an angel. Good luck to you."

Well into the next game, her phone rang, not Layla or Juanita, but Rex. She went into the quiet of the parlor to talk, leaving behind the teasing comments of her dad and brothers. "Oh, who could that be with the jazzy New Orleans ringtone?" "Maybe it's Louis Armstrong," Colt said.

"He's dead, man," Carson corrected.

"I know that! Calling from the grave, I meant."

Good to be home again.

"Rex, I'm so sorry you didn't get to play. If I'd been there with Layla, that incident wouldn't have happened."

"Nothing unusual about me not getting in the game, but it got worse afterwards. I heard Layla trashed the suite. The Dome is cancelling her contract for the skybox. Later, she went to Mariah's Place to see if I hung out there. The guys who did said she offered them a BJ in the men's room if they'd tell her where I lived. She got pretty loud. Mariah had her bounced and told her not to come back because she ran a classy joint."

"I hope you have no enemies on the team who would reveal that information." Simply hearing his deep voice warmed her all over.

"I'm getting along fairly good with Jakarta. We work well together. But, Eric Blixen isn't too happy with me since I don't use the wide receivers as much as Joe. The Sinners won't give it out, and you need a key to get in the lobby. I think I'm safe. I don't want to talk about Layla. We have a bye-week coming up. I know it's a lot to ask, but maybe you could visit for the weekend. We won't be rushed and could—spend some time together."

"You just want me to protect you from Layla."

A laugh boomed out of him. "That, too. I'll pay for the plane ticket."

"No, you won't. I'll let you know when I'm getting into town. I guess Iowa can spare me for a few days."

After that conversation with her father, Tricia believed she went to Rex with her mother's blessing.

Chapter Twenty-Five

As if a man that big could hide, Rex met her at the airport early Friday evening, his eyes hidden by shades and the rest of him dressed in an anonymous tan leather bomber jacket, plain T-shirt, jeans, and brown loafers worn without socks. He seemed a little let down that she'd only brought a carry-on with enough clothes for a few days, and the big black bag she was never without, but he took her baggage and tucked her under his arm happily enough. As they walked up the concourse past the newsstands and gift shops, Layla stared at them with mascara-ringed raccoon eyes from the front pages of the tabloids. Her blonde hair twisted into some kind of awful dreads and her clothes two sizes small, she did appear low class as the bouncers evicted her from Mariah's Place. The headline screamed, *The Stalking of Rex Worthy!* Tricia turned her eyes away from the distasteful display. Rex said nothing about it at all. His nonchalant disguise must have worked because they arrived at his place without being exposed by the paparazzi.

"I thought we'd order some dinner in unless you want to eat out. I mean go out to eat in a restaurant."

Touched by his sudden case of nerves, Trisha stroked his stubbled cheek. This time he hadn't shaved. She liked the feel of roughness beneath her fingertips. "Sure, order some food."

"Thai, okay?"

"Great. No too much of that in Iowa."

She took her bag to his room, making no pretense of staying in the guestroom. On the phone, Rex ordered the spring rolls with peanut sauce, pho soup, shrimp pad Thai, and cow in grass, enough to feed a small Asian village as the selections rolled on. After the delivery, they shut out the world, phones off, television dark, music tuned to an easy listening channel, no news. At the dining room table, they viewed the cars crossing the steep bridge, the ships plying the river, the city lighting up and getting ready to party. With her fingers, she fed him a shrimp and licked away the sticky sauce. Rex impaled a tender beef cube on the end of a chopstick and returned the favor. Neither did justice to the abundance of food.

"I'll put the leftovers away and then—"

"Leave it," he said, suddenly commanding. Rex knocked over his chair in his ardor. He pulled hers away from the table, not like a courteous date, but more like a man in a hurry. Scooping her up, wide hands below her buttocks, he pressed Tricia against his groin. She wrapped her legs around his waist and her arms around his neck. He walked to his bedroom carrying her that way and fell to the covers still on top but taking care not to crush her.

The kissing began, but this time he explored below the neckline, working the bra clasp and stripping her top as he went, that lime aroma of his aftershave rising to her nostrils. His lips, warm and supple, went to her nipples, his hand delved into her slacks, loose from weeks of tension and grieving. He knew where to go and what to do now, recognized her readiness, and brought her to completion with a rapidity that astounded Trish, though she breathed too hard to say it.

"More later," he promised, rolling aside to let her peel off his T-shirt and unzip his jeans, going commando, making it easy for her. The loafers thunked to the floor with the pants. Vaguely, she realized he'd dressed for the occasion as she took him in hand cupping and gently stroking an already urgent erection as he worked off her slacks, pausing only a moment to admire the revealed lace panties before they hit the floor, too.

"Can't wait. Sorry, can't wait." He covered her as quickly as he would a loose ball and plunged deep, set up a rhythm so strong, Tricia felt those pleasurable contractions begin again, building and building. If he went first, she didn't notice because Rex did not stop until she convulsed around him, locking him against her with her legs entwining his hips. They stayed exactly that way for one pulsing minute before he laid his bearded face on her breasts and rested.

"Good?" he asked, his breath tickling her nipple.

"More than."

Rex turned over, taking his weight off her body, and put his hands behind his head. Staring at the ceiling, he pronounced, "This is the best free thing God ever invented."

"Absolutely—when it's with the right person."

He raised himself on one elbow to watch her face. "Am I the right one?—because you are my one and only."

Tricia started to tell him he shouldn't assume the first woman he slept with was his one and only. For her, yes, no one could be more right, but when men enjoyed sex, they generally wanted to play the field. No doubt he loved the experience. "Rex, you should…" A low buzzing noise sounded from the living room. "What's that?"

Rex raised his head. "Intercom. Someone wants inside. Layla?"

"Want me to answer it?"

"No, you stay here. I'll tell her off once and for all."

Wonderfully naked, he strode from the room. She admired that rounded, muscular backside as he went to chase away the dragon. Tricia gloated, just a little. Maybe she shouldn't have. The Texas-sized voice reached all the way to where she lay, nude, filled with Rex's seed, protected only by her birth control pills and the firm belief in his newly lost virginity.

"Honey Lamb, it's your mama and daddy come to visit. Let us in before someone mugs us out here."

"I'll come down and meet you."

"Make it quick. I don't like the way that bum on the corner is looking at Honeybee."

"Homeless person," his sister corrected.

"You brought Rebekah, too?"

"Well, your grandparents said they couldn't make the long drive. I brought a cooler of your favorite foods: my double cornbread, a smoked Texas brisket, and a *tres leches* cake. We won't have to go out at all, just have a nice long weekend visit. Your daddy got a substitute preacher so we could surprise you and help in your time of need."

"Time of need?" He needed for them to go home, safely of course, but he took a second to thank Jesus his grandparents loved Texas too much to leave it.

"To fortify you with Bible verse against that Whore of Babylon, Layla Devlin. Hurry up now. That—that street person is heading our way."

Rex pounded into the bedroom. Tricia had her clothes on and turned down his bedspread halfway to hide the damp spot they'd left on its surface. "You heard?"

"Yes, your mom has a rather loud voice." Sadly, she observed nothing shrunk a pecker even as impressive as the one on Rex quicker than the sound of a mother's voice.

"True. She could call the cows home." He struggled into his jeans, rushing and pinching his privates in the zipper.

Tricia gave him credit for not swearing. He put the T-shirt on and the sockless loafers. "I did not intend to introduce you to my family quite like this."

"Hints?" she asked.

"Praise the Lord and her brisket." Rex left to open the gates to the army of Christ.

Tricia took a seat at the dinner table, filled her plate and one for Rex as if they'd been interrupted at a meal. Good a ruse as any, she supposed.

A chunky older woman with short, fluffy blonde hair and the same hazel eyes Tricia loved in Rex entered the apartment. She held a yellow Tupperware cake carrier by its handle and glanced around the large, open room, her gaze passing over Tricia as if she weren't there. "Let me get everything unloaded first, then we can eat. Took forever to get past Dallas, and we got lost in Houston. I surely hope the slaw and potato salad haven't turned."

Behind her, Rex lugged a large cooler. His thin,

bald father, sickly looking, came next accompanied by a girl around college age, slim and resembling her dad but brimming with good health and a contrary spirit in her amused brown eyes. Short, dark brown hair spiked with red accents framed her small, inquisitive face. Her lips quirked as soon as she laid eyes on Tricia sitting there with the paper cartons of the Thai banquet and a full plate

"I think they've already *eaten*, Mom," Honeybee said, putting a whole other meaning into the words.

Mrs. Worthy placed a hand to her heavy bosom. "Oh my, I didn't see you over there. Rex, you should have said you had a guest over for dinner. Good thing we brought plenty."

"This is Patricia Welles, the woman I told you about." His deep voice sounded puppy eager.

Sue Grace Worthy took a good look at Tricia now. "Oh, the poor, lost sheep with the drug problem. I remember you from the tabloids."

"No, Mom, I told you she saved me. She's not a…"

So, that's how Mrs. Worthy wanted to play it. Tricia rose and met her head on, a hand held out steady as preacher's on Sunday morning. She squeezed the woman's plump palm for a moment and relieved her of the cake carrier. "So pleased to meet you. I lost my own mother recently and am glad Rex still has his. I'll bet this cake is delicious. When Rex invited me for the weekend, I had no idea we'd be having another special dessert. Let me put it in the kitchen."

Mrs. Worthy stood so still she might have turned to salt. Honeybee walked around her and greeted Trish. "I'm Rex's sister, Rebekah. Becky is fine, but don't you ever call me Honeybee."

"I feel the same way about being called Patsy. Tricia or Trish, okay?"

"You got it. We didn't stop for dinner. Mom insisted we drive straight through. Mind if I dig into what you got on the table? I am famished."

"Help yourself."

Mrs. Worthy melted into action again. "What about all the good Texas food I brought?"

"We'll put it in the fridge and eat it tomorrow, but I'd like a piece of that cake tonight," Rex said diplomatically. "Sit down and have anything you want on the table. I'll make some coffee. Tricia, would you put the food away?"

"I'd be glad to—Honey Lamb."

Like most bachelors, he had plenty of empty space in his huge, upscale stainless steel refrigerator. Tricia stowed a roasting pan full of brisket on the bottom shelf and shoved the bowls of sides in next to a single six-pack of beer with one bottle missing. The large cornbread pan and a package of buns went on the counter next to the cake. She didn't want to fumble around searching for dessert plates or a knife and so asked Rex sweetly, "Get the plates for me, dear."

He opened a cupboard and took down five small plates, pottery with an olive branch motif, so perfectly stacked she figured his decorator had placed them there. Without a further hint, he handed her a knife from a wooden block and forks from the drawer next to the dishwasher. Tricia freed the cake from the prison of its airtight container and sliding the knife through the white frosting, carved out generous portions.

Rex leaned her way as he filled a glass carafe with water from the faucet. "I know the Honey Lamb was a dig, but you never called me dear before. Does this mean we are engaged?"

"No. That was a dig, too—at your mother for saying I'm a drug addict and implying I'm a fallen woman, her worst fear for you. I'll behave from now on."

"Oh, you don't have to for me."

She took the plates to the table while he measured coffee into the brew basket of a fairly basic machine. Becky dunked the end of a spring roll into the peanut sauce. Reverend Worthy sipped the lukewarm soup. His wife sat rigid before the many choices, none of them hers.

"The soup is delicious, a different taste, but very good. Try it, Honeybunch. I know you are starving by now."

"I was in the mood for some good brisket, not foreign food." Pointedly, Mrs. Worthy dug into her slice of cake, a largest one Tricia intended for Rex. After swallowing a big mouthful, she announced, "I suppose we should find a hotel after we eat since our son's guestroom is going to be occupied."

"No, Mom," Rex said, sliding himself behind the next biggest piece of cake on the table. "You and Dad take my room with the private bath. Tricia and Honey—Becky can share the guestroom. I'll bunk on the couch. It's as big as bed—not that I've ever used it for that."

"We were planning to hold a prayer vigil tonight to strengthen Rex against the wiles of Layla Devlin. The way she looked at his last game, I wouldn't be surprised if she tried to cast a voodoo spell on him."

"Now, Sue Grace, remember we always told our

black brethren in Africa there is no such thing as a curse. The Lord protects and sustains us." Reverend Worthy slurped his noodles.

"Exactly, that's why we came to pray. I suppose we won't be doing that now." Mrs. Worthy nodded at Tricia.

"Sure we can. I need strength for lots of stuff. Tricia, would you like to join us?" Rex hinted broadly.

She answered, "This is *the* most scrumptious cake. I am really looking forward to that brisket tomorrow. I'll bet it melts in the mouth."

Sue Grace Worthy gave into the sin of pride. "Mine is very tender and never dry. I bake it slowly wrapped in foil for six hours. It bathes in its own juices."

"I must get the recipe." That worked on every Iowa housewife she'd ever met and hoped it applied to Texans as well.

"It's all in choosing a good brisket. Will you be joining us in prayer?"

"Not tonight. I flew in from Iowa only a few hours ago, really tired. Think I'll turn in early."

"Me, too," said Becky. "That drive in the backseat was grueling."

"We went out of our way to pick you up in Denton, Honeybee. We drove much farther than you," her mother pointed out.

"Well, if I have to share a bed with Tricia, I don't want to come in late and wake her. You want to shower first, Trish?"

"Yes, I really do. See everyone in the morning. Can't wait to try that brisket."

Tricia went directly to Rex's bedroom glad his

mother's back turned away from the hall. She grabbed her bag and carry-on. Remembering the squeaky wheel, she transported it to the guestroom by its handle. As she tiptoed across the small space between the bedrooms, Becky grinned at her from a prime dining table viewing spot. Sensing an ally, Trish sent her a quick wave of the fingers before shutting the guestroom door.

She wasted no time in getting the shower running, but what to wear to bed? Her wardrobe did not abound in sexy lingerie, but she'd packed the powder blue baby doll pajamas left over from her college years thinking at least they showed off her legs and Rex might find them cute, but not intimidating. No way would she wear them for Becky. A tank top must do paired with running shorts brought along in case Rex wanted to exercise. That decision made, she propped herself up on one side of the queen-sized bed and deciphered a crossword she'd begun on the plane.

Becky joined her an hour later and offered some advice. "Don't let Mom see you like that in the morning. There's beard burn across the top of your breasts and down one side of your neck but your hair covers that pretty well. Knowing my mother, she'll think it's a rash. Then you are in for home remedies and stories about St. Rex having delicate skin as a baby. Either way, I'd cover up."

"Rex isn't that saintly."

"Not anymore, I guess, but our mother really ground in the guilt when he was growing up. He could relapse. She tried that crap on me, too. I should go to Bible College like her and Dad. The best compromise I could get was Texas Women's University. They thought I wouldn't meet guys there. Ha! Let me tell you, I am the only realist in this family. Glad you wiggled out of the prayer fest so I could, too."

Becky vigorously scratched her scalp, making the red spikes in her hair stand up more outrageously. She stretched luxuriously and peeled off her prim, turtle-necked top with its three-quarter length sleeves. A yellow rose tattoo peeped out of the black lace demi-bra she wore underneath. She dropped her old lady jeans to reveal a matching thong.

"Good thing we practice extreme modesty at home or Sue Grace would have stroked out by now." Becky sat on the edge of the bed. "So you and St. Rex are doing the dirty."

"I wouldn't describe it that way, but yes." Only once, but Tricia felt no need to confess to the Honeybee.

"Nice going. I thought my brother would die an old maid. Layla Devlin didn't have a chance with him really. Mom has warned him about that kind of woman since infancy. But you, you're more subtle. I don't know if you'll last though. Sometime tonight, he's going to confess his sins. You should be number one on the list. Dad is a forgiving sweetheart, but Mom is more the avenging angel type. Be careful."

Becky regarded her nails. "To think I had these painted black this morning. I had to use a bag of cotton balls to get the stuff off before the parents arrived. Mind if I sleep in my undies? I didn't bring the granny gown along. No shit about being tired. I went to a blowout party last night. I'll shower in the morning."

With that, Honeybee pulled the covers over her head and went into hibernation. Tricia turned out the lamp on her side of the bed and lay awake for what seemed like hours. After the homey sounds of kitchen cleanup faded, the murmuring began. She drifted off some time after midnight only to wake abruptly around two a.m. when Mrs. Worthy shouted, "Praise the Lord, Hallelujah!"

Becky opened a bleary eye. "Sounds like St. Rex has been saved again. We should be able to sleep until morning now."

****

The smell of coffee and a light clatter of pans in the kitchen woke Tricia at eight, later than she'd intended to sleep. She rose from bed and took a sleeveless white shell from her bag and matched it with a gingham over-shirt, some white cotton slacks and sandals. Her toenails bore only a light coating of clear polish, unlike Becky's sticking out from under the covers still covered in black as if they belonged to a zombie. Her roommate did not wake as she went into the bathroom, brushed her teeth, put on very light makeup, and smoothed her hair over her shoulders to cover the beard burn. No high ponytails today. She took a deep breath and went to help Mrs. Worthy in the kitchen.

Head propped on the throw pillows, Rex snored on the couch. The plaid throw failed to cover his big, bare feet. Otherwise, he wore the same clothes as last night. Barely bothering to lower her voice, his mother said, "Can you believe this boy doesn't have any eggs or the makings for flapjacks?"

"Most guys don't keep a fully stocked pantry," Tricia remarked.

"Oh, you've done a lot of these sleepovers with young men, then."

"No," she said carefully. "But I have three younger

brothers. My mother always said if she hadn't kept the kitchen stocked, there would no food on the shelves. We could go to Café du Monde for beignets. Everyone enjoys that. From here, the walk is kind of long, but we can take the little streetcar once we get to Canal. It's fun."

"No need to take our chances in the streets. I told Elton last evening not to give that panhandler any money, he'd only drink it away, but my husband is the soft touch in this family. I am not."

"I can tell." Tricia poured a cup of coffee and added sugar and milk from the jug, figuring she clutched breakfast in her mug.

"I'm warming up the cornbread. Nothing better with a glass of cold milk and some orange juice to start the day. We'll have an early lunch. Looks like we're the only early birds. Far from finding a prayer session tiring, I take my vigor from it. My husband is ailing you might have noticed and needs his rest. Rex always did sleep like a steam engine parked in a roundhouse for the night. Nothing wakes him. Honeybee is a slugabed. That's all good because now we have time to talk."

Oh, goody, Tricia thought, but said, "I would like to get to know Rex's family better."

"What you should know is that Rex reaffirmed his belief in the teachings of the Lord last night. He admitted falling by the wayside—having impure thoughts, cavorting with naked women. "

Tricia didn't remember any cavorting though they certainly had been naked. The timer on the stove dinged like a tiny chapel bell. Mrs. Worthy removed her cornbread from the fiery furnace using a dishtowel wrapped around her hands in lieu of potholders. She set the pan directly in front of Tricia. The steam rose tinged with the sting of jalapenos.

"Good wholesome food for a good wholesome boy. He can never get back what you have stolen from him, but the Lord will forgive as long as he walks the straight and narrow from now on. Football playing won't last forever. It's nothing but a game, a trifle, a vanity. From the moment he went to live with my parents, he wanted to return to Africa and complete his father's work as a missionary. He needs the right kind of wife to do that. Now being such a fine young man, Rex thinks he is obligated to marry you. I set him straight on that. If he had taken *your* virginity, I'd have asked the reverend to perform a ceremony before we returned to Texas. There are two kinds of women put on this earth. One kind provides a good time and doesn't expect a ring on her finger. It is other kind you take to wife. Which one do you think you are?"

Tricia closed her eyes, the rising aroma of peppers making them water. Hadn't she believed she must urge Rex to look around before settling on one woman to make sure he made the right choice? But in no way could she see herself as a missionary's wife. If that was truly his dream, she should set him free to pursue it.

She opened her eyes. "I think there are many kinds of women. Like people in general, few are all good or all bad."

Mrs. Worthy's hazel eyes bulged a little at Tricia's refusal to categorize herself.

"Now I understand your mama was sick for some time and you didn't have her guidance, so your behavior is somewhat understandable, but…"

Tricia envisioned Honeybee asleep with the yellow

rose tattoo revealed by her lacy bra and her toenails painted black. "Too much guidance can result in rebellion. Maybe that's what Rex—and Becky—are doing. I got over mine in college. I talked to my dying mother often. She never once made me feel—unworthy. You know what? I am in the mood for beignets. I'm going out for breakfast."

She left Mrs. Worthy with her slack jaw resting on her double chin. Retrieving her black bag from the bedroom, Tricia left the condo with a slam of the door. Walking full steam ahead, she progressed halfway to the café before she realized she'd have to buzz Rex for reentry to his flat. If he wasn't awake, his mother might let her stand outside with the street people. She slowed down, took her time, got her order and carried it to the table behind the palm tree where she and Rex had stumbled across each other. Turning her phone on, she called home more to hear her father's voice than anything else.

Cody answered. "Hey, sis, you marry Rex Worthy yet?"

"No. His family is visiting. I had to sleep with his sister last night."

"She cute or is she big like Rex?"

"Cute if you like red spikes in the hair, a tattoo, and black nail polish."

"That's fine by me. Maybe we'll hit it off at your wedding."

"Not likely to be a wedding."

"There goes my big chance at a tryout for the Sinners."

"Rex will keep his word about that. Could you put Dad on the line?"

"He's out on the tractor. You want me to fetch him?"

"No. I'm coming home tonight. Once I know the time, I'll let you know when to pick me up."

"Look, I got a game this evening."

"Sorry, I forgot. Maybe Colt could come. Go Cyclones."

She disconnected feeling lower than before. The world did not revolve around her. Cody had football, her father his farm. The sugar and caffeine rush from the beignets and latte failed to cheer. In her black bag, her phone buzzed with no special ringtone, not Layla's *Ride of the Valkyries*, not Rex's *Sweet Like This*. She answered cautiously. "To whom am I speaking?"

"Micah Stanley, babe. Look, Patsy, you gotta go back to Layla. We need her fit and ready to film *Scandal!* this spring. I can't get through to her. Some guy named Lee always answers her phone. If he's her new PA, he's doing a lousy job. You see that scene she made at the Sinners game? Now I'm the first to say all publicity is good publicity, but she looks like crap. Not a good image for that sexpot role she has coming up. Name your price, hon, I'll pay it."

"Sorry, Mr. Stanley. I am no longer for sale." Not feeling the least tempted, Tricia drained her coffee cup.

"You want a role in *Scandal!* I'll see you get it. You weren't a bad little actress, but you didn't have the heat, ya know. More girl next door, the kind who doesn't put out. What do you say?"

If only he knew. "No, thanks. I'm thinking of going back to college for my teaching degree."

Micah Stanley barked out a laugh that turned into an old man's cough. "That's as nuts as, what's her name, Dolores Hart becoming a nun. This could be your big break."

"I appreciate the offer, but no." She hung up on one of Hollywood's most powerful directors.

Buying a sack of the donuts as a peace offering, Tricia headed back to the apartment. Rex let her in, no questions asked. She set the bag of pastries hard on the kitchen counter sending up a little puff of powdered sugar from opening. "In case you want to try the local delicacies."

"I do," said Becky, now discreetly dressed again with her black toenails covered by a pair of Skechers and her red spikes smoothed down against her head. She looted the sack of two beignets and sucked up the powered sugar.

"You'll grow fat as a Texas steer if you eat that *and* cornbread, Honeybee. We're getting pretty close to lunch now," her mother declared.

"Not a problem for me. I have Dad's metabolism. It's Rex who will turn to lard because he takes after you."

Mrs. Worthy crimsoned. Her husband patted her pudgy arm. "Love you just the way you are, Honeybunch." Still, he tried a beignet.

Rex huddled over a plate containing a huge hunk of cornbread and some breakfast sausages that must have been hiding in his freezer. Syrup covered both. "You want to go for a run, Tricia, maybe in City Park?"

"Sorry, I won't have time. I talked to my brother while I was out. They need me at home. Not much to pack. I'll get a cab to the airport. You have a nice visit with your family."

"Trish, don't go. We need to talk."

"I would think you talked enough last night to get it out of your system. I know what you want to say. No hard feelings."

Some girls you marry, some you don't. Some women like Mrs. Worthy are fit to go to Africa as missionaries, some aren't and don't want to be. She went to the guestroom and got her carry-on, added her toiletries, and phoned for a cab. She'd leave Rex to his cornbread and his vocation.

Chapter Twenty-Six

Tricia's car arrived from California. Black trash bags contained most of her clothes, though Juanita packed her photos and souvenirs more carefully wrapped in newspapers and placed in boxes. How very little of her own she accumulated while working for Layla. Tricia made a point of driving to Ames immediately to inquire about joining the school of education for the spring semester. Many of her UCLA credits would transfer. At least, she wouldn't have to endure the basic freshman and sophomore classes again. If not enough money remained after her mother's medical bills and funeral expenses were settled, she'd take out a student loan and get a part-time job. In the meantime, she kept her phone off and her laptop closed. No Layla, no Rex, no problem.

The last thing she needed to see upon returning to the farm—a pink Cadillac driven by Doris Dillman. If only it had been a pink cow or a pink elephant, both easier to accept right now. Layla's mother had cornered the cosmetics market in their little section of Iowa twenty-five years ago and never let a competitor get a foothold since. She used her own sad story as a marketing tool: a dowdy housewife, pregnant and abandoned by a philandering insurance salesman husband, blossoms and empowers herself by using and selling fine makeup products. Further proof of success, her daughter, actress Layla Devlin, who used her cosmetics line since appearing in childhood beauty pageants where she inevitably won with her blonde ringlets and unusual eyes highlighted with just the right shade of shadow and liner.

Tricia considered turning around and going into town to hide, but Doris waited on one of the porch rockers despite the nip in the air. At the funeral, Doris offered the usual condolences and a remark that Trish looked peaked and could use a new skin and make-up regimen. Evidently, a polite demurral to her follow-up call had not deterred the woman. A representative wasn't awarded a pink Cadillac for lack of persistence. Sighing, Tricia got out of the car and prepared to submit to a makeover whether she wanted it or not. Maybe she needed one.

As she approached, however, she noticed Doris sat hunched, face in hands. When she raised her usually perfectly made-up visage, a considerable amount of it stayed on her fingers as black smudges and lipstick stains. Her eyes, minimized by puffy lids above and pads of fat below, floated in tears like the pernicious lilac water hyacinths of Louisiana. Overweight as long as Tricia had known her and always a brassy blonde no matter what her age, Mrs. Dillman foretold Layla's appearance in middle age—unless she got sucked and tucked like most actresses. Always full of a brash confidence she'd transferred to her daughter, today the woman was nothing but a mess.

"Please help my little girl," Doris whimpered.

"Sorry, I'm done helping Layla, but come inside and have some tea. It's chilly out here, and you don't want people to see you this way."

"No, I don't. I rang and rang, but no one answered. I would sit out here until Hell froze over to rescue my only child."

"Dad and Carson are turning over some of the fields. Cody and Colt went to classes. I plan to start at State next semester, so you see I'm not going to be available."

Tricia unlocked the door and led the way to the kitchen with Doris trundling behind dressed in an overstuffed pink pantsuit but minus her cosmetic case and samples. How often had Marty Welles entertained the woman in this same kitchen, buying a lipstick or compact because the poor soul had to support herself and a daughter, making her tea, feeding her bundt cake? Automatically, Tricia put on water to boil and took a leftover funeral pound cake from the freezer, gave it a short zap in the microwave, and arrayed the slices on a plate.

Mrs. Dillman waved the offering away. "I can't eat. That dreadful Micah Stanley phoned me to say Louise is in a bad way. Not that I couldn't figure it out by myself, but she won't take my calls. This man, Lee, always intervenes. When you were assisting my daughter at least I got to talk to her sometimes."

Tricia kept her back to the woman as she prepared the tea. One in five calls from Layla's mother was to be accepted on the star's orders. Mommy and Me time Layla called the lengthy conversations. "After all, I owe the old bag everything from the color of my eyes to a ticket out of Iowa." Lee must have received new instructions.

"I know Mr. Stanley exploited my daughter, took her virginity on the casting couch like that awful man in

The Godfather. Maybe I should have remarried. Then, Louise would not have fallen for a father figure. But, he does seem genuinely concerned for her wellbeing."

Tricia eyebrows shot up. Layla had lost her virginity behind a set of Iowa bleachers long before she got out of high school. If anything, she'd used aging Micah Stanley to get ahead.

"I know I said some mean things to your mother about your being only a talentless gofer riding on Layla Devlin's coattails. I guess that's why you don't want to help me now. You know, my daughter's condition is partially your fault. You stole that prime young man she wanted. I could tell by the way he looked at you when he got up to speak at the funeral. A man like that could turn her life around. Now, Louise might die of heartbreak because of you."

Tricia served the tea, shoving one of the pretty china cups her grandmother always used across the table so hard the scalding water sloshed into the saucer and drew a small squeak from Mrs. Dillman's smeared lips. "My mother did not repeat ugly words. She always said they should fall on barren ground and never bear fruit."

"I can't say enough good about your mother," Mrs. Dillman rushed to say.

Nor had Doris spoken any nice words at the funeral. Unmoved, Tricia said, "Cream and sugar?"

"Tea and sympathy?" Mrs. Dillman countered. "Your mother never judged, never failed to offer the helping hand. When others said I'd driven my husband away, she was the first to place an order when I started my business—pearl pink nail polish and matching lipstick. I haven't forgotten."

Her mother never wore either. Years later, Tricia used both to play dress up as a child. The memory made her eyes water. Doris Dillman noticed. She knew where to apply pressure exactly like Layla.

"You are your mother's daughter, so good at heart. I know people think I'm pushy and overbearing. No one will say nice things about me when I'm gone, but what I fear the most is that I'll have to bury my Louise long before that time comes. I am afraid she is flickering out, you know, like that candle in the wind. When the two of you left for California, I was so glad she'd have a sensible friend by her side and that you stayed with her when she made it big. I am so very grateful."

Right. She and Layla had hardly been friends in high school. Only her own fear of going to a big city convinced her to room with the bolder personality unafraid to take on anything, sometimes too unafraid. Tricia met Doris' faded violet eyes, a big mistake.

"Save my daughter for me, please." More tears carried runnels of eyeliner and mascara into the grooves of Mrs. Dillman's fleshy face.

Before she capitulated, Tricia allowed herself one last unkind thought. Doris should have worn the waterproof liner. "I can stay with Layla until mid-January when the semester starts, not a day longer."

****

Tricia arrived back in New Orleans with her black bag and baggage prepared to stay only as long as she promised. Knowing Rex played out of town with the Sinners for the next couple of weeks helped. She wouldn't run into him accidently. There would be no beignets or bars in Layla's near future. Still, the night before she left Iowa, she'd had a dream of being crushed by overweight blonde women sitting on her head, heart, and private parts—Layla, Doris, and Sue Grace Worthy.

Having left her key behind when she quit, Tricia knocked on the door of the condo. It opened a crack. "Pizza?" a husky, somewhat feminine voice asked.

"No, Lee. It's Tricia. I answered Layla's seventy-six voice mails and 222 e-mails begging me to return by saying yes and listing my conditions. She agreed."

"There must be some mistake. I'm taking care of her now. I took away her phone and computer for her own good. I knew she could get into trouble harassing you and that football player."

When his hands left the doorknob and fluttered in agitation, Tricia forced the opening a little wider. "Evidently, she found a way to communicate. Are you still doing your act?"

"Of course. It's a tribute that immortalizes Layla, but I make sure she is sedated before I leave—so she won't hurt herself."

"One thing you should have learned about Layla by now—when she wants pills, she gets them. When she doesn't want pills, she hides them under her tongue and spits them out later."

From the turquoise couch, a dreamy voice said, "Patsy is that you?" A puffy hand embedded with large rings flopped over the back of the sofa and beckoned to her. "Lee-Lee, let my Patsy in."

He stood aside unwilling but unable to disobey his idol. Tricia stalked to the sofa. "Rule Number One: If you call me Patsy one more time, I am gone."

Tricia gazed down on the wreckage of Layla Devlin who wore the sunburst caftan and nothing else.

It fit her fairly well now. In only an additional three weeks, she had ballooned. A frizzy mess of coils framed a face greatly resembling Mrs. Dillman's with those famous eyes sunken into flesh like black olives in the deep-dish pizza they awaited for dinner.

"Rule Number Two: No more food orgies."

"After the pizza, okay?" Layla whined.

"Your last pizza. Rule Number Three: No more pills and alcohol."

Layla groaned. "How am I gonna get by without a little help from my friends?"

"You'll live. That's the important part. Rule Number Four: You will exercise. I've found a personal trainer for you."

"Is he cute?"

"Her name is Selena. A lot of the Sinners' wives use her services to stay in shape. You will not be able to convince her that having sex with you is an aerobic exercise."

"Well, it is. And I bet I could. Don't you think so, Lee-Lee?" Layla offered the hand with the rings cutting into her flesh to the transvestite.

He kissed her dimpled knuckles. "Yes, I do. Lay-Lay, you don't have to lose an ounce for me, and you can do whatever you want. I will always love you. Send Patsy away."

Layla extracted her hand and waved a pudgy finger at him. "Ah-ah-ah, she's Tricia now. See how well I did that, Pat—Trish."

Tricia pressed her lips together to keep from screaming. "A good start. Rule Number Five: You will not stalk Rex Worthy."

Layla pouted her lips, not very voluptuous-looking

now as their pillowy softness had to compete with her jowls. "I think I still have a good chance with him."

"You are so wrong. Rex loves only God. He wants to be a missionary in Africa like his father. Are you up for being a missionary's wife? I know I'm not."

"I played one once in *Masai!* Remember, a great white hunter seduced me inside my husband's chapel, which freed me to find true passion with a Masai warrior. I could act the part to be with Rex."

Tricia shook her head with disgust. "What are you on today? No more Rex for either of us."

Layla stretched her stuffed sausage arms wide. "I could give him something he won't have to pray to God for."

"Not likely."

"Can I still watch the Sinners' games, huh? They took my luxury box away over a teensy bit of damage to the suite."

"If you don't mention his name, we could do that here in the apartment. No sports bars, no unhealthy snacks during the game." Regardless of how things had turned out between them, she could still follow his career from afar—which made her not much better than Layla.

"Any more stupid rules?"

"I'll let you know as the situations come up. Selena will be here in half an hour. Hoist yourself off that couch and put on some exercise clothes."

"Can't go to a gym like this. I have no exercise clothes that fit me."

"Fortunately, one of the amenities of this place is a small gym on the first floor by the laundry room. Since most people who rent here are either partying on

Bourbon Street or taking their kids to the aquarium, it is usually unoccupied and kept locked. The key should be in the kitchen drawer. I'll be back with something you can wear by the time Selena gets here. If not, do some stretches and jumping jacks or something."

"I hate jumping jacks. They hurt my boobs." Like a small child hiding, Layla put a throw pillow over her face and mumbled into it. "Kill me now."

With a great deal of doubt, Tricia left Lee in charge of Layla. She stepped out into the heat and humidity malingering all the way to November and headed into the Quarter where nary a block existed without a T-shirt shop. At the first one encountered, she scored an XXL purple shirt with a festive Mardi Gras theme—masks, beads, and crossed champagne glasses on the front. Took two more searches to find bottoms that might fit Layla's enlarged rump: a pair of men's novelty boxers with "Suck the Head" printed across the rear and a large, red crawfish on the fly. The T-shirt would cover most of the vulgar message.

Returning to the condo, she encountered Selena Jaspers entering. No doubt who the woman was as she'd checked her web site. A statuesque black woman with short-cropped hair showing some gray, Selena owned arm muscles that made Michelle Obama's physique look puny. She showed them off with a tight sleeveless black top that clung to impressive abs. Tricia suspected the long legs beneath her nylon running pants would be hard as an Olympic sprinter's. Only that bit of gray gave away Selena's age because her smooth mahogany skin had not a single wrinkle. It stretched tightly over high cheekbones. Her deep brown eyes gleamed with the fervor of an exercise fanatic. Hard core, just what Layla needed.

"So you are trainer to the wives of the Sinners," Tricia said as they ran up the flights of stairs to the condo. Not necessary to confess she'd come across her name while searching for information on Rex.

"You might say I am intimately connected to them. I was one of Joe Dean Billodeaux's list ladies soooo long ago you were probably in kindergarten back then. He invited six of us to spend an island weekend with him and the team. I thought he might give my business a boost, so I went even if I had to sleep with him. Not that it would have been a hardship, a fine looking man then, a fine looking man now. He didn't know it, but he was already hung up on Nell. Never slept with a one of us, but gave me an endorsement as a trainer. You know Tabby Johnson, the comedienne? She was there, too. Joe got her a gig at one of the clubs he frequented. Friends to this day." Selena showed no sign of being winded as she talked.

"Interesting story. You go on ahead. I'll catch up." As soon as Selena rounded another landing, Tricia slowed to a walk. She might have to do some exercising with them.

The trainer waited at the door doing stretches, not wasting a minute. Tricia let them in to bathe in the aroma of a pepperoni and sausage deep dish. Layla sat at the dining table stuffing her face as if pizza would cease to exist tomorrow, which in her case was true. Selena slapped the greasy wedge from her hand.

"I'm Selena Jaspers, and I'm here to help you. Can't hardly believe you're Layla Devlin. Girl, your curves have turned into landslides. Put on your exercise clothes, and let's get started."

"You can't talk to me like that, you black bitch." Layla grabbed another slice and shoved it in her mouth.

"Yes, she can because I said so." Tricia relieved her of the pizza and firmly shut the box. She held out the bags. "Best I could do on short notice."

Layla considered the offerings. Laughing when she read the slogan on the shorts, she said, "I have to get some of these for Micah Stanley but in a smaller size. He has the skinniest ass. See to that, Tricia."

"When I have the time. Get dressed."

Even in a caftan, Layla managed to sway seductively to the bedroom. "Humph! You joining us?" Selena asked, unimpressed by the star's performance.

"Maybe tomorrow. I need to do a sweep of the condo today. Lee, take the pizza back to your place."

"Actually, I've been spending most of my time here caring for Layla." Lee held the box as if it contained some precious souvenir of the star.

He had turned the actress from a raging, seductive tyrant to an overweight petulant child during his tenure. Which was worse, Tricia could not say. "Take the pizza as a thank you and go before I have Selena toss you out. Or you can work out with us. It won't be pretty."

Shuddering, Lee clutched the box to his chest and resigned his position. After Selena and Layla left for the gym, Tricia did a sweep of the apartment, first cleaning out the refrigerator and cabinets of junk food, then doing the harder part of searching for drugs. The night table drawer, easy and obvious for prescriptions, but she inspected the hems of Layla's sheets in case any pills were inserted there. The tank on the commode yielded well-sealed baggies of pot, and a tangle of purses in the closet a cornucopia of ways to get high.

She flushed so much she feared the plumbing would back up and hoped the fish in the nearby aquarium did not share the same water source.

She got her own exercise heaving bags of salty, greasy, and sugary sweet snacks to the dumpster. Tonight, the homeless would dine better than usual. They could use the calories. As an added incentive, she printed the picture of Layla wearing the sunburst caftan off the internet and stuck it on the refrigerator. So ended day one of the rehabbing of Layla Devlin by Tricia Welles, Patsy no longer.

Chapter Twenty-Seven

Funny how weight is so easy to gain and so hard to take off. Tricia recalled Shelley Winters gaining a bunch for a plum role and lately, Sally Fields packing it on to play Mrs. Lincoln. Convincing Layla she had to be svelte for her spring film wasn't as easy. Nor was dealing with the dreadlocks, all Lee's idea.

"I complained and complained about how frizzy my hair gets in this city. Lee suggested I wear wigs, but they're so hot and uncomfortable. Then he came up with this great idea that I get dreads. It's so New Orleans. He took me to this black hair salon where no white people went. They were so honored. Anyhow, another good thing about the dreads is you hardly ever have to wash them." Layla paused in riding the exercise bike to inform both Tricia and Selena of this.

Tricia wrinkled her nose. "Yes, I can tell you haven't washed them often." Frankly, they smelled of weed and pepperoni.

Selena said, "No white person should wear dreadlocks. Save your breath for pedaling. You got another ten minutes to do."

"There were only five minutes left!"

"It's ten now, baby."

A specially selected hairdresser arrived the next day toting gallons of cream rinse and hair straightener. She started with a deep cleansing wash and ended with a vicious combing. Layla sobbed throughout the entire ordeal. When the hair flowed like molten gold again, Tricia paid the stylist for her afternoon, added a generous tip and a threat. If any of the tabloids got wind of the treatment, her services would never be called upon again, not only by Layla, but by every person Layla knew. Keep quiet and become hairdresser to the stars. Deal.

Even the formidable Selena took Sundays off, but she showed up to watch the Sinners' games with a veggie tray in hand and a choice of hummus or yogurt dip to go with it. She allowed Tricia to put out a dish of dry-roasted peanuts, but nothing else. All of them sipped water with lemon slices since the trainer swore diet drinks upset the metabolism and caused weight gain in the end. She settled on one side of the turquoise couch, Tricia on the other with Layla like the pale, fluffy mayonnaise-laden filling in between a slice of dark rye and healthy light whole wheat.

"I've been a fan of the Sinners ever since I didn't do Joe Dean," Selena said.

"Evidently no one does Joe Dean anymore. He's too old to get it up. In fact, he's too old to play football. They should put in…another guy," Layla sniped.

The pre-game chatter filled the air. The cameras nosed here and there ferreting out interesting shots the commentators could make noise about. They selected Joe Dean's family filling two prime rows near the field. The handicapped boy sat in a wheelchair on the end slot. Nell and her belly took up quite a bit of room right next to him. A reporter climbed into the stands to do an interview. "I wanted to see one more game in person before I'm confined to bed rest again with these twins,"

Nell explained, hands resting on her rounded stomach. "We flew to Miami this morning, the entire gang."

"I guess Joe Dean can still get it up. His wife is expecting twins," Tricia remarked.

"That woman! She humiliated me twice. I hope she dies giving birth," Layla frothed.

"Whoa, there. Hatred releases cortisol into the system. You'll never get rid of your belly fat if you keep this up," Selena warned. Over Layla's head, she raised thin plucked eyebrows at Tricia who gave her a grateful nod.

"Put a carrot in it, Layla," her PA said, dipping one in hummus and offering it to her temporary boss.

The Sinners ran onto the field, and all the Billodeaux children stood to cheer for their dad, even Teddy with the braces on his legs. Nell struggled to her feet and added her applause. Layla hissed but watched avidly as Rex Worthy dropped to his knees to pray. Tricia covered her interest with sips of lemon water and a handful of peanuts. She thought he prayed longer than usual. Other than that, no sign he languished for her or anyone else. He still rode the pine with panache, cheering for his teammates and offering a back slap when they returned from the field after scoring.

Way ahead, Rex did get to play the fourth quarter. He put in a workmanlike performance and made one touchdown with the help of Jakarta Jones. See, he'd put the whole Layla/Tricia mess behind him. No affect on his game at all, Tricia believed. No damage done to anyone but herself.

****

Thanksgiving waddled in on turkey drumsticks wading through gravy. Tricia feared Layla would overindulge if she left her alone for a trip home, and the actress refused a plea from Doris to spend the holiday with her mother in Iowa.

"I won't go back there until I am one-hundred and ten-percent gorgeous again," Layla declared.

Her long legs were the first to recover, now more shapely than before thanks to Selena. Her face thinned, and she could finally get her rings off again. Unfortunately, a good deal of belly fat, though firmer than before, remained around her middle. Tricia honestly wondered if cortisol could be the problem. Layla, forbidden to mention Rex, raged about Joe Dean and at any mention of Nell, a topic that always came up during interviews at the end of the game.

"How are Nell and the twins doing? They ask every time as if she were a bigger celebrity than me." Kept from the disparaging eyes of the paparazzi, Layla felt the lack of publicity. "If we don't go out soon, the world will forget me," she claimed.

On the phone, Trish apologized to her dad and brothers. "I'm so sorry I can't be with you, this year especially. Next year I promise to make all of Mom's recipes for you, her apple crumb pie as well as pumpkin."

Before her father could answer, Colt chimed in on the old extension phone. "That's okay, sis. Mrs. Welch invited us to her house. She's making a pumpkin pie, but Heidi is baking brownies, the recipe that won the 4-H contest, just for me."

She managed to get out a "Great. You go enjoy," when her father said they could stay home if that upset her. In the background, Colt protested, "I don't want an omelet for Thanksgiving."

Tricia put together a meal for herself and Layla: slices of white meat, a small whole wheat roll, fresh green beans with almonds and no sauce, salad with vinegar and oil dressing, and a special treat, low-fat frozen yogurt sprinkled with crushed graham crackers. Afterwards, they exercised.

She knew how Rex celebrated because the Sinners home game featured a cameo of him serving the homeless mashed potatoes in Dallas. Beside him, Honeybee in a hairnet splatted canned green beans onto the trays. In the evening, he ate with his family at a communal dinner in the church hall held for those who had no family or simply wanted to share the meal. The room appeared overcrowded with young women who desired to spend Thanksgiving with their pastor's family. Rex exhorted everyone to remember those in need, especially people who had lost a dear one in the past year. They needed to know they were still loved by another—by others, he meant to say.

Chapter Twenty-Eight

Nell Billodeaux traveled to New Orleans for her last prenatal exam before her confinement to bed rest. Confinement: a term used in ancient times to describe a period of time when a pregnant woman left society to await the birth of a child. More like a jail sentence, two months of bed rest, but she'd promised Joe no drama this time. She would not give birth in a motor home because of a jealous snit, nor would she insist on going to one of his last games near her due date, not even the Super Bowl. Her husband struggled to accept the end of his football career. She meant to give him nothing else to worry about.

Given her age, previous history, and the impending double birth, Dr. Stewart regarded her as high risk. She would deliver by caesarian section under his care at Ochsner one day after the Super Bowl or sooner if she went into labor. Staying at Lorena Ranch for most the time, she'd transfer to the condo in New Orleans a few weeks in advance to be closer to the hospital and away from the turmoil of her other children. All appeared to be going well. She tried to take a deep breath of relief, but the pressure of the babies on her diaphragm prevented that from happening.

Nurse Edith Wickersham Brinsley, dear Shammy always in attendance, helped her from the car. They planned to have an English tea together before naptime.

Shammy's husband, Clive Brinsley, had packed a small cooler with cucumber and turkey salad sandwiches, scones and fruit tarts along with a thermos of Earl Grey tea for their trip, a treat after the checkup. With luck, Joe might be back from practice. Nell had gotten him a large, wet roast beef po-boy with extra gravy for dipping as dainty foods seldom satisfied him. The last person she expected to trip over outside the condo door—Rex Worthy hunched against the wall with his head resting on his knees as if he held up the entire building with his back.

"Rex? Have you been waiting here very long?"

"Doesn't matter. I need to speak to Joe in private. You, too. I didn't want the other guys to hear."

"Get up off the floor and come in. Shammy, would you set up the tea? I tried not to eat before the weigh-in and I am starving."

Her nurse took the hint and busied herself in the kitchen. Nell led Rex to the long, leather sofa in the living room. "What can I do for you?"

"Maybe you heard Tricia left me."

"Joe suspected as much but said as long as you played well he didn't want to butt in."

"I always try to do my best no matter how I feel."

"I am certain you do. Why did Tricia leave?" Nell pondered how best to put it. "Were there sexual problems?' As conflicted as Rex had been about his virginity, the possibility of not being able to perform in bed entered her mind.

Though his face glowed red under his stubble, Rex shook his head. "No, we were doing great. Then, my family, my mother, showed up for an unexpected visit."

A key turned in the lock, and Joe entered with one

hand held behind his back. He whipped out a bouquet of pink and lavender roses and presented them to Nell. "How are you and the babies doing—and why in hell are you here, Worthy?"

Before Rex got his mouth open, Nell said, "These are so lovely. I think a little bit of Brian Lightfoot is rubbing off on you."

"Nothing about Brian is ever going to rub against me. You know, you still can't get blue roses. Someone should fix that. I stopped at the florist on my way home and lavender is the best they could do. Lavender is too gay for a son, not that Brian isn't a good guy in his way."

"Could be two girls, you know. Or did Dr. Stewart break down and tell you the sexes of the babies?"

"No, he sure didn't. That's why I bought both colors." Joe sniffed the air and changed the subject swiftly. "Do I smell roast beef?"

"We have scones and cucumber sandwiches, too. We'll have something to eat after we talk to Rex. His family, most especially his mother, showed up when he and Tricia were together."

Rex clenched his hands between his knees. "I swear my mom knew the second she walked in the door with her cake carrier. That evening she prayed over me and got the details, I mean not about what we did, but all about Trish. I had a hard night and overslept. Tricia went out for beignets and packed up and left as soon as she got back from the café. She didn't give me a chance to explain anything. Her phone is always off. She won't answer e-mails. My mother says it's all for the best."

"I'll just bet she did," Nell muttered, possibly thinking of her own mother-in-law.

"Yeah, never sleep with a woman when your mother is around. Nell and me used to go off in the cane fields to get away from mine," Joe reminisced.

"Not in front of the boy, Joe!"

Still flushed, Rex continued, "I know Tricia thinks I only want to marry her because she is my first, but it's not that way. Sometimes you just know when a person is the right one. I tried talking to her father, but he said the Welles women can be very hardheaded. If Trish made up her mind not to have me, I should leave her alone."

"I'd say it's pretty hard to romance a woman in Iowa from here," Joe said.

"No, she's back in town and working for Layla again. He told me that much. I could go over there, but don't want Trish to think I'm stalking."

"Why would she do that once she shook free of that—that…" Nell scrambled for a word that wouldn't bring the roses to Rex's cheeks. "That monstrous woman."

"See, that's what I mean about Tricia. Layla's mother begged her to help her daughter. She wouldn't go back for money or an acting job, her dad said, only because of a mother's tears."

"Too bad your mother couldn't shed a few and give the girl a break. So why are you here again?" Joe looked toward the kitchen where a microwave dinged and a tea kettle whistled.

"I want to quit football."

Joe's head jerked around. "*C'est vrai?* You can't mean dat—that. The Sinners are having their best season ever. We already have a lock on the playoffs. I can smell my fifth Super Bowl ahead just like a roast beef po-boy. It will be your first time. You get a ring even if you don't play."

"It's your Super Bowl, not mine, Joe. Football is only a game I'm good at playing. If I can't marry Tricia, I'd just as soon go to Africa, maybe work with the Jimmy Carter foundation. I don't think I have it in me to be a missionary, though my mama has been pushing that idea since I was thirteen. People are more important than a sport."

"Amen. It took Joe years to figure that out." Nell's stomach growled. She covered her belly in embarrassment.

"For sure my wife and kids are more important, but man, it's the Super Bowl, my last. You're my backup. I need you there in case, just in case. Next year, the Sinners expect you to lead them."

"You and the Sinners don't need me. Tricia doesn't need me, but maybe some African kids do. I'll finish out the season, then try to get out of my contract so I can move on. I'm keeping Nell from her meal, I can tell. Just wanted to let you know my plans."

"No, eat with us. We need to talk some more," Nell insisted.

"She's the psychologist," Joe said. "I'm team captain. Have some food. I can split that roast beef po-boy with you, I guess."

"From Johnny's?" Nell nodded. "I'm in."

Shammy, listening to every word said lest her patient get upset, added an extra place at the table and divested Nell of her bouquet, quickly dispatching it into a vase to serve as a centerpiece. The sandwiches and sweets ringed a large platter. Two of the Royal Doulton teacups from the ranch and so carefully packed by dear

Clive sat across from each other. The roast beef po-boy, severed in half, resided on plainer dishes with individual dunking cups on the side. Nell inhaled the bergamot-scented steam of her tea and heaped a plate with delicate goodies. "Wonderful," she said.

"Yeah, wonderful. You want a beer, Worthy?"

"That would be great."

After Nell took the edge off her appetite with several small sandwiches, she said, "Now before you rush off to Africa, I'd try another tactic with Tricia. If she won't speak to you or respond to e-mails, why not express yourself in a letter, handwritten, sincere, so rare she must open it, and will treasure it forever."

The men, making a mess of the tablecloth with gravy drippings, stared at her. "What would I say?" Rex asked with the leaking sandwich half-raised to his mouth.

"Say what is in your heart. When we are done here, I'll give you some of my good stationery and a pen."

Rex gulped. "Maybe I should write it on a legal pad first, like a draft. You could read it and see if I did all right."

"By all means, write a draft, but it must be your words, not mine." Nell pressed her fingers to her lips to suppress a small burp. "I really must lay off cucumbers soon." She helped herself to a strawberry tart and a blueberry scone.

"I am glad to see we have a good appetite," Nurse Shammy said. "Finish, then it's nappy time for you and the babies, and I'll be off for my daily walk."

Before submitting to nurse's orders, Nell supplied Rex with a yellow legal pad and a few pencils. She laid a box of thick, creamy white paper with gold foil-lined envelopes next to his plate. He finished inhaling the roast beef po-boy and took his dish and empty bottle to the sink like a well-trained son. Shammy didn't remove the leftover desserts in case Rex needed something more to keep him going. She put Nell to bed and left in her walking shoes. Joe settled in front of the TV, flipping through channels while his substitute put words on paper, struggling as much as he did when trying to complete long passes.

Sheets from the yellow tablet balled up on the floor. Two pencils lost their points under the pressure of Rex's grip. Once, he pulled a miniature Bible from his shirt pocket and copied a verse. Finally, he exhaled loud enough for Joe to hear over the noise of a sports channel.

"You done? Want me to read over it?"

"No, thanks." Rex took up the pen and a sheet of the fancy paper.

He botched his first attempt and tore it to pieces. Finally, he folded his missive into an envelope. "I think that's the best I can do. Thank Nell for me, would you?"

"Sure. See you at practice."

Rex let himself out. Joe turned off the television and went quietly to the bedroom he shared with Nell. She lay on her left side curled around her belly. The second he sat on the edge of the round mattress, she opened her eyes.

"Sorry, didn't mean to wake you."

"Only dozing. I really can't get comfortable. Is Rex gone?"

"Yeah, he left most of a legal pad on our floor. Didn't think he'd ever get it right."

"Really? I want to see."

For a heavily pregnant woman, Nell got out of bed fairly fast. Belly leading, she went to the table and began laboriously picking up the drafts. "Tricia, my one and only love. Awww. Your eyes are the color of the summer sky. Oooh!"

Joe smoothed out one of the crumpled sheets of paper and read a few lines. "You'd really want to get a letter like this?"

"What woman wouldn't?"

"I mean I could do this, too, but I show how much I love you every day."

"So how would you describe my eyes?" Nell fluttered her lashes.

"I don't know. Sweet as chocolate kisses and the same color, too?"

"Not so good."

"I'm more a man of action than a guy for words. Shammy is out. Rex is gone. You are awake. Two months of bed rest starts tomorrow. It's gonna be a long time for both of us. We could take it slow and easy." Joe smoothed his long-fingered hands over her belly. The babies sent up a flurry of kicks as if their, or maybe Nell's, heartbeat went up a notch.

"I'd like that, man of action, I truly would."

Chapter Twenty-Nine

Tricia noticed the envelope stuck in the side of the door as she and Layla returned from the gym. Thanks to her long legs, Layla reached it first and scowled. Tricia saw her own name written on it in a heavy, masculine hand.

"I believe that's addressed to me. Help yourself to a bottle of water and some fruit." She plucked the letter from Layla's grasp.

"I hate fruit unless it is baked in a pie." The actress flounced over to the turquoise sofa and flopped onto its cushions. Her long, sweaty blonde ponytail hung over the arm.

"As we well know. Suit yourself. I'll be in my room."

Heart pounding and not only from the exercise, Tricia closed and locked her door. She knew, simply knew, who had written her name on that envelope. Rex appeared to have accepted her decision after a flurry of phone calls and e-mails. Her father said Rex made an appeal to him, but he'd sided with his daughter. Dad did want to know what went wrong. She put it succinctly—his mother. "Heaven knows your mother put up with a lot from mine," he'd answered. She supposed he understood.

Opening it carefully, not wanting to mar the envelope, she took out the luxurious paper and read.

Tricia, my one and only love,

You would say that is impossible for me to know until I see other women. I have not and will not. Sometimes, a person can be positive about something without having to test it all the time, like believing in God or believing in us. Yes, you are beautiful with eyes blue as the summer sky, but my love for you goes deeper strengthened by the sacrifices you made for your mother and the concern you have for your family. Even returning to help Layla, not for wealth or success, but because her mother asked it of you speaks of your goodness.

My mother agreed with you, claiming I need not marry a woman just because I lay with her. Do you believe I would feel the same about marriage if Layla had been my first? You can answer that yourself. I have no idea what else Mama said to you. She never lies but sometimes rearranges the truth to her liking. Since I turned thirteen, she thinks I wanted to be a missionary. Mostly, I was homesick for my family and wanted to return to them in Africa instead of living with my hateful grandparents who would not let me study Spanish or bring home a black friend. I do want to help people, but in a secular way. To have you by my side while I accomplish that would be my finest dream. I hate mentioning any of those who would come between us in this letter, but did need to explain.

I turned to the Bible for better words. This is how I feel:

Place me like a seal over your heart,
like a seal on your arm;
for love is as strong as death,
its jealousy unyielding as the grave.

It burns like blazing fire,
like a mighty flame.
Many waters cannot quench love;
rivers cannot sweep it away.

If one were to give
all the wealth of one's house for love,
it would be utterly scorned.
Tricia, I love you. I want to marry you. Please give
your consent.
Rex

Tricia opened her phone and called the man whose signature song was *Sweet Like This*.

****

Layla Devlin still sprawled on the couch in her new spandex workout clothes when the doorbell rang. It woke her from an exercise-induced sleep. Tricia usually bolted to answer, trying to intercept pizza deliveries, drug dealers, and Lee, but this time she wasn't swift enough. Layla got there first hoping for some forbidden fruit. And there he stood, Rex Worthy in suit and tie carrying an armful of lavender roses.

"Oh, darling boy, for me?"

"No. For Tricia."

Layla held her arms out at her side to display her wares, a newly toned body. "But, I've got my glitter back now. I know I wasn't at my most appealing last time. We can still…"

"Yeah, I remember the glitter." A small shudder shook Rex's broad shoulders. He peered over Layla's head, his eyes fastened on a vision.

Layla turned to see what entranced him. Tricia twirled from her bedroom like that woman who got a baby by Clark Gable—Loretta Young. If she had lived then, Clark would have had an affair with Layla Devlin, but she would not have given birth to the child. The patsy wore a sky blue dress that swirled around her knees and a strand of pearls at her neck. Her hair hung loose and straight over her shoulders, not a hint of frizz in it. She had a glow about her that makeup could not duplicate. Layla hated her more than ever. Tricia ranked right up there with the Billodeaux bitch and Joe Dean.

Rex offered the lavender flowers to the humble PA. "Because they had none in blue to match your eyes."

"Oh, beautiful." Trish put them in water and carried them to her room. "I'll be right back."

She returned with only a small evening bag in her hand and a light wrap draped over her arm. "Layla, Rex and I are going out to dinner. I made up a plate with a cooked chicken breast and some boiled veggies for you while you napped. All you have to do is it nuke it. Fix a salad if you want, too. Sugar-free Jell-O for dessert."

"I'm not interested in Jell-O unless it has a shot in it."

"You are so close to your goal, only ten more pounds. Don't blow it. Act like a grownup and behave yourself tonight. I'd like an excuse to go home early."

"Yeah, I'd like that, too."

"Just say the word."

Layla remained sullen and silent. The couple left without another word. For a few minutes, wrath consumed the actress. She went to Tricia's room, removed the flowers from the vase, and stomped them into the carpet. Her eyes lit on the black bag, the one containing all her needs and comforts. She dumped it out on the bed, searched very pocket and crevice, no drugs but aspirin and Midol turned up. About to trash the contents, Layla stopped in the process of breaking the top off a stick of lipstick and mashing it into the bedspread. Lilac with a bit of sparkle, it belonged to her—as did the phone Tricia confiscated upon her return. She must have taken her own with her, but no matter at all.

With the phone in her own hands again came freedom—to call her supplier, to order as much takeout as she could possibly eat, to contact Lee and set up a good time. She hadn't been out in weeks. Oh, the power of the little instrument. But no, she wanted to stay gorgeous and clear-headed to plan her revenge—against Tricia and Nell. Layla made a couple of calls. Lee wanted to celebrate her restored fabulousness by doing a duet with her in his act tonight. She could squeeze into her sexiest gowns now. Let the paparazzi photograph her all they wanted. Layla Devlin was back and determined to triumph over her enemies in a big way.

****

Tricia and Rex shared a sumptuous meal of seafood and champagne, but decided on Café du Monde for coffee and dessert. It seemed like their place, the place where they first got to know each other. After that, they strolled along the esplanade on the top of the levee, the famous Moon Walk, Rex leading her away from the street performers wailing out songs on old saxophones and even the plaintive scratch of a dilapidated cello. Music playing in the distance, he selected a bench near a pool of lantern light, got down on his knees with the mighty Mississippi serving as a dark, moonlit backdrop, and offered her a ring.

"There are sapphires a darker blue, but I wanted this one to match your eyes. Please say yes."

Tricia gazed on a ring chosen with care. The blue did match her eyes. Small diamonds surrounded it. The stone was a good size, but not ostentatious. She realized he had enough confidence in her answer and their future to include a wedding band of alternating diamonds and sapphires, all set in platinum.

Because she didn't answer, he added, "I bought the rings right after my family left town. Nothing they said changed my mind, but I hope I changed yours with my letter."

"It did. I'm sorry I wouldn't give you a chance to explain. You, the ring, all of this seems impossible when you could have a movie star or fulfill yourself as a missionary."

"What I want is a life with you, Tricia. Nothing else. Say yes."

"Yes."

Flashes surrounded them like an attack of lightning bugs. The danged street performers must have phoned in a Rex Worthy sighting to the paparazzi for some additional coin. They'd crept up on the couple in the dark but had the tiny bit of decency to hold off until she accepted—or maybe Rex on his knees simply made a better shot. From out of the night, one rough voice asked, "What's your name, honey? You the same babe he carried up to the hotel room? You still working for Layla Devlin?"

"Come on, Trish, let's get out of here." Rex barged through the photographers taking out a few of them with a straight arm as he might for a Jakarta Jones run.

"Trish, is that short for Patricia or your real name?"

a paparazzo who'd received an elbow to the stomach gasped. "I thought you went by Patsy."

"They never give up," Tricia told him.

Coming off the steps leading down from the levee, they lucked out on hailing a cab. Rex had them locked in his building before the entourage of photographers caught up. Some might stake out the place all night. Others would troll the Quarter for scandals in the making. In the safety of the apartment and his arms, Tricia said, "We didn't have time to seal our promise with a kiss."

"I can think of something better—unless you want to wait until after we get married."

"When do you think that will be, Rex?" Tricia's lips curved into a coy smile.

"Um, next week? We could fly to Vegas on Friday and be back in time for Sunday's game."

"No, I don't want a big, fancy wedding, but I want a church and my family and yours to be there. Iowa can be nice in April or May."

Disappointment showed in every line of his stubbled face. "That long?"

"But, I didn't say I wanted to wait any longer to celebrate." She backed him toward the bedroom working on his tie and buttons along the way. This time, Rex had not come prepared to undress in a hurry. She clawed off his jacket and shirt, worked the T-shirt over his head, the slacks and briefs from his body. His shoes fell down beside the bed, loafers filled with his socks.

"Let me," he said, reaching for her.

But Tricia *had* come prepared. "No, I can do it faster." She whisked the dress with the built-in bra over her head. Beneath it she wore only blue lace panties. Shedding those and kicking off her heels, she pushed Rex back on the bed. Watching her strip had him readied him. She climbed on top. "No missionary position tonight."

"Was that missionary position last time? I didn't think it involved your legs wrapped around my backside with your heels kicking me like a bucking bronco."

"Modified missionary, let's say." Straddling his hips, she rubbed along his shaft, closing her eyes and feeling his strength beneath her.

"Wait," Rex said. Her eyes opened. His arm dangled off the bed and found his suit jacket. He fumbled the ring box from a pocket. "I didn't have the chance to get this on your finger." He put the sapphire there now.

"Oh, Rex Worthy. I place the seal of my love over your heart." She leaned forward and kissed his chest. "And on your arm." She laid her lips on his remarkable biceps. "And your lips as well."

When she rose again, she took him deep inside her body and began to move. Her eyes closed again. Rex kept his open. He watched Pretty and Perky bob with her motion, her dark hair form a veil around them, her mouth open as she began to pant. He waited for the signs that she reached climax and held himself back until that moment because he wanted them to do it together in one perfect joining.

****

Tricia refused to stay the night. "I do have an obligation to Layla, and you know what the tabloids will say about you if I leave here at dawn."

"I don't care." Reluctant to let go, Rex held her firmly in his arms.

"Well, I do."

He did a slow release and watched her dress. Putting on enough clothes to be decent, he waited until the cab came to take her back to her hell of a job. Too bad she wouldn't consider Vegas next weekend, then all this pretense would be over and done.

New Orleans and its denizens were still wide-awake as the cab passed along its gaudy night time streets. A couple of sleepy paparazzi followed to learn her address, but didn't harass her any. Letting herself into the apartment, Tricia hoped Layla had gone to bed. The place was dark, and she tiptoed to her room considering if she should wear the ring tomorrow or not, certainly not to workout with Layla, but how she wanted to show Selena. With a flick of the light switch, the devastation of her belongings crashed into view. Well, the contents of her bag could be put back into order, bedspreads were washable, and flowers only temporary delights. She saved one of the least ravaged blooms to dry and put it in the locked drawer of the desk with Rex's letter and the newspaper clipping of him carrying her. Nothing could ruin this evening, not even finding Layla Devlin gone astray in her absence.

Chapter Thirty

Though Tricia slept lightly expecting a call from the police or a bartender to come pick up her charge, Layla found her way home alone around four a.m. Selena arrived at eight sharp as always and personally rousted her client from bed, rolling Layla from the sheets with strong, black arms. Complaining and using the N word without restraint, the actress struggled into her tight exercise clothes still unwashed from yesterday since Tricia hadn't done a load of laundry and all the other outfits smelled just as bad. Her PA held out a glass of tomato juice garnished with a celery stick.

"Hair of the dog?" Layla said hopefully.

"You wish. It's a Virgin Mary. Enjoy the celery."

"Speaking of virginity, how is Rex? I assume you have taken his by now."

Trisha held back as long as she could. Taking her hand from behind her back, she showed the ring to Layla. "We're going to be married in the spring."

"The hell you are! I'll do something for Rex so spectacular, he'll take that ring right off your finger and put it on mine—but I'd want something bigger." Layla tipped over the tomato juice, making a mess for someone else to clean up.

Tricia let the red puddle spread on the floor like blood at a crime scene. "Rex isn't into spectacular—though we came pretty close last night. Since Selena is here, why don't you go ahead and get started. I'll catch up."

"I have a headache, the classy kind. Lee and I polished off two bottles of champagne last night, but no drugs, I swear. I went over to his club, and we did a duet on stage together. The paparazzi bulbs were popping all over the place. Then, I was horny, so we got it on at his place," Layla boasted.

"Plenty of paparazzi to go around," Trisha commented, not bothering to explain.

"You got lots of alcohol calories to burn off and ten pounds still to lose." Selena snapped Layla's greatly reduced backside with a dishtowel. "How about we jog down those stairs?"

"I haven't had breakfast!"

Tricia tossed her a granola bar. "You poured the rest on the floor. Enjoy."

Selena hustled Layla out the door, then turned to say, "I've had some nasty clients in my day, but this one wins the gold medal in bitchiness. If you weren't paying me a bundle, I'd be out of here today. But, great ring, great guy. Congrats, Tricia. I hope you two are as happy as Joe and Nell."

"Thanks. I'm sorry about what she called you."

She didn't think she could hope for better than what Joe and Nell had. Fewer children certainly, but definitely a family of their own, a home far away from Mrs. Worthy, and if that meant living in Africa, so be it.

****

Christmas approached garlanding the French Quarter in red and green in spite of the mild warmth of the days and setting the oaks in City Park alight with thousands of tiny white lights at night. Tricia and Rex went to see the display and discussed the usual quandary couples faced—where to spend the holidays. He had one more regular season game, then the playoffs.

Finishing at the top of their division, the Sinners gained the advantage of playing in the Dome for the first of the contests to go to the Super Bowl. If they made it through that gauntlet of great teams, their home city had the contract for the big event. The team couldn't ask for a better chance. Joe Dean, full of fire he hadn't shown in the last couple of years, aimed to win that trophy. Rex got little playing time, but enough to keep him on his toes, just in case, as Joe said.

Holding hands, the couple strolled by the oaks on a balmy winter night. No fear of getting mugged when a girl walked with a guy as big as Rex, but she'd had the good sense to leave her engagement ring at the apartment locked away from Layla's wrath. Gradually, Tricia learned the ways of New Orleans and grew to love the place.

"I talked Layla into going home to Iowa now that she's back to her fighting weight again. She trash talks to me more than Mike Tyson before he bit Holyfield's ear in that boxing match. I could use a break."

"Why do you stay?" Rex put a protective arm around her slender shoulders at if the evening grew chilly or bad people lurked in the shadows.

"I gave my word. You know how that goes."

"I do. You could come home with me. My mom stuffs the turkey with her special cornbread. My dad and sister are happy for us. Mom says she's resigned. Best we can do for now."

At the remembrance of the cornbread and Rex's

mother, Tricia did shiver a little. They hadn't had an encounter since she walked out on Mrs. Worthy's brisket and the engagement made the front page of the tabloids with a rather sweet picture of Rex on his knees and her face so full of joy. The headline read *Rex Finds his One and Only* in one paper and *Worthy to Marry his Damsel in Distress* in another that recapped the story of his carrying her to the elevator along with that photo. At least, they'd spelled her name right, Welles with two e's, and used Tricia, not Patsy. In show biz, that mattered. Layla ripped up the first copy Trish cut out. She and Lee doing their duet only made the inside page. Tricia couldn't quite figure out if her fury was directed at them or simply at being upstaged. No telling with Layla. Anyhow, she'd stashed away several copies along with her ring.

"Thanks, but I want to spend Christmas with my family. You know, check up on Carson, make sure my Dad is okay. I'll see about booking the church this spring for the wedding. I know this is mean, but I think your mother will still try to break us up if I go there."

Rex kissed the top of her head. "I can't say for sure, my one and only, but no one can do that to us."

"I fear all this is too good to be true. Something bad will happen, if not your mother, then Layla."

"Christmas is a time for miracles. Accept ours."

****

A few days before Christmas, Tricia and Layla flew first class to Dallas, then caught the puddle-jumper to Iowa with the actress complaining all the way about leg room and being prevented from ordering an alcoholic beverage. Trish delivered Layla into her mother's fleshy folds at the gate. She laid eyes on her just one more time during the vacation when the actress blocked four people sitting in back of her from seeing the Christmas pageant by wearing a dramatic, but overly large hat. The Welles family skipped the hot chocolate, cookies, and autograph session in the church hall afterwards. Tricia bet Layla took seconds on the refreshments. They drove home surrounded by acres of fallow cornfields lightly dusted with snow and glowing in the moonlight. The four men generated enough heat to warm the cab of the truck, but tomorrow, Tricia thought she'd light a fire in the parlor for the family to gather around while they opened their presents.

With her bank account bursting from her enhanced salary and Micah Stanley's generous monetary supplements, Tricia watched with pleasure as her family received their gifts Christmas morning. The fire crackled and reflected in the shining balls on the tree burdened with handmade ornaments accumulated since the children were tiny. Her mother never threw one away, no matter how crude or homely. Considering she'd had three sons that description applied to a lot of them.

For Carson who had lost his gut and red-rimmed eyes, a box held a check for his first year of college tuition and a new laptop to use at the university. For Cody and Colt, the same laptop plus the latest iPhone. Ecstatic, Colt used the home phone to call Heidi Welch with the news. As for her dad, he rarely asked for anything but another year of good health. A large gift certificate to the John Deere store had to do.

A heavy box arrived from Rex a few days before Christmas. When Tricia opened it, she held up a hefty Bible with leather bindings and gilded edges. Her dismay must have shown because Colt immediately piped up, "If I gave Heidi a Bible, she'd hit me over the head with it."

"What did you give Heidi—a kiss? They come pretty cheap. I'll bet that Bible cost a bundle," Cody said sensitive to his sister's reaction.

"Naw, he got her a little, bitty gold locket on a dainty chain from Walmart," Carson revealed with his pinkie crooked in derision.

Colt reddened. "At least I have a girlfriend. More than you guys can say."

Tricia read the inscription on the marbled inner cover of the Bible. "To my One and Only Tricia, This Good Book contains pictures of all your favorite Old Testament stories, ones from the New Testament, too. In the center are pages where we can record the births of our children. With much love, Rex."

Eyes filling with tears, she announced, "This is a great gift after all. Now go shave, all of you. Letty and Heidi will be here soon."

Seeing the way her father's blue eyes lit with happiness that she had accepted Letty and in fact suggested the two families celebrate together, Tricia knew she'd given him a more wonderful gift than money could buy. She wouldn't be around to take care of him in the future, but Letty Welch could do the job just fine, maybe better. Really, she felt a little ashamed of her gift to Rex, a hefty donation to his charitable foundation. He'd appreciate it, but cash seemed so impersonal.

"One more present." Her father took out a large oblong box he'd hidden way in the back of the tree. "To Tricia from her mother."

She tore off the wrappings to reveal Marty's wedding gown, cleaned, sealed, and put away for the marriage of her daughter. Not designer or couture, Tricia's maternal grandmother had made it in a rush. Why she never caught on that her birth was pending as her mother told the story of staying up nights to get the dress finished she didn't know. Perhaps, that had been her mother's way of telling her. The woman she'd called Nanny, sewer of the gown, passed away from cancer so early in her childhood she barely remembered her. Opening the bag for the first time in twenty-five years, Tricia shook out the gown.

"Why, it looks like Kate Middleton's gown from the royal wedding."

"Yep, so old it's new again. I can't tell you how beautiful your mother looked on her wedding day. The pictures didn't do her justice. But she always said you didn't have to wear it unless you wanted." Still, Tricia saw the hope in his misty eyes.

"I do. It's lovely." She sat there with the long lace sleeves and bodice draped over her knees, the simple, full white skirt pooling at her feet. "I'll wear her pearls, too."

The doorbell rang and sent the men scattering. Cy answered the door to greet Letty burdened with two casserole dishes. Heidi, wearing a tiny gold locket with her merry red Christmas attire, carried a chocolate cake.

"Seems I have to go shave, but let me help you with those dishes first. Trisha has the turkey in the oven and two pies made."

"You don't have to shave for me, Cyrus Welles. I like the rugged look."

From her seat in the parlor, Trisha observed Letty

plant a kiss on her father's cheek, and she longed for a touch of Rex's bristle beneath her hands. She stood up, holding the dress against her body to see if it fit. Letty returned from the kitchen and poked her head in the doorway.

"I brought the green bean casserole and the whipped potatoes like you asked. Thanks for inviting us. It means a lot. Look, I know I am not your mother, never can be, but I'm handy with a needle. I can make any adjustments that dress needs." Letty cocked that jet-black head of hair. "Won't take much you are so very like her."

"Thanks, I appreciate that offer. Let's get the table set. We drag out all of Granny's best china and silver on Christmas. My mom insisted the men wear coats and ties for this one meal of the year. You'll be surprised how well they clean up."

"Can't wait to see that. Just tell me what else you want me to do. I'm your gal, too."

The women had set a beautiful table with a linen cloth and green candles in short silver holders by the time the men returned spruced up and ready to eat. Tricia noticed her father hadn't shaved, starting a new custom perhaps.

"How come Dad doesn't have to..." Carson complained. Cody elbowed him.

Colt told Heidi, "I don't mind shaving. Sometimes I do it twice a day."

His brothers snickered, but their father called the table to order before the teasing intensified.

"Let us pray. Dear Lord, we thank thee for the bounty set before us. This year we miss our wife and mother, Martha Welles, but know she sits at your table now. We are grateful to be free of debt thanks to our beloved daughter, Patricia, who sacrificed for us and has been rewarded with a wonderful life ahead. We are happy to welcome new faces to share our meal today. For what we are about to receive, our deepest gratitude. Amen."

"Amen! I call a drumstick," Colt shouted.

Tricia smiled, feeling the warmth of her family, her great good luck in meeting Rex. Still, she worried. She simply wasn't good enough to deserve such happiness.

****

At the end of the trip, Layla waited impatiently for Tricia at the airport. Her PA noticed at once a weight gain of at least five pounds put on over the holidays but said nothing. Selena would handle it. Though Tricia had withdrawn from Iowa State because of her upcoming wedding set for the first week in May, she did plan to enroll at UNO to be close to Rex. How close she could not say. She only knew in fifteen days she would be free of Layla forever and living elsewhere.

Back in New Orleans the new script for *Scandal!* waited, and Layla immersed herself in the role while Selena sweated the last pounds off her frame. She looked toned, fit, even a little muscular beneath her curves. Rex and Tricia met away from the apartment to avoid any more scenes. He wanted Tricia to move in with him after the fifteenth. She refused.

"You need to keep your mind on the playoffs and the Super Bowl. Neither of us needs more tabloid headlines."

Hangdog, he said, "I guess this means I'm celibate until after the big game."

"Didn't say that, did I? Remember, people can

have sex anytime, anywhere."

Rex brightened considerably. "Where will you be staying after you get rid of Layla?"

"I'll find a place, maybe just stay in a hotel for a few weeks and look around."

"Why don't you go stay with Nell? Joe says bed rest drives her nuts, and she'd like some company. They have four bedrooms, only two occupied."

"I hardly know them well enough."

"No, but I do. I'll arrange it."

As it turned out, the Billodeauxs were happy to have her. When she bid farewell to Layla, the actress lounged on the turquoise sofa and barely raised her eyes from the script.

"Selena will come twice a week now until you leave for L.A. Do you know when that will be?"

"When I feel like it."

"Okay. Don't let Lee lead you astray."

Layla flicked her lavender-coated nails at her. "You know I don't do drugs or alcohol when I'm working, only men. Why don't you just go? Leave your forwarding address in case anyone cares which I highly doubt."

Tricia scribbled the address on a sheet of paper from her small notebook tucked in one of the pockets of the black bag. "I'm staying with the Billodeauxs. Please don't call or bother them in any way. Nell is on bed rest until the babies are born."

"Rather you than me sitting around with a pregnant woman all day. Are you still here?"

"Not anymore." Tricia shouldered her black bag, picked up her laptop, and gripped the handle of her luggage. Now that she thought about it, she could donate the oversized bag to charity. She no longer had to lug Layla's life around with her. Feeling lighter and happier, Tricia marched out the door toward freedom.

Layla splayed the script over the back of the sofa and stretched for her phone lying on the coffee table. "Hey, Lee-Lee. My patsy is gone. I need you to get something for me. No, not drugs. I'm working right now. My drug use is strictly recreational. I want a gun for my protection now that I'm all alone. Yes, I know how to use one. Didn't you see me in *Point Blank Range!* where I played the sexy lady cop. I took training so I'd know how to handle a pistol. Something small but lethal. Yeah, bring it by tonight and be prepared to stay."

Wouldn't be long now before she showed Rex Worthy what she could do for him that wimpy Tricia Welles could not.

Chapter Thirty-One

The Sinners disposed of an exhausted wild card team with ease and worked their way through the rest of the playoffs with a respectable win each time. The French Quarter burst into drunken revelry when they claimed the right to go to the championship game, not that its denizens needed an excuse. Joe Dean Billodeaux played brilliantly like the final burst of a skyrocket. Rex Worthy quietly rode the pine.

Nell Billodeaux fretted about her confinement and missing the Super Bowl in person. During the pre-game show, the camera panned across her children in place to see the game live with Knox Polk, Corazon, their son, Brinsley, Mawmaw Nadine and Pawpaw keeping them in line. Nurse Shammy allowed Tricia to bring requested beignets into the condo to tempt Nell's flagging appetite and cheer her up though eating two gave the twin-bloated woman heartburn.

"Be still. One more day," the nurse kept telling her patient.

Tricia did her best to be good company. However, she planned to go to the Dome for the second half to congratulate or console Rex as needed even if he never left the bench.

****

Layla Devlin obtained a gun and bought a costume in advance of her planned festivities. On Super Bowl day, she purchased a large bunch of Mylar Best Wishes balloons in pink and blue. She spent the afternoon in Lee's dressing room perfecting her makeup with his help and viewing the game on his small television. In acting, timing mattered. She watched Joe dominate the first half though the Colts and their young quarterback played hard, especially on defense. The Sinners were up two scores to none when she got into a cab and rode to the address Tricia had given her.

The doorman, Gregory according to his nametag, left his computer console to open the entry for a very sexy Raggedy Ann carrying a balloon bouquet. The sexiest Raggedy Ann ever, Lee assured her. Layla wore a wig with long red yarn braids topped by a white cap. Her breasts bulged out of a white apron over the blue dress that ended six inches above her knees. Red and white striped stockings clad her magnificent legs halfway up her thighs. Red bows serving as garters drew the eyes upward from her coy black Mary Jane shoes.

Lee had outdone himself on the make-up. With her lips coated in scarlet, he'd extended black lines on either side making a happy bowed smile that nearly reached the two perfect red circles on Layla's cheeks. He'd used his own glittering eye shadow extending it up to her brows plucked into two thin lines and painted black. Long false eyelashes fluttered over marks drawn on her lower lids to give his Raggedy Ann a starry stare.

"Oh my, I could eat you up you look so sweet," Lee exclaimed.

"Later for that. Do I look like Layla Devlin?"

"Darling, I would recognize you anywhere, but no

one else. Even though I know Patsy treated you abominably and Nell humiliated you, I do think it's so wonderful of you to make peace with them this way. Oh so cute and original, so gracious for a famous star to reach out to those little people who wronged her."

"Yeah, hand me those balloons and call a cab."

While Lee took care of that last detail, Layla stowed her pistol in the elastic waistband of Raggedy Ann's very short bloomers. Now by the look in the doorman's eyes, she knew he thought he beheld a stripper moonlighting for a balloon delivery service. She fluttered her false lashes. Didn't matter because Raggedy Ann would not be on his computer's "no entry" list while Layla Devlin most assuredly was. "Delivery for Nell Billodeaux in the penthouse apartment," she said in a little girl's voice.

"I can take them up and spare you the trip," he said.

And grab the tip, Layla thought. She recognized his kind, always scheming for extra bucks like Tricia. "Oh no, I have to sing and dance for the lady to cheer her up."

"I don't think she's going to like that during the game, but she could use something to take her mind off her surgery tomorrow. You know about that?"

"Sure, everybody in New Orleans knows." The commentators had done nothing but yammer about Nell and her precious babies leading up to the game. Would Joe Dean be able to keep his head in the game? Evidently, because all of them said he played like he was thirty again and Rex Worthy didn't stand a chance of getting into the action.

"Wait with me till halftime. Her husband send

those?"

"I guess. How's the game going?" she asked, keeping her voice childish.

"Down to less than a minute until the half. Joe has the ball again. Go, Joe! Make it three up." The doorman took a look at his screen. "Want to see?" he offered.

Layla bobbed her red-wigged head and crowded close enough for the doorman to cop a feel if he wanted, but considering the gray tufts in his hair, he probably had no interest. Joe stepped out of the pocket. One of his long spirals barely left his fingertips when a tackle hit the quarterback hard against the shoulder from the rear taking him down. A Colt deflected the ball before it reached its destination. As the play ended and the clock ran out, Billodeaux still lay on the turf. A couple of trainers ran out and helped him up. He cradled his right arm.

"Oh, I hope he didn't break his throwing arm!" Layla declared. Because then *she* wouldn't be the one who offered Rex Worthy the chance to win a Super Bowl and received his everlasting gratitude.

"Word will come pretty soon. You want to wait and see? I don't know if the Sinners can win if they have to depend on Worthy."

Now the petulant child, Layla said, "Rex is a great quarterback. I love Rex. I want to go up now."

"To each her own, I guess. Joe was much more popular with the ladies in his early days. I tell you, I should have put in a turnstile to control all the comings and goings from his apartment back then. Now, I have to keep an eye on all his kids when they're around. Times do change." Gregory escorted Raggedy Ann to the elevator and punched the appropriate floor. "You tell Miss Nell I'm rooting for her, too, now."

Layla gave him her exaggerated bowed smile and put a hush-hush finger in front of her red lips. "Don't tell her I'm coming. It's a big surprise."

A horse-faced nurse with short, gray hair answered her rap on the door. She seemed puzzled at the intrusion. "Did Gregory allow you to come up here?" the woman asked, stern as a nun.

"I have a surprise for Nell Billodeaux," Layla trilled and executed a cute curtsey while holding out one side of her lace-rimmed apron.

"Who is it?" Nell called from her bedroom.

"I'm not quite sure. Do you feel well enough for company?"

"Give me a second. I got overexcited when Joe was injured and need to go. Tricia, help me up."

Delightful, both of her nemeses in the same room, no need to herd them together at pistol point. Layla followed the nurse through the leathery living room to the first bedroom on the right. With one hand behind her back, she worked the pistol free of her bloomers.

"Let me make sure Mrs. Billodeaux is decent," the nurse said and preceded her into the room.

Yes, in acting timing matters. As soon as the starchy woman in white cleared the door Layla pushed through and aimed her gun at the center of a huge, round bed. Only a big dent and a lot of cushions occupied the middle. She swung her weapon to the side and focused it on Tricia guarding an inner door. "Where is the tiny bitch?"

Trish took one look at the lavish breasts dominating the costume and shouted, "It's Layla with a gun! Lock the door!" A sharp snap told them Nell followed the orders.

"That won't do you any good. If you don't come out, you fucking pixie, I'll shoot the other two."

"I can't hear what you're saying," Nell said in a muffled voice.

"You two, over there." Layla edged closer to the bathroom door. "Come out or I'll shoot them."

"What?"

"For Christ's sake, open the door or I'll shoot!" Layla swore, her scarlet lips nearly touching the wood.

The door burst open hard, catching her on the side of the face. Nell, her voluminous white nightgown flying, launched herself on top of the movie star and carved grooves through Raggedy Ann's carefully applied makeup with her nails. "Don't call me a frigging pixie!"

Her move might have worked if Layla hadn't been in peak condition and Nell sluggish with twins. Releasing the balloons that sailed toward the ceiling, the actress rolled on top of Nell's thighs and began punching her chest and belly with her left hand, the gun held high out of the pregnant woman's reach in her right.

A strong grip grabbed her wrist. Layla squeezed off two shots that punctured a couple of balloons and dug holes into the ceiling. The grasp loosened for a moment with the noise. She attempted to shoot over her shoulder, awkward with Nell bucking beneath her. With the third blast, the hand let loose of her gun arm.

"No, Shammy!" Nell humped beneath Layla again trying to knock her off her legs.

"Shut up, you cunt, and get back into bed."

Nell stilled. "Need help getting up," she whispered

weakly.

"I won't fall for that get closer ploy again." Layla rose sinuously, backed away, and motioned to Tricia who held the fallen nurse in her arms. "Patsy, put the pixie to bed."

"What about Nurse Shammy? She's bleeding."

"I could care less. Hoist the prego up. We need her to call Joe during halftime and say she's in labor and having trouble with the birth. See, then Rex gets to play. You'd like that, huh? I'd be willing to kill to help his career. I'll bet you wouldn't because you don't love him as much." Tricia eyed her the way she did when she suspected Layla of being high. "I'm not on drugs. I know what I'm doing."

"Right."

"Go on, dear. Help Nell. I'm fine. I do believe the bullet passed right through my arm. We can take care of it later." Shammy waved Tricia away with her good arm, but the grayness of her face belied her words.

Moving cautiously the way a person would around a mad dog or a wild horse, Tricia propped the nurse against the side of the bed and gave Nell a hand up. Fluid gushed onto the floor wetting the hem of the nightgown. Disgusted, Layla leapt back to avoid getting her Mary Janes wet. Her red yarn wig, loosened in the fight with Nell, canted to one side, its cap gone.

"My water broke," Nell said very matter-of-factly.

"Another gross reason not to have kids. Get into bed. You have a call to make."

"I told Joe to finish his last game no matter what. I need to get to a hospital."

"Then, you'll have to change his mind, won't you? Tell him to get over here or you and his twins will die."

On the wall-mounted flat screen across from the bed, the halftime show began with a tribute to ragtime and jazz. One of the ancient Preservation Hall musicians sat at a piano in a circle of light and banged out the *The Entertainer* while a chorus line dressed as ladies of the evening cavorted around him.

"Patsy, give her a phone and let's see how convincing an actress the fairy queen is. I love this song. It's from *The Sting*, one of my favorite movies. Wish I could have slept with Robert Redford before he got old and wrinkled." With blood running down her cheek from Nell's deep scratches, Layla relaxed against the wall thoroughly amused and in complete control.

Chapter Thirty-Two

Joe Dean sat on the examination table and grunted once when the doctor popped his dislocated shoulder back into place. "Give me a shot for pain and tape me up. I'm good to go."

"You'd better consult the coach about that. We should do some x-rays before you mess up this shoulder anymore."

"Doc, it's my last game. I don't give a damn."

Coach Marty Buck sauntered over, his flattop matted down from wearing a headset and Sinners cap and sweating the plays. "What's the verdict?"

"I can play," Joe insisted. "We do short passes and use some of the trick plays. Let me finish the game."

Out in the Dome, ragtime gave way to Dixieland and leggy flappers danced in the locker room's monitors. A nervous assistant ran up with a portable phone. "It's for Joe. His wife is calling. You want him to take it?"

"Give me that!" Joe snatched the phone. "What's wrong, sugar?"

"I'm—I'm in labor. My water broke, and the babies are coming fast. Tricia went to the Dome to watch the end of the game—and Shammy is out getting me some ice cream I wanted."

"Have you called an ambulance? Try to get Shammy on her cell."

"She left it here. Please, Joe, Tinker Bell needs you at home right now."

"Are you delirious? You hate being called Tinker Bell."

"Listen, you stupid coonass, I need you to come to me."

How many times had Nell told the kids not to call each other stupid? As for coonass, she never used that term. Of course, women in labor might say anything and not mean it. No sense in taking chances and wasting time on the phone. Decision made. "Be right there."

Still wearing the lower half of his uniform, cleats and all, Joe slid from the table bare-chested. "Someone help me get my jersey on. I need an ambulance after all. Nell is in labor. Give me a minute to talk to the team, then I'm a gone pecan."

The doctor nodded. "Probably for the best he doesn't play with this injury. I'll authorize the ride, but the crew needs to be back when the game starts again."

"Okay, okay. Say what you want to the team, then get going," Marty Buck said as grim-faced as a man who saw his fifth Super Bowl ring circling the drain and about to be flushed.

Joe climbed up on a bench to address his fellow Sinners. "Look guys, my shoulder is busted and Nell is in labor. I know y'all can win this one without me. I expect you to fight as hard for Rex as you do for me. Rex, may *le bon Dieu* be with you."

"What?" Rex looked up at his mentor blankly.

"The Good Lord, Rex. What, you don't speak French?"

"He's always with me."

"Right. Do your best for the team."

"I always do."

"Yeah. Go Sinners! Fight, fight, fight!" Joe punched the air with his good arm.

The team returned the cheer. They watched Joe leave with despair upon many tough faces. Rex didn't look any happier.

The ride to his condo took fifteen minutes with the sirens blaring and the traffic light since the citizens of New Orleans gathered around their sets to view the game, eat some damn good food, and consume excessive alcohol. He bolted into the lobby of his building, tearing up the carpet with his cleats and simply not caring.

The astounded Gregory said, "Mrs. Billodeaux received her balloon bouquet. The entertainer is still up there singing and dancing for her."

"Say what?" Joe said over his injured shoulder as he punched the button hard willing the elevator to arrive faster. It came quickly as if summoned by his determination. "Doesn't matter." Only Nell and the twins mattered.

He soared non-stop to the penthouse, got his key in the lock of his condo and entered calling out, "Nell, you in the bedroom?"

"Yes."

Her voice shook, and his wife gave a small gasp. Joe Dean rushed to her side as if he'd decided to run the ball like Rex Worthy and charged right into an unexpectedly hard defense. A grotesque Raggedy Ann with red wig askew and an eye swollen shut, held a small pistol in his direction. Blood dripped onto her impressive chest and down her pure white apron from deep scratches on the left side of her face. Loose pink and blue balloons floated lazily around the ceiling in crazy festivity. Tricia knelt on the floor swabbing a wound in Nurse Shammy's arm with an alcohol wipe. In the round love nest of their bed, his wife practiced her Lamaze breathing and stroked the gold locket containing his curl that hung around her neck.

"You really in labor, sugar?—because all this is insane."

Nell nodded but didn't reply. She concentrated on her panting.

"Relax, Joe. You need to be here so Rex can have his big chance." Postal Raggedy Ann gave him a lopsided grin.

He recognized that throaty, undisguised voice, "Layla?"

"You guessed! See, nobody needs to die here, though I wouldn't really mind if certain people expired." She glanced at Nell and swung her one-eyed glare to Tricia. "We can go our separate ways once Rex wins the game. If these women hadn't attacked me, everything would be fine, but your midget wife slammed a door into my face and clawed me. I'm glad she's suffering now, her own fault. I hope she has a long, hard labor."

"I warned you back in New Mexico, Nell is fierce."

"Not so feisty now, look at her all bloated and heaving like a sweaty dog. And you preferred *that* to me." Layla pouted her cherry lips.

Joe refrained from saying Layla looked like the ultimate psycho chick. He'd known some in his day, and she took the grand prize. "My wife needs to get to the hospital. She's high risk and is scheduled for a section. I'll stay here with you. Allow her to go—for the sake of our tee-tiny babies."

"Jesus God, I hate kids, so don't go there. Your swarm put me off you forever. If I let her go, she'll call the cops."

Mentally, he thanked *le bon Dieu* for little blessings and went to take his wife's hand.

Nell stopped puffing as the labor pains let up for a minute. "Sorry, Joe. The babies are coming fast like the girls did after the motor home accident. I didn't mean for this to happen again."

He squeezed Nell's hand. "Hey, this ain't my first two-step, *cher*. I can deliver dem 'xactly like last time. I'll wash up just in case, me." There, he'd gotten his wife to smile a little with his cute Cajun routine.

"Keep the bathroom door wide open. No searching for any weapons in there. You done with the old hag yet, Patsy?" Layla backed away from Joe's long reach as he passed.

Tricia smoothed antibiotic cream from her big black bag over both sides of Shammy's wound and tied a clean white handkerchief tightly around it. "Would you like something for the pain?"

"Not aspirin or anything that will increase the bleeding," the nurse directed.

"Hydrocodone?"

"That would be good. Only one."

Tricia delved into her bag again and drew out a prescription container. She shook out a single pill and put it in Shammy's hand. "Joe, could you bring some water?"

"Have you been holding out on me, Patsy? Where did you keep them hidden? I need a painkiller and some cleaning up myself. Me, next." Layla held out her hand, and Tricia deposited one pill in her palm. Like a spoiled child, her former boss said, "More!" Tricia shook out three extra pills.

Finished scrubbing up to his elbows, Joe brought water in two of tiny paper cups Nell insisted were more sanitary than glasses. How he wished he had something lethal to break and use against Layla.

Layla seized her cup and washed the pills down in one swallow. "Wish I had a grapefruit juice chaser," she said. "That really gets the drugs flowing."

Their family nurse accepted her water more gratefully. "Can you really deliver a baby? I will talk you through it but am in no condition to do so myself. Wobbly in the knees, I'm afraid."

"Am I Cajun? I know the drill, but stop me if I'm doing it wrong." Joe flipped the covers off of Nell and raised her sopping gown. "*Mais cher,* you crownin' already."

Nell smiled feebly. "I thought so. Here comes another pain."

Layla turned her eyes from the awful sight of a bulging vagina to the TV screen. "Hey, they have a Louis Armstrong impersonator up now. He's pretty good with that horn. I like the business with the handkerchief and mopping the sweat from his brow, but when are they going to get back to the game?"

"Still have Bradford Marsalis and Harry Connick, Jr. to perform," Joe said casually to keep Layla calm. "Give me a nice big push now, sugar. Here comes the head."

Still watching the halftime show with her back against the wall, Layla swatted away Tricia's hand when she attempted to clean the scratches with an alcohol wipe. "Wait till the pills kick in before you touch me with that shit again."

Harry Connick, Jr. appeared behind a piano with Bradford Marsalis in front playing a soprano sax.

"Remember to rotate the shoulders, Joe," Shammy prompted.

"I got it. Pant for me, Tink. Now push again." The baby girl, covered in cheesy vernix, slid into his hands. "Bigger than Jude or Annie. Good work, little mama."

Layla wrinkled her nose at the sight. Tricia rushed into the bathroom and grabbed heated towels off the rack to wrap the baby. "You got a scissors and any string in that bag of yours?" Joe asked.

"Scissors, yes. Would shoelaces do? I have white and black."

"I think so. Don't matter if they're black or white. See, we gotta tie the cord in two places and cut between."

Tricia did the tying. Joe cut the cord. The baby howled as Trish wiped her down with one towel and wrapped her in another. "Better than the paper towels we used the last time, *cher*," the proud daddy said. Nell gave him a grin that turned to a grimace as another pain hit. She held on hard to her locket.

"Shut up! The game is starting again. There's Rex." Layla pointed at the screen and jumped up and down, his hyperactive personal cheerleader. Her breasts bounced like a Jell-O mold hitting a cold plate. Joe barely noticed. Nell began another round of labor pains.

Chapter Thirty-Three

Rex knelt in prayer. In the background, he heard the announcement that injured Joe Dean Billodeaux was out of the game and on his way to the hospital. The smattering of applause and a chorus of boos hardly penetrated his concentration. He asked God for the strength to do his best for the team. When he rose, the normally loud stadium sat eerily quiet as if each and every ticketholder waited to see what he could do.

Rex glanced toward the block of seats where the Billodeaux family sat. Joe's girls cried. His mother glared at the backup quarterback as if he'd personally been responsible for the injury. A kid who knew about adversity, Teddy in his wheelchair gave him a thumbs-up. The other boys nodded in support. But, where was Tricia? She should be here by now. He'd like to feel her presence supporting him all the way. No choice but to get out on the field and try his hardest when his turn came. Howdy kicked the ball to the Colts. Their opponents, newly invigorated by the change in the Sinners' quarterbacks, scored in four plays.

Rex trotted out to do his best. In four plays, he lost the ball to the Colts. Their quarterback, not much older than Rex, threw a long pass into the end zone for another touchdown as the third quarter ended. At the top of the fourth quarter, Rex, feeling the pressure to break the tie, tried his own long pass a la Joe Dean

Billodeaux. Picked off, the Colt's cornerback ran the ball back to the fifty-yard line. Their offense surged onto the field and completed a series of runs and short passes for their third score.

No longer tied, the weight of the massive Dome seemed to press on Rex's wide shoulders. He lost the ball again on a fumble. Boos rumbled round the stadium like waves bashing against the shore. The Colts began a leisurely progression down the field running time off the clock—but they moved a little too slowly. Adam Malala ran down their receiver, popped the ball that came out high, caught it, and ran for the Sinners goal. He didn't get very far before being brought down, but Rex knew a reprieve when he saw one. A profound steadiness filled him as the two-minute warning sounded. Finally, he found his rhythm: a short pass to Jones, a run by himself past the fifty, an unspectacular shovel pass to another of his running backs, then to Jones again who took off and scored. The clock ticked down to seconds. Time out!

****

Layla filled the bedroom with her shrieks of joy. Nell screamed again and again, but not for Rex. Her pains let up for a moment. "Something is wrong, Joe. I know it."

"Jesus God, Shammy, I see feet," Joe said.

"A footling breach birth, Mother Mary have mercy. We must get the child out as quickly and carefully as possible to prevent cord prolapse."

"I'll tear Nell apart if I try to get in there. It's not like catching a ball, no." Joe stared at his big hands, so effective on the football field, and wished they were smaller.

Shammy looked at Tricia's slender fingers as the PA cradled the first baby. "Tricia must do it."

The time out continued. Layla momentarily lost her focus on Rex. "I can do a C-Section," she claimed with great confidence. "I played a doctor once."

"It's the hydrocodone speaking," Tricia said.

"Is not!" Layla cried. "Get me a knife." No one followed her orders.

"Tricia, do you have any lubricants? That might help," Shammy suggested.

She placed the baby into the crook of nurse's good arm before delving into her bag. "Hand cream and sun screen—and latex gloves. I've had to clean up after Layla's escapades in some pretty grungy places. Sorry I didn't offer them sooner, but they are a small size and wouldn't fit Joe."

"Go into the bathroom, wash well but quickly and get those gloves on. Hurry!"

Tricia took off her engagement ring, laid it on a curved night table, and went to prepare for delivering Joe's next child. The Sinners lined up by the goal and diverted Layla from her murderous thoughts.

"Mr. and Mrs. Rex Worthy can do anything." She snatched up the sapphire, putting it on rather clumsily with the gun clutched in her right hand. Having fingers thicker than Tricia's, it went only as far as her knuckle. "No worries. We'll have it sized. Oh, I'm beginning to feel so warm and fuzzy."

"He's going for two points, and he'll run it. The Colts know it, too," Joe muttered, but turned his head back to his wife's struggles.

"Listen, Tricia. You must insert your left hand into the vagina and use your middle and index fingers to gently depress the upper jaw to flex the neck. Rest your palm on the baby's chest. Use your right hand to pull a shoulder down toward its pelvis. Joe, you can help by putting pressure on the uterus from the outside."

Glad to have something to do, Joe took up his position using his big palms to apply pressure. Tricia inserted her fingers into the distended vagina. She passed the baby's hips and continued to his surprisingly wide shoulders, making progress every time the contractions ceased.

"No arms in the way?" Shammy asked.

"No, I think they're crossed on his chest, but his shoulders seem big for a baby."

"Work past them with your left hand and tuck that chin. Grab a shoulder with your right and do your best to bring him down gradually. Rotate those shoulders if you can. Don't go too fast. Sudden decompression can injure the brain, but second twins usually do well in a breech birth. We'll pray for that," Shammy directed over Nell's agonized cries.

Rex caught the snap and fake-pumped toward Eric Blixen in the end zone. He tucked the ball and went over the top of the Colt's line. His team pushed from behind. Extending his arms, Rex broke the plane with the ball and tumbled to the other side with his free hand raised to God. Layla did a victory dance, waving the gun carelessly and firing off a shot. Joe's infant daughter startled and began to cry. On the bed between his mother's legs, Joe's new son joined her with gusto. Shammy stuck out a leg and tripped the wildly celebrating actress. Layla's arms wheeled to regain balance. The gun pointed now at Shammy, then at Tricia crouched over the newborn.

And Joe went over the top, too, across the end of the bed and crashing into Layla's side. He took her down, his first full-body tackle in a long pro career. The pistol popped another balloon and sailed through the air before landing on the far side of Nell. Beneath Joe's weight and muscle, Layla squirmed like a trapped python. Tricia tied off the baby's cord with slippery fingers and made the cut severing him from his exhausted mother. She laid him on Nell's warm hip.

"Trish, you got anything in that bag to restrain her?" Joe asked as he used his big left hand to hold Layla's behind her back because his right shoulder hurt like hell.

With two sticky fingers, Tricia probed the open mouth of her oversized purse and hauled out a pair of plastic restraints. "These should work."

"You carry handcuffs?"

"Layla is often very difficult. Better mine than a policeman's."

"I'll sue you for treating me this way! Get off! I have to go to Rex and tell him I'm the reason he won the Super Bowl. I'm going to be Mrs. Rex Worthy, not Patsy." Layla spat at them.

Joe finished cuffing her and rolled the actress over on her back. He picked up the scissors used to cut the cord, snipped off one red yarn braid, stuffed it in her mouth, and hauled her to her feet. He returned Tricia's ring with a bow. "You are the world's greatest PA."

Suddenly, Layla's one good violet eye widened. She let out several muffled screams and stamped the floor. Nell had the gun pointed directly at her. "Let me kill her, Joe."

"Now, sugar, you know you get irrational when

you're pregnant," Joe said soothingly.

"Don't call me sugar. I'm not pregnant anymore. I'm..."

"Bleeding," Trish said. "Shammy, she's bleeding."

"Could be just a vaginal tear or more seriously a rupture. Are the afterbirths whole?"

"I don't know, I don't know," Trisha and Joe said nearly simultaneously.

"Put pressure on her abdomen. Get an ambulance here at once."

"Done." Holding her cell phone rather gingerly, Tricia told the 911 operator exactly what they needed and where while Joe pressed against his wife's belly and the babies cried.

"Joe," Nell said. "As soon as the ambulance and police get here, I want you to go back to the Dome and claim your half of the victory."

"No, Tink, I'm riding with you."

"The children are there. You tell them I'm going to be fine and they have a new sister and brother, six of one, half a dozen of the other now."

"Twelve. We're done. And I'm done as a football player."

"All the more reason to enjoy your last victory. I promise you I won't die."

"You're a Billodeaux. Remember, you have to keep your word."

Chapter Thirty-Four

Strange to walk into the Dome with no one cheering for him. Joe needed to get used to the idea. The mass of reporters crowded around Rex as black and red confetti rained down on him. All eyes turned to the Sinners' new quarterback. Then, Joe heard a single voice shout, "It's Dad! He's back." Sounded like Dean who had a grown man's voice and the height to see over all the people on their feet.

Around the arena, a chant started. "Joe, Joe, Joe." Signs dropped down from balconies. "We love you Daddy Joe." "God Bless, Joe." "We'll miss you, Joe." And his favorite, "Good-bye, Joe, We know you gotta go have some fun on the bayo," a play on the words in the song, *Jambalaya*. All of them love letters from his Sinners' fans. The spectators on the field made way as he joined Rex on a platform for the trophy presentation. He gave his backup the firm handshake and the manly hug.

"You done good, Rex."

"Thank you, sir. I'll try to keep up the good work."

They held the trophy high, one quarterback on each side. Joe thought he spotted Connor Riley's wife, Stevie, in the throng of photographers. *Sports Illustrated* cover for sure.

"Joe." Rex turned away from the mikes. "Where is Tricia? Did she decide to call things off and go back to

Iowa?"

"Hell, no. She just delivered my new son. Hang on to her. The woman can do anything as long as she has that damn black bag along."

Rex winced slightly at the profanity. "I intend to. She's my one and only, but where is she?"

"Was right behind me. There with my parents and kids. Let's get them all up here."

Joe's family crowded several league bigwigs off the platform. Rex tucked Tricia tight under his arm as if to make sure he wouldn't fumble this play. "You saw the ending?" he asked.

"Between delivering babies and fighting off a crazed Layla, yes. A big day for all of us."

"Huh?"

"Later. They want you to say something about your victory."

Rex stepped close to the mike. "Uh, I couldn't have achieved this victory without God, the love of my fiancée, Tricia Welles, and Joe's two touchdowns. If I can be half as good a quarterback as Joe Dean Billodeaux, the Sinners will win a sixth Super Bowl."

His popularity rose to new heights in that moment, but soon after, the crowd started calling for Joe again. Rex stepped back, giving Joe the stage.

"Y'all know this is my last game with the Sinners. I won't be signing on with any other teams because I don't believe they could match the quality of the men I've played with over my long career or the fervor of the Sinners fans."

He paused, waiting for cheers to die down. "See, now, that's what I mean by fervor. Had to look dat word up, me, but it fits." Laughter.

"Seriously, this is the best day in my life. I'll be getting the fifth Super Bowl ring that has slipped through my fingers these last few years thanks to an assist from Rex Worthy. He'll serve you well. My wife gave birth to our twins today. The babies are doing fine, but Nell had a hard time of it. Your prayers would be appreciated."

Rex lost no time in bowing his head and moving his lips. Tricia did the same. A reporter shouted from the throng at the base of the platform, "What did you get, Joe?"

"Another beautiful daughter and a broad-shouldered boy. You know my son Dean at age seventeen is showing lots of talent as a quarterback. I figure by the time Dean is ready to retire, this new son will be starting his pro career. The Billodeaux boys are gonna dominate the league for the next forty years."

The male reporters laughed, but one of the female commentators called out, "Names and weights of the babies?" Women always asked that.

"Not sure about the weights, but Nell carried them full term. They're pretty hefty for twins. Considering how and when they came into the world, I think we will be naming the girl Edith Patricia for the two women who helped in her delivery."

"Edith, really?" he heard his ever particular niece, Anastasia Marya Polasky, better known as Stacy, say.

"Yes, Edie in honor of our family nurse."

Joe glanced to the side of the stage where Shammy's husband, Brinsley, stood beaming beside Corazon and Knox Polk who had helped hike Teddy's wheelchair onto the platform. The butler had no idea his wife laid injured in the hospital. That knowledge would come soon enough when Joe could get down there and tell him.

"As for the boy, only one name will do—Rex Worthy Billodeaux. T-Rex the Cajuns are likely to call him."

Behind his father, short, bespectacled Trinity said, "Cool. Wish I had a nickname like that."

"Does Mom know about this?" Jude Emily questioned.

Joe smiled. Now came the hard part. "No more questions. I want to get over to the hospital. Just let me say…" He choked on his final words. Tears he'd meant to hold back ran into the grooves at the sides of his mouth. He tasted salt and sorrow over the end of his football career. "Just let me say good-bye. Hey, I think I need me a champagne shower before I go."

Unexpectedly, a second rain of confetti drifted down above the stage. Each red piece carried his lucky number seven in black. His kids scrambled to grab the souvenirs of their father's last game. Fans did the same. Joe left the platform under a confetti cloud.

He stopped by Brinsley. "Your wife is in the hospital with Nell."

"You do mean at the hospital, sir."

"No, Layla Devlin shot her when she tried to defend Nell. I think she'll be fine, but get yourself over there. Let Knox and Corazon handle the kids. Tell Nell I'll be right along as soon as I do the champagne thing with the team. They'll be let down if I don't."

Of course, sir. I am—what do you always say?— the gone pecan."

****

By the time Joe showered and changed, having

bathed in much more of the champagne than he drank, too much time had passed. Although reporters still waited, he pushed through with help from Rex and Adam, Howdy, and even Brian Lightfoot who disliked getting his street clothes rumpled. He clutched a bag he'd been keeping in his locker, something to show Nell. They piled into a waiting limo and steered for the hospital to see the babies, join their wives who waited there, and head out for other parties Joe had no intention of attending.

He left his friends standing at the window that allowed the viewing of the babies. Full term and weighing in at six pounds, seven ounces for the girl and six pounds, nine ounces for the boy, neither twin needed an incubator. While Tricia, Cassie, and Winnie cooed over them, Joe moved down the hall to find his wife's whereabouts. Brinsley, looking deadly serious, intercepted him.

"Shammy okay?"

A small smile tweaked Brinsley's stern demeanor. "Oh, yes, the old girl is sturdy as London during the Blitz. It's Miss Nell. She had to have surgery to stop the bleeding, rather serious I am afraid."

"Where?"

"She is awake and aware but somewhat weak. They used an epidural."

"Where, Brinsley?" Joe wanted to take his butler by his very proper lapels and shake him until his buttons popped.

"Only trying to prepare you, sir," his butler said, pointing out a room.

Prepare him for what? Joe didn't stick around to find out. He ran to Nell's bedside quicker than he'd ever covered ten yards in his life. A No Visitors sign hung on the door. Hell, he wasn't a visitor. He was a husband, a lover. Joe slammed the door open and felt the pain in his shoulder. Should have that looked at while he was here, but later.

"Tink, you okay?"

"Good as can be expected right now."

She did sound weak. A couple of bags of fluid fed into her arm. Could one of them be blood? Beneath the covers, Nell appeared small and frail except for the deflated hump of her belly. The tears he'd left behind in the Dome returned, pushing to get out like flood waters against a levee.

"Remember, you promised not to leave me. Especially with twelve kids."

"I wouldn't do that to you. Sit down. I have to tell you something."

Not liking where this was going, he sat and tried to postpone the bad news by holding up the bag and opening it for her. He laid out one small pink afghan and a slightly larger one in blue, both edged in white. "From Madame Leleux's chest. I tell you that old lady always got it right."

"Joe, there won't be any more children."

"*Cher,* we got enough. Twelve, this way, that way, all ways, like she said. We can take the twins home in these. Can be chilly on the bayou in February." He shivered a little himself, dreading what might come next.

"I had a rupture. They needed to do a hysterectomy, just the uterus. I still have all my other parts."

"That's—that's good, I guess." He said what

always preyed on his mind. "No cancer?"

"None."

Joe exhaled, his big shoulders heaving. A couple of those damned, humiliating tears escaped. "Can we still—you know?"

"Have sex? Absolutely. The doctor says you won't be able to tell the difference."

"Then, Tink, I can't wait to try it out. You say when. I'm still your man, your one and only as Rex would say."

Chapter Thirty-Five

Tricia believed Iowa put its best foot forward for her wedding. The rows of young corn and small clumps of soybeans danced in a light breeze under a sky the color of her sapphire ring. Wildflowers edged the fields along the roads the limo took transporting her and the family to the church where Reverend Worthy would preside over the service. Meadowlarks sprang upward in the pastures as the large vehicle passed raising dust.

All of her men looked so handsome in tuxedos today despite their insistence that if Rex could have stubble so could they. Colt's grew in rather light, but her father had the start of a short beard. At the steps of the simple red brick church with its white spire, Letty Welch fussed with the arrangement of Tricia's gown and veil. She'd added two inches of lace to the bottom because Trish stood taller than her mother and had taken in the bust a bit to account for smaller size, probably because her mother had been pregnant, though Tricia didn't mention the fact. Letty made a new veil very similar to the one worn by Kate Middleton in the royal wedding and now held in place by its own small diamond and sapphire tiara, a wedding gift from Rex after many consulting phone calls back and forth to Iowa. Marty's pearls circled Tricia's neck.

Rex asked Joe to be his best man and of course, all her brothers had to be groomsmen. That left Tricia with a bridesmaid shortage. During her years as Layla's PA in Hollywood, she'd formed no female friendships, always too busy for that. She'd long parted ways with high school acquaintances. Needing four, she'd asked Becky, naturally, and Nell seemed a good choice for matron of honor after the ordeal they'd shared. A woman who could handle that and deal with twelve children nothing would upset. Finally, she'd included Letty and Heidi since it seemed likely they'd be family in the future. Nell would pair with Joe, Heidi with Colt, and after some jockeying for position, Carson agreed to take Letty and leave the Honeybee to Cody who appeared intrigued by rumors of her tattoo. Their heads, crowned with circlets of baby's breath and blue statice, the ladies wore sapphire to match the bride's ring and carried bouquets of white peonies spiked with blue delphiniums and a few pink roses.

Letty arranged a drift of white calla lilies on Tricia's arm, the same flowers Marty held in her wedding pictures, and called on her daughter to carry the short train of the gown into the church where they met Nell and Rex's sister. Ida, the perpetual church organist, her aged but sharp eyes on the aisle, began loudly pumping out the traditional wedding march. The men lined up at the altar and the matrons and maids began their progress between the rows of guests.

"Look at Mom! How pretty she is," Lorena exclaimed from the third row of the church where the Billodeaux family spread out on the bride's side. A brilliant smile lit Nell's face, erasing the pain lines of her long recovery. A grin from Joe standing next to Rex answered her.

"Hush," Nurse Shammy said, decked out in a blue

suit bearing a large jeweled brooch rather than wearing her customary white. "You will wake little Edie." Beside her with a spit up rag draped over the shoulder of his immaculate suit, Clive Brinsley uncomfortably held the baby boy who would always be known as T-Rex.

The true wonder was that Mrs. Worthy's sobs didn't wake the infants or drown out the entire service. She bawled from the time Tricia appeared at the head of the aisle until the service finished, more as if she attended a funeral than a joyous wedding the other guests said. Rex, eyes on his bride, didn't take notice. His maternal grandparents, pried out of Texas to attend, sat stiffly beside Sue Grace, only too aware of the hulking Sinners players sitting behind them, a good many of them black. "Get over it," Honeybee advised them as she accepted a dance invitation from Jakarta Jones later at the reception much to their horror.

Before the festivities in the church hall began, however, the bride and groom walked among the tombstones behind the church. Tricia placed a lily on each of her grandmothers' graves and the rest of the bouquet on her mother's resting place. "Mom, he looked past Layla and noticed me," she murmured.

"Layla never stood a chance," Rex said as he helped her back to the hall where folks waited to toast them with sparkling cider since the church didn't allow alcohol on the property. He had a bottle of the best champagne cooling in the limo for their ride to the airport among other surprises.

They'd agreed to keep the wedding and reception simple and put what might have been spent on a lavish affair into the Worthy Foundation. Still, the church ladies who catered the event outdid themselves with vats of swedish meatballs, pyramids of crustless sandwiches, and a vast bowl of ice filled with shrimp flown in from New Orleans that they'd spent hours steaming, peeling, and deveining. The wedding cake, professionally but locally made, kept up the theme of restraint being plain white and decorated with fresh blue and pink flowers and tiny bits of fern. Leftovers were to be taken to the firehouse and police department since their cars and trucks blocked the road and their men patrolled the fields around the church to keep out the paparazzi.

A local DJ provided the music, which tended toward slow, romantic numbers, the chicken dance, and the hokey-pokey. Ida Lutz amazed the audience by doing a fairly good slide jazz piece on the old piano in the hall.

"Good clean fun for everyone," Mrs. Worthy said primly to the elderly pianist.

Ida called out, "One more round of the hokey-pokey, guys." She leaned toward Sue Grace and remarked as the Sinner players lined up to dance, "You ever seen so much prime beef on the hoof? Look at that footwork. No wonder football players always do great on *Dancing with the Stars*."

Mrs. Worthy huffed away. She'd had little to say about the arrangements due to her own refusal to participate in the planning, but Sue Grace had contributed a roaster full of barbecued brisket and a pan of her special cornbread. She went to stand beside her offerings in order to accept the compliments.

Tricia didn't allow Rex to pay a cent for the wedding. Her civil suit settlement from Layla's lawyer more than covered expenses. The last time she'd seen the actress in person, the cuffed Layla slept curled up on the floor of Joe's bedroom having finally fallen under the soporific effects of the hydrocodone which could have kicked in sooner for all their sakes. The tabloid mug shots spared her nothing, showing the star with a scratched and swollen face and smeared, grotesque make-up worthy of a zombie movie.

Layla's attorney got her out of jail on two million dollars bail and followed Doris Dillman around as she pled with all those Layla had harmed. Her daughter suffered from mental issues and needed treatment, not incarceration, she claimed. Shammy's settlement alone would have allowed her and Brinsley to retire in style for the rest of their lives, but neither wanted that. Childless, and having the Billodeauxs as their only family, both wanted to remain useful and on Lorena Ranch to the end of their days. Joe and Nell granted that wish and gave them land to build a larger home than their cottage if they desired.

As for the Billodeaux's own payoff, which they hardly needed, it went into Camp Love Letter and a trust fund for the twins in case either suffered long-term damage from their delivery. So far, no sign of cerebral palsy or autism in either child, but Nell cautioned it was early days yet. Joe, ever the optimist, claimed T-Rex already had a steady gaze and good hands and Edie her mother's big, brown eyes and remarkable spunkiness. He tended to be right as if wishing hard always made it so.

With unexpected comments on the tip of her tongue, Doris Dillman made her way over to the bride and groom. Since the entire small congregation had been invited, they could hardly leave her out. She squeezed Tricia's hand with her pudgy fingers.

"You know Louise would have loved to be here, but she is still receiving treatment. How lovely she would have looked in one of those sapphire bridesmaids' gowns. You were such a good and understanding friend, she'd have walked proudly in your wedding to such a fine young man."

Tricia and Rex exchanged glances. Now they knew Layla came by her delusions honestly. Both had done their best to forgive, but some time had to pass before they forgot.

"A tragedy Micah Stanley wouldn't wait for my daughter to recover and recast her part in his upcoming movie, his loss. She will have other chances once she is out and well." Doris stared resentfully at Nell Billodeaux who "danced" with Teddy in his wheelchair.

"That woman should have been sued for what she did to the great Layla Devlin's face. To think we had to sell off the Hollywood mansion to meet all those trumped-up claims, not to mention the cost of the plastic surgery. Well, I once built my life up again from scratch and so can Louise. I know you'll always be there for her. Have a blessed married life." Finally, her damp hand fell way from Tricia's, and Doris returned for a third helping at the buffet.

"That was scary. You about ready to go, my one and only wife?" Rex said.

"I am, wherever you want to take me."

Ida got everyone's attention with a crescendo on the piano and proclaimed the bridal couple about to leave. The guests filed out carrying their traditional little net bags of rice to throw.

The stars shone above and the fireflies below, but Tricia and Rex left without any other fireworks or fanfare. The local police cruisers stood ready to escort them safely to the airport. Rice pelted down as they ran to limo, and Mrs. Worthy began another crying jag.

Honeybee flirted with Cody by pouring rice down his collar and offering to help get it out again. The Reverend Worthy beamed at his son, now a married man and so happy, by the looks of him.

Leaning against each other, Joe and Nell stood among their twelve children. "You know where they are going?"

"Africa for two weeks. Rex wants to show Tricia where he spent his childhood. They'll take in some of the big game parks, too, but he has to be back for minicamp training. Not me."

"And after that?"

"The condo in New Orleans for now, a bigger house later, and maybe a place outside of Austin far enough away from his family for Tricia's comfort and close enough to his dad if he needs help."

"Sounds wise. So a new married life begins. More children will come into the world, but our family is complete."

"My career is over. His is only beginning. We're just an old married couple now. No more excitement for us."

Nell detected the hint of sadness in Joe's voice. "You really think *that* with twelve children to raise?" She drew his silver-streaked head down close to her lips and toyed with the curl on his forehead as she whispered, "If you want excitement, just wait until I get you back to the hotel. Ever done it with a matron of honor in all her regalia?"

Joe answered that honestly. "You know I always tried to avoid married women, but you're an exception. If you're ready to leave, then so am I, sugar."

A word about the author...

Once a librarian, now a writer of romance, Lynn Shurr grew up in Pennsylvania Dutch country. She attended a state college and earned a very impractical degree in English Literature. Her first job after graduating really was working in a burger joint. Moving from one humble job to another, she finally buckled down and got an M.A. in librarianship.

Lynn found her first reference job in the heart of Cajun country. For her, the old saying, "Once you've tasted bayou water, you will always stay here," came true. She raised three children not far from the Bayou Teche and lives there still with her astronomer husband.

When not writing, Lynn likes to paint, cheer for the New Orleans Saints and LSU Tigers, and take long road trips nearly anywhere. Her love of the bayou country, its history and customs, often shows in the background for her books.

Contact Lynn at www.lynnshurr.com or visit her blog, lynnshurr.blogspot.com.

Other Wild Rose Books by Lynn Shurr